## 'I have brought your bride price.'

Aro reached out, captured her hand, and placed a gold and iron ring on her fourth finger.

The ring weighed heavy, but Lydia made no attempt to pull away. Aro bent his head and his lips brushed hers for the traditional betrothal kiss, the acceptance that he would now have rights over her body. The touch was feather-like, but it did strange things to her insides, made her wonder what it would be like to be kissed for real by this man.

Lydia regarded her left hand and the iron and gold that now encircled her finger. Her *arra*, the symbol of the money he had paid for her. This was no midnight fancy brought by furies. The weight of the ring made it a reality. She had started off down a path and had no idea where the end might be.

## Author Note

One of the many delights of researching Ancient Rome is discovering traces or hints of modern-day customs. Although I knew about some of them, I was surprised to find many marriage customs had survived or had been adapted from the Roman marriage celebration—from betrothal rings to bridal wreaths made from verbena and sweet marjoram (during the Roman Empire orange blossom and myrtle) and brides being lifted over the threshold, to name but a few. However, some of the more pagan references, such as the orange veil to symbolise Juno's loyalty to her husband, the Herculean knot around the bride's waist, and the reading of bloody entrails to determine the success of the marriage, were abandoned long ago. As with other celebrations, the early Christian church can take some credit for retaining certain customs as they attempted to keep them familiar for the converts.

Hopefully you will enjoy reading this tale of Roman romance as much as I enjoyed writing it. I would love to hear from you. I can be contacted either through my blog—www.michellestyles.blogspot.com—my website www.michellestyles.co.uk, or write to me care of Harlequin Mills & Boon.

# SOLD AND SEDUCED

Michelle Styles

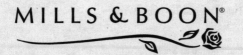

MILLS & BOON®

First published in Great Britain 2007
Harlequin Mills & Boon Limited,
Eton House, 18-24 Paradise Road, Richmond, Surrey TW9 1SR

© Michelle Styles 2007

ISBN-13: 978 0 263 85170 0
ISBN-10:    0 263 85170 2

Set in Times Roman 10½ on 13½ pt.
04-0407-82622

Printed and bound in Spain
by Litografia Rosés S.A., Barcelona

Although born and raised near San Francisco, California, **Michelle Styles** currently lives a few miles south of Hadrian's Wall, with her husband, three children, two dogs, cats, assorted ducks, hens and beehives. An avid reader, she has always been interested in history, and a historical romance is her idea of the perfect way to relax. Her love of Rome stems from the year of Latin she took in sixth grade. She is particularly interested in how ordinary people lived during ancient times, and in the course of her research she has learnt how to cook Roman food as well as how to use a drop spindle. When she is not writing, reading or doing research, Michelle tends her rather overgrown garden or does needlework, in particular counted cross-stitch.

**Recent novels by the same author:**

THE GLADIATOR'S HONOUR
A NOBLE CAPTIVE

To Maddie Rowe, who is not only a
Bad Influence but an inspiration.

# *Chapter One*

Rome—68 BC

'Lydia, come and look. A man is arguing with Gallus the porter.' Sulpicia rushed into the *tablinum,* causing the thread on Lydia's spindle to snap.

Lydia Veratia placed her spindle down with gratitude and went to stand next to her sister-in-law at the living-room window. Anything was better than the tedium of spinning, even watching her father's volatile porter argue.

'What's it about this time?' Lydia asked, peering out between the shutters. Gallus stood gesturing to an unfamiliar man. 'Fish sauce again? Or has Gallus picked a fight with a stranger?'

Sulpicia cupped her hand to her ear and leant further out the window. 'Something about a delivery of wine.'

'But that was taken care of two Nones ago.' Lydia peered down at the man towering over the hapless porter. His sandalled feet were planted firmly as if he were on the deck of a ship. The cut of his dark blue cloak and his embroidered tunic showed he was no mere servant. The man glanced upwards and Lydia caught the fullness of his golden gaze. A half-smile appeared on his lips. He inclined his head in her direction. Lydia banged the shutter closed and withdrew to the other side of the room.

'Undoubtedly Gallus can solve the query. I am forbidden from such things now.' She forced her lips upwards to show her father's edict no longer hurt. 'I am to be a proper Roman lady, and stay at my spindle while Father searches for an appropriate bridegroom.'

'Publius has sent another tablet,' Sulpicia said, coming to stand next to Lydia. She tucked her head into her neck and glanced up through her eyelashes. 'He wants to know if that last cargo of *liquamen* has been loaded or if it has been delayed yet again.'

A small pain started behind Lydia's eyes. She should have known Sulpicia would have an ulterior motive in finding her, something she wanted done. Normally by this hour, her sister-in-law would be at the baths, gossiping with her cronies or listening to the criers in the Forum giving the latest news of the war against the pirates. 'He should ask our father.'

'But Cornelius has been ill. I don't want to worry him, and it is ever such a small thing.' Sulpicia gave a tiny pout and put her hands over her expanding belly. The kicks from the baby she carried were clearly visible. 'You can find out for me, Lydia. Publius says the factor is refusing to release any more money until the cargo arrives. I just want to know when it was shipped. I'd search myself, but I have no idea where to begin looking and you know where everything is in the study.'

Lydia rubbed the back of her neck. She refused to give in to temptation. She had given her word.

'I told Publius before he left that he should guard his *denarii* well. Sometimes shipments of *liquamen* take time. The amphorae are an awkward shape. Besides, the more mature the fish sauce is, the higher the price in Corinth. Ofellius has a good reputation.'

'Publius was being careful.' Sulpicia gave a demure smile. 'He had a few unexpected expenses. It could happen to anyone.'

'Publius spends money far too easily.'

Sulpicia fluttered her eyelashes and laid a manicured hand on Lydia's arm. 'Check for me…as a special favour. The baby is due in a few months, and I possess as much grace as one of Hannibal's war elephants.'

'Father has forbidden me to go into his office. Women should be attending their household duties and not seeing to shipping lists. His temper is so uncertain these days. He has become a different man since his illness.' Lydia fought to keep the bitterness out her voice.

'Our father doesn't realise how you saved this house when he lay ill. You will be in and out before anyone notices.' Sulpicia lowered her voice to a conspiratorial whisper. 'Gallus is busy with that man. Find the tablet and bring it here. If you won't do it for me, consider how upset our father will be when he finds out about Publius's debt. It might even bring on another attack.'

When Sulpicia put it like that, her request became more tempting. It would mean Lydia would have less time to spin, and she could check on the status of several cargoes. Her father meant well, but he had not recovered his former vigour.

Things slipped or became misplaced. Gallus had been grumbling about having to find missing scrolls this morning. Lydia tapped her finger against her mouth. The news that her brother had reverted to his spendthrift ways might indeed send her father back to his bed. 'Publius ought to have been more careful.'

'I'll do your spinning for you, Lydia.' Sulpicia dangled the abandoned spindle from her fingertips. 'No one will know you were there. Cornelius has gone to the Senate. One quick look. That is all I ask.'

Lydia took a look at the huge pile of wool next to her stool.

'I will do it for you, Sulpicia, but only this one time.'

Enough of this delay and excuses from a porter.

Quintus Fabius Aro glowered at the closed door. How many days had his men been forced to kick their sandals? His ships stay idle in Ostia, waiting for the promised cargo of Falerian wine?

The money he'd receive from the wine would enable him to carry out the final stage in his plan. He'd finally be able to honour the vow he'd made on his father's deathbed. Aro's hand tightened on the hilt of his dagger. The Fabii would again be one of the first families of Rome.

The antechamber with its intricate mosaic floor and fully frescoed walls reeked of wealth and privilege, but when he looked closely at the central tiger motif, Aro spotted the signs of money trouble—a tile missing in the tiger's right eye, water damage on the fresco by the window and the marks of a charcoal brazier in the corner. Veratius Cornelius was not as well off as he pretended.

A grim smile stretched across Aro's face. Good. It served the cheat right. Nobody made Fabius Aro look like a fool.

Eighteen months ago on the deck of his favourite trireme, the *Sea Wolf,* he had bargained with Veratius Cornelius—a cargo of next year's Falerian wine in exchange for passage for himself and his spices to Corinth. It was time for the senator to make good his promise before the winds changed and it became impossible to sail for North Africa and Cyrene.

Three times he had sent his men, and three times they were sent away with the same assurance—the scroll had been mislaid and the wine would arrive tomorrow.

Now the senator would have to answer to him.

Aro cocked his head, listening. The inner room had been silent when the porter first showed him in. But there was a distinct scratch of stylus against papyrus. Aro lifted an eyebrow. Obviously, Veratius Cornelius believed his unwelcome guest had departed and had decided to resume his work, coward that he was.

By Neptune's trident, he should have made Veratius Cornelius swim for it when he rescued the man from the sinking ship, rather than wasting precious time and effort saving his worthless hide. He should have recalled his father's bitter statements about the Veratii and the way they twisted the truth.

'Where is the Falerian wine you promised, Veratius Cornelius?' Aro strode over to the door and flung it open. 'We had a bargain, you and I.'

He stopped and stared. Instead of the grey-haired senator bent over his tablets and scrolls, a woman dressed in a dark blue gown sat at the table. Her dark brown hair escaped in curling tendrils about her heart-shaped face. At the sound of the crash, her hand stilled, frozen in the act of making some note. Her hazel eyes widened, but she recovered quickly, hurriedly shoving a scroll under the pile of tablets that littered the table.

'Who are you? Honestly, Gallus gets worse and worse.' She arched one perfectly plucked eyebrow, but Aro noted the smudge of ink on her cheek. 'This is a private office. Leave at once!'

'You are not Veratius Cornelius.'

'No. I'm not.' She inclined her head and rather pointedly made a note with her stylus.

Aro waited for her to say something more, but all her attention appeared to be on her writing.

'You are alone.'

'Do you always state the obvious?'

'I have business with Senator Veratius Cornelius.'

'Many people have business with him. He is one of the leading senators in Rome.' She pointedly shuffled the tablets and gestured towards the door. 'You will have to wait your turn.'

Aro tapped his fingers against his thigh. He refused to be dismissed that easily, as if he were a lost messenger boy. Exactly who was she? Veratius Cornelius's wife? His mistress? And why was she here in Veratius Cornelius's office?

'It is imperative I speak with him.' Aro kept his tone measured and his eyes fixed on a point somewhere above her head. 'I'm Fabius Aro.'

He waited for the response and recognition that he deserved as head of the Lupan House, one of the most successful trading houses in the western Mediterranean.

'The name means nothing to me.' She sorted through another tablet. Her lips curved upwards, then she fixed him with the full force of her hazel stare. 'You might want to try his negotiator who deals with such things.'

'I already have. He sent me here.'

'He wasted your time.' She gave another nod towards the door. 'Pray don't waste any more.'

Aro ignored the invitation to leave. Veratius Cornelius would have to return at some point, and he intended to find out why the senator felt he could cheat him. It made little sense. There again, a high-born lady as this woman clearly was had no call to sort and shift through tablets and scrolls like a scribe.

'You're not supposed to be here.'

'I'm Lydia Veratia. I have a right to be here.'

The words were quick, too quick, and accompanied a slight toss of her hair and a defiant look. Aro stroked his chin. He doubted her words were the whole truth. Wherever Lydia Veratia was supposed to be, it wasn't here.

'Your father has no idea you are searching through his papers.'

'You are spouting nonsense.' She lifted her chin and met his gaze, challenging him, instead of cowering as most women and many men would have done. 'Of course I have permission. Why do you think otherwise?'

'You failed to scream. You kept silent instead of calling for the porter.' Aro ticked off the reasons on his fingers, beginning to enjoy himself as a look of discomfort crossed Lydia's face.

He reached over and tweaked the tablet from her hand. A

shipping bill for *liquamen,* with the seal of the house of Ofellius attached. He would be tempted to wager that the fish sauce would never arrive at its destination. Ofellius had a tendency to use that particular seal for cargoes that mysteriously vanished.

'In fact, you want everyone to remain ignorant that you are in the senator's inner chamber, searching through his private scrolls.'

'Do you always deal in myths and legends?' She snatched the bill back, and rose. She was taller than he had expected, the top of her head about level with his nose.

'Shall we call the porter and see?'

A look of discomfort passed over Lydia Veratia's face.

'It is far from necessary,' she mumbled to the floor.

'Tell me when I might expect the senator and I will tell no one, I promise.' He forced his features into a pleasant smile, but continued to watch Lydia like a hawk. If he could get her on his side, it would make it much easier to find Veratius Cornelius. The coward, skulking while he sent a woman to do a man's job. 'My ship waits for the wine he promised to deliver over three weeks ago. We had an agreement, your father and I. Or is it as worthless as the bill of sale you hold in your hands? Mark my words, the fish sauce will not arrive in Corinth. When dealing with that trading house, you need to get your money first.'

She jerked her head up at the statement and her eyes blazed, full of fury.

'My father made no such agreement.' Her hand hit the table, causing the scrolls to jump and a pile of tablets to crash to the mosaic-tiled floor. 'Impossible, I would know if he had.'

'Do you know all of your father's business?'

'Most of it. He…he confides in me,' she said in a quiet voice. 'And…and you are wrong about the *liquamen*. It has been delayed. That's all.'

She shrugged and her shawl slipped, revealing the delicate cream of her neck. Her hand immediately rearranged the shawl and the brief glimpse was no more. A gesture designed to distract. He had seen other women use it too many times before to allow his thoughts to wander, but his blood stirred at the sight.

'Shall we find your father and discuss the matter? You show me I am wrong.' Aro put his hands on the table and leant forward. The colour drained from her face. 'You must know where he is and when he is expected to return. Or is that something else he decided not to share with you?'

'That is not any of your business.' She picked up the stylus and gestured towards the door. 'Go now or I really will call the porter. I can't think why you were left here on your own. What did you bribe the porter with?'

'The porter did not need any silver. He listened and understood.' His body tensed as he watched her eyes flicker about the room. What was she going to try now? What would she do to distract his attention this time? He was hard pressed to remember the last time he had faced such an intriguing and infuriating opponent. His reputation ensured everyone he encountered treated him with the respect he deserved as head of the Lupan House. 'Your father owes me a valuable cargo, and therefore it is my business.'

'We have failed to establish if he owes you anything.' She tilted her head to one side. Her lips curved upwards, but her knuckles showed white where her hand gripped the stylus. 'You offer no proof. You merely demand.'

Aro made a show of straightening his cloak, giving the deliberate impression he had time to spare. Neither Lydia Veratia nor her father must guess how precarious the situation was. Another hour and he'd have missed today's tide.

Each day's delay brought him closer to the time of the fierce north winds when it would be dangerous to set sail. Falerian wine was worth more than its weight in gold, but even in his younger days, when amassing a fortune was all-important, he would not have risked his men on such a venture once the winds started to blow. His success depended on judging the sea correctly, getting the cargo to market and, more importantly, keeping his men for the next voyage. However, this money would ensure he could pay for a fixer and be enrolled in the Senate. His vow to his father would be complete and his branch of the Fabius family would once again rank among the elite.

'We made a bargain, your father and I, eighteen months ago out on the sea. Gold plus a cargo of Falerian wine when I should require it if I transported him to Corinth. I had thought it finished, but discovered that one of my captains failed to take the cargo. He has only just returned to Rome from Egypt.'

The white of her teeth showed, followed by a sudden flash of recognition in her eyes. 'You are the pirate who demanded ransom after my father's ship was slightly damaged in a storm.'

'No, I am the merchant who gave your father shelter on board my vessel when his own ship was floundering, taking on water.' Aro pronounced each word with care and through gritted teeth. He had gambled with his life and his ships, fought other crews to reach a port first, seldom hesitated to seduce a beautiful woman, but he had never resorted to piracy. 'If we had not been there, your father would have drowned. I lost two experienced men in the storm, saving his precious store of spices.'

'My father has paid enough, more than enough.'

'You are an expert in these things? How? Are you your father's scribe?' Aro's voice betrayed his incredulity. But Lydia continued to look at him with level eyes. Aro opted for an indulgent smile, one he knew had charmed many of the women in the seaside resort of Baiae. 'I would have thought your head would be full of other things—running a household, ribbons or perhaps one of the poets, not the dull bookkeeping of a shipping house.'

Instead of a simper or a flirtatious laugh, Lydia Veratia drew her eyebrows together and frowned. She tapped her forefinger against a stack of tablets.

'I know the going rate for a passage to Corinth. It is not too difficult to discover. It is in the region of thirty *denarii,* rather less than what you charged.' Her voice held a distinct note of ice. Lydia Veratia's back straightened and she raised her chin, challenging him.

'There are charges and there are charges.' Aro pressed his lips together to form a firm line. The last time someone had dared question his prices, the paint had barely dried on the decking of his first ship. 'I risked my life and that of my men to rescue your father and his cargo.'

'I may be a woman, but I am not a simpleton. Pray don't treat me like one.'

'I never said that you didn't have a mind,' Aro retorted quickly. 'I would have thought you'd have preferred to use it for different pursuits.'

'How I use my mind is no concern of yours, but as it happens I prefer business to spinning. My father values my counsel.' Lydia bent her head and sorted through some tablets, her tongue caught between her teeth.

'The Falerian wine has gone elsewhere. Sold to the highest bidder last Nones.' She sorted through a stack and held one out. 'All perfectly legal. You should be content with the going rate for passage to Corinth. You did receive a higher commission on the spice, I believe.'

Aro reached out and grabbed her wrist, holding her there, preventing her from moving. He had enough of Roman treachery. If Veratius Cornelius thought because Aro was the head of a merchant house rather than a Roman senator that he could cheat him, he was sadly mistaken. His father's words haunted him. 'What do you mean—sold?'

'Let go of me!'

'Not until you tell me to whom and why the cargo was sold. It was not your father's to sell. We had a legally binding agreement.'

'I said let go of me! It is none of your business who purchased the wine.'

Lydia moved her wrist and tried to break free of the broad-shouldered man who had invaded her father's inner sanctum, but his fingers held her fast, preventing her. Large. Dangerous. Untamed. She was so close the flecks of gold in his tawny eyes were clearly visible.

She bit her lip. She should have called for Gallus when he

first burst into the room, but that would have meant alerting Gallus to her presence and awkward questions from her father. She had no wish to inflame his temper. No, it was too late for regrets.

She moved her wrist sharply downwards and, as suddenly as the man had grabbed it, he let go. Her skin tingled where his fingers had been. She rubbed her wrist, trying to rid her body of the feeling.

'But it is very much my business, much more so than yours,' he said quietly, but he did not move away from her. Lydia held her body still. 'Most matrons are attending their spinning rather than shuffling scrolls in an office. Why do you know so much about your father's business? And you still have failed to explain why you wish to keep it a secret from him.'

The rage grew within Lydia. There was much more to her world than spinning and gossip at the baths. She was not one of those empty-headed women who lived only for pleasure. Over the past six months, besides running the domestic side of the house, she had learnt how to manage her father's business affairs and handled them quite well in her opinion. She did not need some ship's captain telling her how she should be conducting herself.

Selling the Falerian wine had been a master stroke. Pompey had swept the pirates from the Mediterranean, and therefore her father's bargain was finished. Publius had always proclaimed the man who stood before her was a notorious pirate. The Falerian wine had sat in the warehouse for nearly a season, forgotten. When her father lay ill and the bills for the doctor had been presented along with Publius's mounting debts, it seemed the most sensible thing to do. The pirate, if he lived, would never dare claim it.

Problem resolved. The honour of the Veratii saved.

Staring up at the man's tawny eyes, his warm breath fanning her cheek, Lydia felt a sense of unease pass over her. Perhaps she should have sold something else, but it had seemed to be the only way at the time. Her father had to live. The doctors and soothsayers demanded money. Publius had lost a fortune at the gaming tables.

No, she had done what she did because she had to.

How did she even know this man was telling the truth? It might be that he had heard the tale and decided to claim the goods for himself. She drew a steadying breath. Yes, that was it. It had to be.

'I mean you no harm,' he said. 'I want what is rightfully mine.'

'Pompey has got rid of all pirates.' Lydia pressed the skin on the bridge of her nose. This man was taking an awful risk by showing his face. A line of crucified pirates stretched for several miles down the Appian Way. 'The pirates have stopped menacing the seas and people no longer need fear them.'

'For that I am grateful.' He gave a mocking bow, a flourish with his hand. His cloak moved, revealing the hard muscular length of his leg, muscles that had come from hard work, not the gymnasium at the bath. 'The Cilian pirates have been a menace to honest traders for years. We honest merchants suffered grievously.'

'You are not a pirate.' Lydia's hand clutched her throat. The sudden possibility that Publius had lied to her grabbed her insides. The room swayed and then righted itself. Had she made a dreadful mistake?

'Would I be here, openly in Rome today, if I were?'

'How would I know?'

'Do I look such a fool that I would appear in Rome with a price on my head?' The man lifted his eyebrow. A half-smile appeared on his full lips. Lydia had no doubt most of her friends would be swooning by this stage. He had bedroom eyes and his legs put those of a gladiator to shame. 'I can assure you my life is worth far more than a cargo of fine wine.'

Lydia pressed her lips into a firm line. He made it sound plausible. It would be suicide for a pirate to boldly enter Rome, particularly one as well known as Publius claimed her father's rescuer was. He had to be an impostor. Lydia heaved a sigh of relief. That was it. An impostor who had heard about the bargain her father had made.

'I don't know what you might or might not do.' She crossed her arms and returned his stare. 'It is of no concern of mine. What proof do you have that the wine was even intended for you? It could be you somehow heard about this wine and are attempting to get it through trickery.'

'The lady wants proof, and proof she shall have.' He gave a bow and drew out a tablet.

Lydia's heart sank as she saw the first seal. A wolf's head. 'You belong to the Lupan House?'

'I am the head of that trading house, yes.'

Her heart sank further when she examined the seal next to the wolf's head. Her father's. This was indeed the man. He did hold the right to the wine, the wine she had sold without her father's knowledge or consent.

Lydia caught the tip of her tongue between her teeth. Things were going from bad to worse. The docks buzzed with whispers about the rise and rise of the Lupan House. It was said that the head of the house was blessed by the gods, a true son of Neptune. A man with the touch of King Midas, all his cargoes turned to gold and little wonder with the prices he charged.

'You should have told the porter. You should have told me who you were.'

Fabius Aro made an annoyed noise at the back of his throat. Lydia cursed her ill luck. Why hadn't Publius told her the truth about the wine? If she'd realised, she would have never sold it. To alienate one of the most powerful trading houses in the Mediterranean was beyond stupidity. What was worse—Publius had to have known.

'Where is my wine?' Aro asked again. This time his voice held a note of menace.

'Sold, I told you.' Her hand twisted her shawl tighter.

'Then Veratius Cornelius owes me the gold from the sale. He has sold something that belongs to me. And I could have received three times the amount in North Africa than I could in Rome for that wine.'

Lydia swallowed hard. Triple the amount. He had to be lying. She risked a glance upwards at his features. They were set harder than ever. He was telling the truth. She should never have given in to temptation. She should have sold one of the estates in northern Italy instead. She blinked. Anything but the wine.

'It will take some time to get the money,' she began, willing her mind to think up a good excuse, to buy time.

'Time is not something I have. I have buyers up and down the African coast waiting for this wine. I will have to purchase it from wherever I can or risk facing the north wind.'

'You will need to speak to my father about this.' Lydia winced as she said it. She would have to explain the situation to her father, and risk his wrath. The question was how to break it to him, what to say. The doctors had said that he was to be kept quiet, and allow nothing to disturb him. She was positive she could find a buyer for her mother's estate, if she was allowed a few weeks.

'And we are back to where we started from. I must speak with your father.'

'Who wishes to speak with me?' Lydia heard her father's voice call out. 'Who dares invade my inner sanctum without my permission?'

# Chapter Two

Lydia winced at the sound of her father's voice. So much for Sulpicia's prediction of getting in and out without his knowledge. Everything would be exposed.

She glared at Aro, standing there, brushing a speck of lint off his tunic. Unconcerned. It was all his fault. Everything. If he had come for the Falerian wine when he was supposed to, none of this would ever have happened. How very like a pirate to be underhanded. Even as she thought the words, she knew she was being unfair.

'Gallus informs me my presence is required urgently,' her father's voice boomed. 'He has run all the way to the Senate. I had to excuse myself during Cato's speech on the necessity to limit fish ponds in Rome. There had best be a good reason.'

'There is a man here, Father,' Lydia called out. There was no point in hiding. She had to face her father and take whatever punishment he deemed appropriate. She hated to think what a confrontation with Fabius Aro might do to him. He had barely recovered from his last attack.

'Ah, Veratius Cornelius, at last we meet again.' Aro broke in before she had a chance to say anything more. His voice sounded lazy and easygoing, nothing like the intense man she had been arguing with. 'I trust life has treated you well since we last parted in Corinth. As I promised, your spices went for twice what you expected.'

'Aro, Fabius Aro. You have come for your wine, no doubt. About time too. Cobwebs are gathering on the amphorae, but there again I suppose you will get a better price for it.' Her father entered the room at a slow shuffle. He paused in the doorway to straighten his toga, highlighting the broad purple stripe. His features hardened when his gaze lighted on her. 'Lydia, you are neglecting your spinning again. Do you not remember what we discussed only yesterday? Forgive my daughter, Fabius Aro. The young women of today, they will ruin the Republic. In my youth, women always left business to the men. As Cato was saying this morning, where will it all end?'

Lydia tried to ignore Aro's arched brow and superior expression. But she inwardly winced, her earlier boast revealed for the lie it was. She twisted her belt around her hand. She could hardly begin explaining about how her father had encouraged her before he suffered from his ill health, but since his recovery had seemed to have forgotten. Sometimes, Lydia could almost believe the soothsayer who said a demon had taken charge of her father's body.

This was definitely the last time she helped Sulpicia and Publius out. Next time, Sulpicia could approach her father herself. Today was getting worse by the heartbeat. Early this morning, she had begun to hope that at long last things were beginning to return to normal, that her father would once again start managing his business affairs, that she could go back to the baths and discuss the latest plays, poetry and scandal with her friends, instead of worrying about which merchant should be paid first, and when the grain should be harvested. It had been such a long time since she had the time to do more than have a quick scrape down with a *strigil* and a rinse off. She had intended on keeping her promise, but now all her father would be able to see was she had broken it at the first opportunity.

And there was the small matter of the wine…

Her father started towards the desk and stumbled. Lydia's heart turned over. Her father was a shadow of his former self. She could see that Aro saw that as well. Gone was the large man with an even larger appetite for life, and in his place was this shrunken man with watery eyes. She watched Aro closely to see his reaction, but his face was a blank slab of marble. He stood there with his hand upon his dagger.

'There appears to be a bit of trouble with the shipment,' Aro said. 'I wonder if you might help me solve it.'

'Trouble? What sort of trouble?' Veratius Cornelius cocked his head. 'I placed those amphorae aside just as I promised I would. A Veratii does not attempt to break a promise, even one given on a rain-soaked deck.'

Lydia shifted from foot to foot. She had to tell him. Now. She had to confess and risk undoing all the progress he had made.

'The wine has been sold, Father.'

'Sold? Why and under whose order?' Veratius Cornelius's face flushed. He reached out and laid a trembling hand on the table. 'Who would do that? Which misbegotten slave dared do such a thing? Tell me and he shall be punished. Whipped within an inch of his miserable existence.'

Lydia stepped backwards. The last thing she needed was her father exploding. But he had to understand that it was the only way they could have survived.

'I took the decision to sell the wine, Father.' Lydia tucked a strand of hair behind her ear. A small gesture, but enough to keep her hands from shaking. She ignored the man standing a little way to her right and concentrated on her father. She had to make her voice sound slow and calm. 'Publius agreed with me. It was the right thing to do.'

'You sold the wine,' he father repeated in an unbelieving voice.

'Yes, and the gold is spent.' Lydia felt the edge of the table jab into her thighs. She hated the expression on her father's face. She wanted to curl up in a ball and hide. 'It was wrong of me not to tell you before—'

'When did you plan on telling me you had done this, Lydia?' Her father's voice cut her like a lash. 'Taken my seal without asking and sold something you had no right to. By Jupiter Maximus, you need a husband who will control you. I should never have listened to you or your brother. You will not have a say in who you marry.'

Lydia's throat refused to work. She wanted to explain, but her father was not giving her a chance. The doctors and sooth-sayers had wanted more than fresh air, then there was the apothecary. Her father had turned towards Fabius Aro now, all fawning and apologetic.

What should she have done? Allowed her father to die? Or if not to die, to live disgraced? Her father's position as a senator was important to him, to the whole family. She refused to allow him to lose that simply because the Fates had decreed him to fall ill.

'I did it for you, Father,' she whispered, but he gave no sign of hearing.

Instead, he turned towards Aro, his silver head bowed low.

'If you will give me until the next Nones, I will get you the money,' Veratius said. 'My honour demands I find the gold for you, and you will have it as soon as I can manage. My reputation and that of my family is at stake. It is my sincere regret that this has happened.'

The merchant crossed his arms. Lydia could see the bulging muscles of his forearms. Unlike her brother or father, here was a man who worked for his living. His face had only become harder, and more marble-like.

'I regret that I don't have the time.' Fabius Aro's voice held no warmth. 'You gave me your sacred word, Veratius Cornelius. You staked your honour on the amphorae of wine. My men died for you and your spices.'

'I did not think that my idiotic daughter would take it into her head to sell them.' Her father banged his hand against the table. His eyes held a wild trapped look. 'What did you do, Lydia, buy a new silk gown with the money? What was the thing that couldn't wait?'

'I…I…' Lydia wondered how to explain without alerting Aro to the state of her father's ill health. If that became common quayside gossip, all hope of any more concessions and deals would be gone. Worst of all, the censor could remove her father's dignities and they would be left without any status. 'Father, I did what I thought best in the circumstances—'

Her father's peremptory gesture cut her words off.

'Thinking is never good for a woman,' her father said. 'No man will have you if he thinks you are interested in a man's work. Why can't you be interested in the womanly arts of housekeeping?'

'I did what was necessary.' Lydia stared at the mosaic on the floor rather than let her father see how much his words pained her. She had done so much in the past months when he lay ill in bed. Had he not even noticed? Did he think his vast empire ran by itself? Publius had departed for the east with Pompey and never a backward glance, but the decisions had to be made then. Her father's life had depended on it. Lydia retrieved a set of scrolls. 'Every transaction is written down. The money was not squandered.'

Her father barely glanced at the scrolls. A lump formed in Lydia's throat. 'You shall have your money, Fabius Aro, but you must give me time to raise it.'

'I have already wasted enough time.' Aro's eyes glittered gold. Lydia could see the distinct resemblance to a wolf. 'I should have you declared a debtor, Veratius Cornelius. Today. The censor will have something to say about a senator who can't pay his debt.'

'Don't do that!' Lydia cried. 'You must not blame my father. He knew nothing. He has just found out. We will raise the money somehow. Father, there is my dowry—the estate in northern Italy. If the sale is handled properly…'

Aro shook his head. His eyes appeared harder than amber.

'Is there one thing that will change your mind? Something you will take in exchange?' her father asked.

'There is nothing you have that I need. Or want!'

At those words, her father buried his face in his hands and sank to the floor. 'Ruined. Ruined, I tell you. All from giving my children so much.'

Lydia gently raised her father up, but he shook off her hand. She stared back at Fabius Aro who stood there with an unyielding face.

A shiver ran down Lydia's back. The merchant had something planned for them. Something unpleasant. Fabius Aro would ruin them. All because she had sold the cargo. She had to do something. Now before it was too late. Her father was not strong enough to withstand prison.

'If you seek to punish someone, punish me,' she said. 'My father acted in good faith. He set aside the wine for you. It is I who sold it without his knowledge. I made the mistake. If you must blame someone, blame me.'

She caught her breath and waited. He arched an eyebrow. His eyes roamed over her face, her figure, undressed her. Lydia forced her body to remain still. She refused to show her terror.

'Perhaps there is something after all.' Aro fingered his chin. 'An intriguing idea.'

'What is that?' her father asked, raising his head.

'Your daughter's.'

'My daughter is not part of this conversation,' her father said. 'Lydia, you may depart. You have done too much already.'

Veratius Cornelius drew himself up. His voice held some of its old booming magic. There was nothing for her to do except to leave and hope. Lydia started towards the door. She had to obey her father, but she was reluctant to leave. It was her fate they were discussing.

'There are many things I would dispose of, before I sell my children,' her father said, not even bothering to glance at her.

'I speak not of slavery. I speak of *coemptio,* of marriage between a Roman citizen and a patrician woman.'

Lydia's sandals skittered into each other. She paused, her hand on the door. She couldn't go, not now, not when her entire future was at stake.

Marriage? Surely, the Furies had touched Fabius Aro. She was the daughter of a senator and he, a merchant. Wealthy, powerful, but not of the noble class. Lydia risked a glance at his face. His countenance gave nothing away, just the firmness of his jaw and the deep golden hue of his eyes. He was undeniably attractive, with his black hair and broad shoulders and pleasing smile, but marriage was another chariot race. It went beyond physical attraction. This was about her family's future.

'My daughter and you? Marriage with a plebeian?' her father barked.

'You indicated earlier she is unmarried.' Aro's voice was cool, unhurried.

'There are several different possibilities I am currently examining.' Her father's mouth bore a pinched look. Lydia's stomach clenched. She did not want another of his attacks, but she felt powerless to intervene. 'None involving a plebeian.'

'I have need of a wife.' Aro pressed his fingertips together. His gaze did not waver from her father's face. 'Your daughter is unmarried.'

'Nevertheless, all suitors must be considered, balanced

against one another.' Her father twitched the corner of his toga. 'The Veratii can trace their lineage back to Romulus and Remus.'

'I have the same number of ancestors.' Aro coolly lifted an eyebrow, and Lydia saw the steely-eyed determination in his face. 'You will marry your daughter to whoever best serves your needs and purposes. Don't bother denying it. It is the way Rome has always worked.'

'You are not a true Roman,' her father spat with a curling lip. 'You are a sailor, a trader. You sully your hands with physical labour.'

Aro flinched; his eyes narrowed. The intensity of his gaze increased. Fierce with a controlled fury, but in the next heartbeat it was masked. Her father's words had struck a raw nerve.

'Does it really matter who I am?' He expelled a breath with a hiss. 'You are in serious difficulties and I am offering a solution.'

'I would have my daughter marry well, increase this family's prestige.' Her father straightened, his face as red as a centurion's cloak. Beads of sweat stood out on his forehead. 'Not to a ship's captain.'

'I am a merchant, the head of a trading house.'

'It is much the same thing,' her father said.

'If that is the way you feel…'

Lydia saw Aro begin to adjust his cloak.

This was all her fault. No one else's. In another heartbeat, Fabius Aro would leave, and everything would be exposed and disgrace would follow. The censors would come and her father would have his senatorial dignities removed.

The shame would kill him.

Already the colour had drained from her father's face, leaving him grey. She had to find a way to save him before another attack started. The doctors had warned the next one could be fatal. Her mouth became dry. She swallowed rapidly.

'Father, be reasonable. You know many of our friends invest in ships.' Her voice sounded high and unnatural to her ears.

Her father made an irritated noise in the back of his throat.

'Lydia Veratia is the only thing you have left to bargain with.' Aro leant forward, his face level with her father's. 'Your daughter in exchange for the Falerian wine, wine you purchased your life with. Which honest merchant will carry your cargoes of grain and olive oil if they know you to be a cheat? Tell me—what is the going rate for daughters of impoverished senators these days? Senators whose dignities have been taken away by the censor?'

Lydia forced her body to stay upright. She should never have sold that wine. She should never have listened to Publius's bland assurances about pirates. It was not hers to sell. Now she had to pay the price. She refused to let anyone else pay for her mistakes. She had to act. Her family's honour was at stake. Once lost, it would take generations to restore.

'Does it matter, Father?' Lydia heard her own voice from a long way away. 'Shall we be sensible about this? We do not have the gold Fabius Aro requires. I sold the cargo. We must accept his offer. I will become his wife in a *coemptio* marriage.'

'Lydia, how can you say such a thing?' Her father turned towards her, astonishment in his voice, but she could see relief in his eyes. The purplish hue started to fade from his face.

'If your daughter raises no objections…'

Lydia watched her father bow his head. She hoped he'd understand why she had done this. She had to buy time. Time to raise the gold, to fix her inadvertent mistake. He could now negotiate the betrothal, and a *sine manu* marriage where she remained under her father's guardianship. It would give her time to sell her mother's estates in northern Italy for a good price. A betrothal was different from a marriage, and could be easily broken. Or, if worse came to worst, her father could arrange for the divorce. It would be a business arrangement, rather the hoped-for meeting of equals.

Her heart panged slightly. Some day, she wanted a true marriage like her parents had enjoyed before her mother's death. She wanted to have children and bring them up properly so that in due course they could take their place on the senate's floor. But that couldn't be helped now. The Fates had decreed that she must save her family's honour.

'As my daughter raises no objections…' her father paused, straightened his toga, and stood with his shoulders back, the very picture of senatorial dignity '…I agree to your offer of marriage.'

'We shall formalise the agreement tonight.' A smile flicked across Aro's face. 'I am positive we can arrange terms.'

'Very well, if that is your desire.' All the blustering had gone out of her father. He turned towards her and she could see the lines etched on his face. 'Lydia, you must allow me to discuss business matters in private. It is not seemly for a woman to be discussing the finer details of her marriage.'

'As you wish.' Lydia turned to go. From the look on her father's face, she knew that she could not risk further disobedience. She had to trust he would be able to negotiate a good settlement.

Aro caught her hand, raised it to his lips. The briefest of touches, but it sent pulses of warmth throughout her body. She swallowed hard. It bothered her that her lips tingled. She had done this for her father, not because she was attracted to this man, this merchant.

'You have saved your father's honour. A Roman woman at her finest.'

'You gave me no choice.' Lydia snatched her hand away and tried for as rapid an exit as her dignity would allow her.

'Lydia, your face is as white as a Vestal Virgin's robe,' Sulpicia remarked when Lydia returned to the *tablinum*. Her greyhound, Korina, lifted her brown and white head and padded silently over to her, nudging her nose under Lydia's hand, demanding adoration.

'It's nothing, Sulpicia.' Lydia gave Korina's head a stroke and tried to regain control of her thoughts. If she concentrated on something other than her problems, she might regain her poise.

'Has the cargo been lost?' Sulpicia caught her hands together and made her eyes wide, her usual gesture when she wanted something. 'Don't keep me in suspense Lydia. Tell me what has happened to the *liquamen*.'

Lydia blinked. In her shock at the betrothal, she had nearly forgotten why she was in her father's study in the first place.

'No, no, the cargo was loaded on the day after the last Ides. The loading tablet was where I thought it would be.' Her stomach became less knotted with every word she uttered.

'Provided the ship reached Corinth, Publius will have his money from the cargo. I suspect the next tablet you receive will tell you that the cargo has arrived safe and sound. Ofellius is reputable and charges a fair price, unlike some I could mention.'

Lydia wrapped her arms about her waist and tried to forget the other merchant, the one she had promised herself to—Fabius Aro with the penetrating eyes. Was it any wonder Fabius Aro prospered when he drove such hard bargains? And now she would have to pay the price.

'I knew you wouldn't fail me. Thank you, my sweetest and dearest sister.' Sulpicia leant forward and kissed Lydia on her cheek. 'While you were out, the apothecary delivered a jar of pills. You are not ill, are you?'

'No, no, they will be for Father.' Lydia forced her lips to turn upwards. 'He promised to send over the medicine, in case there is another attack.'

'I have had Beroe put them on your make-up shelf. They are there when you want them.' Sulpicia's gaze searched Lydia's face. 'But I feel there is something you are keeping from me. Something you discovered in the office. Is it bad news about Publius? We are sisters now, Lydia. You can trust me.'

Lydia drew in a great breath. She had to say it, see how Sulpicia would react.

'I am to be betrothed.'

'Betrothed? But that is wonderful news. Who is the lucky junior senator? Someone I know?' A gleam came into Sulpicia's eye and she clapped her hands together. At the sound, Korina gave a joyful bark and started to chase her tail. 'For too long, this house has been silent. We can have a wondrous party to celebrate. It should match my own betrothal to Publius in splendour. What a pity he isn't here. He does so love parties. There will be so much to plan. The house will positively hum with excitement for the next few months. When is it exactly?'

'I don't believe you know my intended.' Lydia bit her lip and regarded Korina's ears. 'The party is to be kept quiet because of Father's health.'

'Who is he, then?' Sulpicia leant forward, the spindle lying forgotten at her side. 'It can hardly be some great state secret. I am your sister-in-law. I have a right to know who this family seeks to ally itself with.'

'Fabius Aro.'

Sulpicia tapped her mouth with a perfectly manicured hand. 'I know most of the Fabii, but don't recall this one. Is he very young? Is that the problem? A younger spouse can be useful. Much more vigour than an old, worn-out man.'

'He's not a senator,' Lydia said and started to pace the floor. When she reached the charcoal brazier, she stopped and turned. 'He's a merchantman, a trader.'

'You mean he's a plebeian.' Sulpicia covered her mouth with her hand. 'You gave just two names, not three. Worse than a plebeian, he could be a former slave. Oh, Lydia, I am so sorry. Whatever can Cornelius be thinking of? The Veratii marry patricians. It is what they have always done.'

'Fabius Aro is a merchant.' Lydia raised her head. She had not done anything to be ashamed of. She had acted in good faith. If Publius had told her the truth, then the crisis would have been solved in another way. 'He's the driving force behind the Lupan trading house.'

'You mean you are betrothed to the Sea Wolf?' Sulpicia gasped and leant forward, eyes gleaming. She patted a spot by her side. 'Lydia, I have heard tales about him. They say his temper is twice as fierce as a storm at sea. He is not a man you want to cross. Marriage to such a man might be difficult. But then he is handsome. Women flock to his bed. He was the toast of Baiae two seasons ago, with his looks and money. They say Cadmunia—you know, the notorious friend of Clodia Metellia—even tried to bribe his porter so she could make her introductions in bed.'

'How do you remember such things?' Lydia shook her head.

'It was a big scandal at the time. My brother does business with them.' Sulpicia waved an airy hand. 'I am not simply a pretty face, you know. I do listen. You never know when it will come in useful.'

'Do you know anything else? Anything not scandalous?' Lydia asked, going over to sit beside her sister-in-law.

'He has come out of nowhere. Nobody knows his background. His family could be anyone. Some say he is the son of a god, and that is why the seas part for him. Others that he has demons working for him. In any case, his temper is legendary as is his seamanship. He was the first to reach Rome with the grain harvest for the last three years running.' Sulpicia's cool hand reached out and grabbed Lydia's, pulling her down on to the couch so they were at the same level. Sulpicia's expensive scent tickled Lydia's nose. 'I probably shouldn't have said anything, Lydia, but you are my sister now and you need to know about your potential bridegroom.'

Lydia disengaged her hand from Sulpicia's. She tried to think, but her head pounded. The Forum always buzzed with the latest rumour or whisper. And Sulpicia took great delight in embroidering the tales.

'Fabius Aro demanded the betrothal take place tonight. My father has agreed to his terms.'

'Tonight? It took my mother and me three months to prepare for my own betrothal banquet. Tell him you need time.' Sulpicia leant forward. 'You need to find a way. Let me speak with my father…'

'Time is not a luxury I have.' Lydia felt a great bleakness rise up within her. If even half of what Sulpicia had said was true, she had made a bad bargain. 'There are other things he needs to attend to.'

'He could do them and have the betrothal dinner later.'

'I know you are trying to help, but everything has been agreed.' Lydia rubbed a hand on the back of her neck, suddenly weary. 'There is a debt to be paid. Publius was mistaken. Fabius Aro rescued my father from the storm.'

'But I thought it was pirates.' Sulpicia flushed red. 'Publius told both of us it was a notorious pirate. How could he make a mistake like that? The head of a trading house? Isn't it just like a man? That gold is gone, spent to clear Publius's debts. Not that it was his fault. Those dice were unfair. He will pay it all back on the *liquamen*, you will see. His luck will turn. Fortune favours him.'

Lydia stood up and dusted a few of Korina's hairs off her gown. She had had enough of feeling sorry for herself. If she could keep her mind occupied on the small things, maybe she would stop worrying about the bigger thing. 'There is no point in sitting around and commiserating, Sulpicia. I have a betrothal to prepare for.'

# Chapter Three

'Could you have chosen a more disreputable place to drink, Piso?' Aro remarked when he had finally run his most senior captain to ground.

The bar was typical of Piso's watering holes, Aro thought crossing the narrow room. Dark even on the brightest day, and lit with too few lamps. The frescoes portrayed gaming with dice and knucklebones, an activity replicated on the tables that were dotted about. Despite it being only the seventh hour, the bar was full of the flotsam and jetsam of humanity— labourers intermingled with branded slaves and other more dubious characters. The barmaid behind the counter also did a brisk trade in the pleasures of the flesh. The elaborately embroidered toga she wore and the explicit frescoes on the back wall proclaimed it.

Piso stood up, disentangled himself from one of the women and indicated a stool next to him.

'You can learn things here. The barmaid is an old and valued friend.' Piso gave a wide smile and signalled for another cup. 'Have you come to pay me the money you owe me? That wine was sold to Ofellius, weeks ago.'

'Why should I owe you anything?' Aro remained standing and kept his face without expression. 'It is you who owe me. Veratius Cornelius did not sell anything.'

'But the wine has been sold to Ofellius.'

'The bet was Senator Veratius Cornelius sold the wine to Ofellius. He didn't. You should pay attention to the wording of any bet.'

'I should know better than to bet against you. You have the luck of the gods. I had thought the *denarii* were mine this time.' Piso laughed and then he leant forward. 'If Veratius Cornelius didn't sell the wine, who did?'

'You should be seeing to the fitting out of your ship, not seeing to the knucklebones and listening to Forum gossip.'

'My men know what to do. Not everyone is like you, Aro. Some of us like to take refreshment and enjoy life.' Piso drained his cup of wine and wiped his mouth, giving a satisfied sigh. 'When do we load the Falerian? We can set sail before nightfall. The wind is still blowing in the correct direction. A risk, true, but with your good fortune… By all the gods on Mount Olympus, you are the luckiest man I know.'

'We don't.' Aro tossed a pouch of coins into Piso's lap. 'You were correct about the wine. It was sold. Congratulate me. Instead of acquiring the wine, I marry.'

'You're doing what?' Piso's large hands fumbled with the purse, spilling two coins on the table.

'Getting married to Senator Lucius Veratius Cornelius's daughter.'

'A joke is a joke, Aro.' The colour drained from Piso's face and he took a gulp of wine. Aro sat down on the stool opposite Piso, enjoying his friend's discomfiture.

'This is no laughing matter, my old friend.'

'Marriage? You? You have always maintained that marriage is for weak-minded fools who have nothing left to lose.'

'Do I look like I am joking?' Aro narrowed his eyes at the reminder of his view on marriage.

Piso shook his head slowly.

'Good, then you may wish me good fortune and join me at tonight's betrothal feast.'

'I would rather face the rocky shoals in the teeth of a gale than face marriage to a respectable Roman matron.'

'I have faced the rocks outside Corinth in one of the worst storms Neptune has thrown up and lived,' Aro said with a shrug.

'By Hermes, I thought we were paying a visit to Poseidon's nymphs that day. You saved my life and the rest of the crew with your superb navigation.' Piso held out his hand. 'See, it shakes from the memory.'

'We made it through safely. Trust me now.'

'But marriage? That is a whole other venture.'

'And what makes you believe that the gods are not with me this time?' Aro raised his cup of wine to his lips and tasted the overly sweet wine. 'They were with me then, and they have not yet deserted me.'

'If you need a woman that badly…' Piso gestured towards the barmaid who sauntered over, her thin tunic leaving little to the imagination '…why not take Flora here or use one of the higher-class houses of pleasure? What was that little matron from Baiae called? It is what you told me to do when

I made a fool of myself over that little serving girl in Athens. You remember, the one with the big eyes and the greedy fingers?'

'I have had enough mistresses. I desire a wife.' Aro banished from his thoughts how Lydia's gown had hinted at her curves, the brief glimpse of her throat and the way her lips had parted ever so slightly when his lips had brushed her hand. Physical desire had nothing to do with the reason he had made his offer. It was a business transaction. It solved several problems. Most importantly, it eliminated the need to pay for a fixer. Senator Veratius Cornelius had enough influence with the censor to ensure he would be elected to the Senate. The sparkle in Lydia's eyes was incidental.

'Why?'

'You're not a Roman.' Aro began. His hand touched the ring he wore on a chain about his neck, his father's signet ring. A ring he would not wear on his finger until he had fulfilled his sacred vow, until he had restored the honour of the Fabii.

'For that—' Piso gave a laugh '—for that, I get down on my knees and thank Hermes and the other gods every night, that they saw fit to make me Greek.'

'If I were Greek, I wouldn't have chosen this bar to drink in.' Aro regarded the various workmen, branded slaves and sailors who intermingled in the bar—the usual waterfront mob.

'We Greeks know excellent wine when we taste it, and Flora is pleasing to the eye and not too pricey on the purse.' Piso tapped the side of his nose. 'Tell me, why now? Why not earlier this year when that Roman widow was pursuing you all over Baiae? She was a patrician. What has changed?'

'Sulla's reforms are being done away with,' Aro said. 'I told you about this last Ides. The dictator's shadow was not very long.'

Piso wipe his hand across his face. 'Why do you need to be in that particular pit of snakes and schemers? You have enough money and estates as it is.'

'I vowed to regain everything Sulla unjustly took from my family and I intend to keep that promise.'

'How so? How will marrying this woman give you anything you don't have?'

'Marrying a Veratii will give me the votes I need to enter the Senate without having to resort to a fixer.' Aro tapped his cup against the table. 'Lucius Veratius Cornelius controls enough tribes to make men wary about voting against him. He has promised to support me. He wants his daughter married to a senator. When you think what the going rate for a fixer is… The loss of the gold is cheap compared to what I have gained.'

'Romans are slippery characters. There is many a man who has come to grief with a Roman woman. I would not trust them further than I could throw them.' Piso took a swig of his wine. 'Which is why I stick to barmaids and women of easy virtue. You know where you and your money stand with them.'

'I am not a seaman, facing his first voyage. I have navigated around senators before.' Aro regarded the dregs of wine in his cup, remembering the negotiations he had had with Veratius Cornelius after his daughter finally left the room. 'We drew up the contracts this afternoon. The betrothal takes place this evening, and the wedding tomorrow. I have been to see the priest. For a fee, he has agreed the auspices are excellent for tomorrow.'

'A toast to the favoured couple, then.' Piso snapped his fingers and the barmaid refilled their cups. 'I drink to your happiness, my old friend.'

Aro ignored the cup of wine. Happiness was not part of the arrangement. 'To the marriage.'

'You have taken our seats,' a gruff voice said behind Aro.

Piso started to stand up, hand on dagger. Aro gave his head a shake. He had no wish to start a fight here, in this crowd. Without turning towards the speaker, he pointed to an empty table. 'There are a few free seats over there. Why not avail yourself of them?'

'These are our seats.'

The entire bar went silent, held its breath. Aro saw Flora stop wiping the cups. Not a single dice or knucklebone was tossed.

'I wasn't aware that there were names on the stools.' Aro kept his voice steady, unconcerned. 'Piso, were you aware of such a thing?'

'No idea.'

'These are our seats.' A heavy hand went on Aro's shoulder.

Piso winced, but remained where he was. His hand shifted slightly and Aro saw him tap three fingers on the table. Three men, that was all. He had been in worse situations before. Then Piso said, 'You really shouldn't have done that.'

'I would ask you to remove your hand. It is well that I am in a good mood today. We are celebrating my betrothal. Come, share a cup of wine with us, and forget this unpleasantness.' Aro's body tensed. He would give the man another heartbeat and then he'd respond. If he reacted quickly, he could regain the advantage and Piso and he might yet walk out alive. 'There is no need for a quarrel. I am sure there is plenty of wine to go around. Flora, find these men a table and a jug of honey wine.'

'There is no place here for the scum from the Lupan House,' the low growl replied. 'This is where Ofellius's men drink.'

'I drink where I please.' Aro jabbed his elbow back. He heard a loud grunt as he connected with the man's midriff. 'Nobody tells me what I do.'

Seizing the advantage, he charged his shoulder in as he rose and lifted the man off his feet, throwing his would-be assailant's body across the table and on to the floor where Piso hit the man with a flagon of wine. His companion with a purple puckered scar halfway down his face drew a dagger and started to thrust forward, but Aro blocked him with his forearm, and the blade hit his arm purse. Aro drew back his fist and connected with the man's jaw, sending the man thundering back into the bar. An amphora crashed on to his head and the would-be assailant lay still.

Aro crouched, waiting for the next attack, but the curtain to the bar swayed. The attacker had fled. Everyone else in the bar turned back towards their drinks. Within six heartbeats, the noise of dice, knucklebones and good-natured banter once more filled the room.

'I told you, you shouldn't have done that,' Piso remarked conversationally to the now prone assailant. 'You don't want to make the Sea Wolf angry. It's not good for your long-term future. Let alone your health!'

'Shall we go?' Aro tossed two *denarii* to the barmaid. 'I have seen enough.'

'Did you get a look at the men?' Piso asked in an undertone.

'Ofellius's men. He will regret it.' Aro pressed his fingertips together and tapped his mouth. 'The question I want answered is why now, when we have been at peace for so many months? Why does he wish to restart the hostilities? There is more than enough trade for both houses.'

'Ofellius wants the respect you enjoy.' Piso stepped over the prone man and tossed a few coins to Flora.

'You really do choose the most extraordinary places to spend your time.' Aro said as they entered the street and headed back towards Aro's villa on the Aventine. 'Maybe next time, somewhere less rough, where the wine is better.'

'You could have a point there.'


Lydia straightened the folds of her pale blue gown for the fourth time. She touched her hair, now confined in the latest style: artfully cascading waves.

Beroe, the tire-woman she shared with Sulpicia, insisted the waves were much better than her more usual knot at the back of her neck, from which her hair kept escaping. Beroe had sent her out with strict instructions not to touch her curls or the wine dregs she had applied to her lips and cheeks. Lydia tried to explain Fabius Aro did not care about the looks of his bride, but Beroe objected—all men cared about *was* the figure.

She glanced about the atrium with its pool of water reflecting the light from the several strategically placed oil lamps.

The jasmine had started to release its perfumed scent, giving a whole feeling of unreality to the scene. Could she really be waiting for her bridegroom? Only this morning, she was overseeing the carding of wool and worrying about the shortage of olive oil.

A wet nose nudged her palm. Lydia reached down and stroked Korina's silky soft ear.

'Korina, I thought you were safely shut in my room. It can't be helped now. Better find out if Fabius Aro is a dog fancier or not, before the marriage. Not that it matters, but I would like to think I can take you with me.'

Lydia resisted the temptation to curl a tendril of hair around her little finger. It should not matter what sort of man he was. She had no choice. She had to fulfil her father's promise, until such time that he was able to release her and she would be able to return home, honour intact. What was it that Sulpicia proclaimed? Marriage for a patrician was not a meeting of hearts, but a meeting of purses. Love, generally, had nothing to do with it.

Lydia crossed over to the household shrine, held her hands up in supplication and offered up a prayer to the Lares and any other god that might be listening that tonight would go well and that some day she might experience the sort of marriage her mother and father had had.

Korina raised her head, and her ears perked up. Lydia put a hand on her collar to restrain her. Her stomach twisted in more knots than she thought possible.

'Easy girl.' Lydia did not know if she was speaking to the dog or herself.

The sound of unfamiliar voices and footsteps filled the

small atrium. Lydia swallowed hard and turned to face them. The time had come all too quickly.

Fabius Aro was in the lead with a crowd of men behind him. His dark hair curled slightly about his temples. Instead of a toga, he wore a richly embroidered blue tunic, and a dark cloak was thrown about his shoulders, fastened with a large gold brooch. The very picture of a successful businessman. Lydia wondered if he had deliberately decided not to wear a toga. The tunic was slightly longer than the one he had worn earlier, but did nothing to disguise his muscular calves.

A small thrill sliced through Lydia. While he was not as classically handsome as some, there was a certain quality about him, a raw sort of power. She could easily picture him commanding a ship.

'Lydia Veratia, I had expected your father to greet us,' he said quizzically.

'He is busy in the dining room.' Lydia hesitated, wondering how much he'd guessed. Her father had retired to the dining room early, with a few carafes of wine and some old friends from his gymnasium, the ones that did not have other better invitations for dining. She wondered what her mother would have thought of this. Her mother revelled in her reputation as a gracious hostess. 'Shall I send word for him?'

She motioned to Gallus, who bowed low before disappearing into the villa. Aro stood there, flanked by his men—none of whom made a sound. Lydia resisted the temptation to fiddle with her hair as the silence between them grew. What did one say to one's nearly betrothed?

Korina had no such hesitation and nudged his hand, demanding attention. Lydia lunged forward, made a grab for Korina's collar, but encountered Aro's warm fingers instead. She jumped backwards as if they had burnt her. Aro's eyes flashed. He reached down and patted Korina on the head.

'She has the lines of a good hunting dog,' he said. 'Is she yours?'

'She comes from good stock.' Relief flooded through her. They could stay on safe subjects. 'Senator Gracchus bred her. But she has never hunted. I have had her as a companion since she was a puppy.'

Lydia watched the black curls on the top of his head as he fondled the dog's ears. Korina, the slave to affection that she was, turned over on her back and wriggled, inviting him to stroke her tummy. He knelt down.

'Then you shall not be parted from her.' A smile tugged at his mouth as he straightened, brushing his hands against his tunic. 'I remember greyhounds from my youth. Loyal and faithful creatures. We had several, but they were lost when we left Rome.'

'Did you live elsewhere?'

'Is your father coming out to greet us?'

Lydia frowned. Out of the corner of her eye, she saw Gallus return, but her father had not yet emerged. She couldn't keep Aro standing here like some errand boy. 'Several close friends from the Senate and a number of my father's clients arrived early to celebrate the betrothal. Undoubtedly, one has detained him. Shall we join them in the dining room? The cook does a very good lark's tongue.'

'I regret, no. There is much to be done. I want my ships to be ready to make the next tide after the wedding.' He inclined his head. 'Arranging to be married was not on my agenda for today.'

'Nor mine.'

She lifted her eyes and met his gaze. There was something dark and unfathomable about his eyes that seemed to peer deep within her soul. With an effort she turned her gaze towards the atrium's pool and the reflection of the dancing oil flames.

There was a great shout of laughter and her father emerged, his scarlet dining tunic slightly askew. He made an elaborate bow towards Aro. Then they exchanged pleasantries. Lydia started to twist her hair, but remembered what Beroe had said and instead pressed her palms together. Her slight hope that the contract was not settled was dashed when her father started to say the ritual words, demanding the bride price. Lydia cheeks grew warm. Would either of them admit what she was bought for?

'I have brought the *arra,* the symbol of your bride price.' Aro reached out, captured her hand and placed a gold-and-iron ring on her fourth finger.

An augur moved forward from the men who accompanied him and recited the words, making the betrothal official.

The ring weighed heavy on her finger, but Lydia made no attempt to pull away.

Aro bent his head and his lips brushed hers for the traditional betrothal kiss, the acceptance that he would now have rights over her body. The touch was feather-like, but it did strange things to her insides, made her wonder what would it be like to be kissed for real by this man. She risked a glance upwards and saw that his gaze fastened strictly ahead on the augur, not her.

Then with a few more words from the augur, the ceremony
was over. Her father turned his back and disappeared into the
dining room again. Shouts and laughter drifted out on the
evening breeze.

Lydia regarded her left hand and the iron and gold that now
encircled her fourth finger. Her *arra,* the symbol of the money
Aro had paid for her. This was no midnight fancy brought by
Furies. The weight of the ring made it a reality. She had
started off down a path and had no idea where the end might
be.

'And what day has the augur set for the ceremony?' she
asked around the lump in her throat.

'Tomorrow afternoon. The auspices are good.' He lifted
an eyebrow in surprise as if she should know the answer. 'I
have little time and need to attend to the loading of cargo in
the morning.'

'So soon?' Lydia's knees threatened to give way. She had
thought she'd have some time to prepare herself for the
marriage, perhaps even buy the time her father needed to find
the gold. She should have known her father's escape from the
house had hidden meanings. Why hadn't he warned her? She
looked up into Aro's face. 'Tomorrow is tomorrow.'

'Your father agreed.' There was no softening of his
features. The planes of his face were hard, and his eyes reflected the golden light of the oil lamp. 'The estate in northern
Italy is to be your dowry.'

'It was my mother's.'

He laid a hand on her upper arm and heat radiated from
it, filling her icy-cold body with warmth. It bothered Lydia
that she should desire his touch. His thumb stroked along the

line of her jaw, sending tingles throughout her body. His amber eyes held a thoughtful expression.

'You need not worry. My fortune is vast enough that I won't pilfer your dowry. You will be able to bequeath it to our children.'

Lydia stared at Aro, uncomprehending for a heartbeat.

'I had never considered children.' Lydia strove for a calm voice. Children? She had never even thought about the possibility. The very idea made her throat tighten. He meant this to be a marriage in the fullest sense.

'Those are my terms.' The warmth in his eyes disappeared. He crossed his arms over his chest. 'Unless, of course, you have the gold to pay for my Falerian wine.'

'I…I…'

'Why did you offer to marry me, Lydia?' His voice was low, lazy and flowed over her like warm honey. 'Your father did not wish it.'

'There was no other solution. I sold the wine and used the gold.' Lydia spoke to his sandals. How could she explain her impulse? How could this sea captain, who was little better than a pirate, understand her need to protect her family's honour? 'I had to do something.'

'You intended it to be a ploy, didn't you?' His fingers gripped her chin, forced her face upwards so the full glare of his golden eyes could search her face. 'Something to buy your father time to raise the gold. Many men have tried to cheat me and have failed.'

'I don't shy away from my responsibilities. I have given my word. It is simply that I had expected more time. It takes days to get the bridal clothes ready.' The excuse sounded weak and feeble to her ears.

'You were married before, your father informs me,' he said. Gone was the gentle persuasion, and in its place an un-compromising tone. 'Your bridal clothes are packed in a trunk, or so your father says. There is no reason that your father knows of why we cannot be married immediately.'

'My father has told you many things.' Lydia plucked at the skirt of her gown. They must have discussed the date during the negotiations. She wished she had chosen a less obvious reason. A betrothal could be broken without too much diffi-culty, but a marriage—that was something else again.

Her mind refused to work. She had run out of excuses. This man appeared to have out-manoeuvred her every step of the way. She'd have to agree and throw herself on the mercy of the gods—not that they had shown any mercy so far.

'I will make you a good wife, Fabius Aro. I will abide by our bargain.'

His eyes travelled up and down her gown, lingering on the swell of her breasts. The heat in Lydia's cheek grew. His lips drew upwards. 'Yes, Lydia. You will.'

# Chapter Four

Lydia's hand touched the unfamiliar weight of her bridal headdress. It was hard to think that the Vestal Virgins wore the six padded hairpieces every day of their lives. The weight made her headache worse as she left the temple of Venus and started back towards her father's house. She had lingered as long as she dared at the temple, asking the goddess for her blessing on her future and the impending wedding, but secretly hoping for a miracle, a solution to their problem.

The goddess remained silent.

Last night her dreams had been filled with men who had turned into snarling ravenous wolves and back again. And gold spilling from wine amphorae, but, whenever she tried to touch it, it vanished. Her hair plastered to her forehead, sheets damp with sweat, she had woken to the chorus of cockerels crowing.

Dawn on her wedding morning. The whole house bustled with activity and she had not been able to draw a breath. Everyone had a question or a problem she had to solve. Then her father appeared, accusing her of being late for the procession to the temple.

The metal collar felt sticky around her neck and the veil of flaming orange kept blowing into her mouth. The scent of sweet verbena and myrtle from the bridal wreath did nothing to calm her nerves. She paid no attention to the curious gazes of the onlookers, but kept her eyes demurely downwards as befitted a bride of the Veratii. She would not give any cause to gossip about her in the Forum or to speak against the family.

She could do this. She tried to tell herself it was no different than when she married Titus, but she knew she lied. Then, she had faced the marriage with, if not happiness, at least contentment. She had known Titus since childhood. Even then, after the marriage, for those few days they were together before he left on that ill-fated voyage with her father, he changed, became proud and autocratic, instead of the submissive boy she had bossed about when they were growing up.

Her fingers twisted the iron-and-gold ring that encircled the fourth finger of her left hand.

Fabius Aro was something else entirely, if Sulpicia's lurid tales were to be believed. How he battled Neptune's fury and won. How even the sea obeyed him for fear of his temper. If Titus had become arrogant and disregarded her counsel, she hated to think what Aro would be, what he already was.

But Titus's touch had never made her feel alive in the same way as Aro's had last might. The memory of his mouth touching her lips last night and the gentle pressure of his arms sent a pulse of warmth through her.

She stumbled on a cobblestone and her father's firm grip

on her elbow tightened, guiding her towards the smoother part of the street.

'Child, I hope you will remember me and your former home,' her father said in a quavering voice as they approached the villa. 'Visit me when your husband permits. Keep our family business our own. Promise that.'

'I promise.'

'Thank you, my daughter.' He pressed her hand to his withered cheek, held it there. A glimmer of tears shone in his eyes. 'You will always be a true daughter of my house.'

The back of Lydia's neck prickled.

What exactly was her father hinting at? What hadn't he told her? How like her father to make a seemingly casual remark and expect her to continue on as if nothing had happened.

She had to know the whole truth.

'Father, I am marrying *sine manu,*' she said, with an uneasy laugh. 'You will retain legal control over me. I will be able to visit whenever I wish and I will wish to do so often, have no fear of that. Aro will have no say over me.'

'Hush, child. Do not make much of a little thing. I have no doubt your new husband will be a reasonable man. He does want the connection to the Veratii after all.'

Veratius Cornelius patted her arm, but his eyes sidled away from her. Lydia bit her lip. Her father had not answered the question. Her father and her brother shared the trait of wishing to avoid any unpleasantness. She had lost track of the times she had sorted out creditors simply because one or the other had been unavailable. Was this another one of those times?

'Father, what do you mean—my husband is a reasonable man?' Her voice trembled on the last word.

'This is no time for such talk, child. See, your bridegroom and his entourage arrives. Show me, you of Veratii blood, how we rise above such things.'

She looked where her father pointed. Her breath caught in her throat. She had expected Fabius Aro to wear a tunic again, but he was dressed in a toga of such fine linen that it could be netting as it moulded to his muscular body, accentuating rather than concealing. The brilliant white highlighted his golden skin, his black hair and his unfathomable eyes, which seemed to be flecked golden. A wolf was a good description for him. Powerful and untamed.

He strode towards them, flanked by his witnesses, four of whom were white-haired senators, resplendent in the togas with broad purple stripes around the hems. Lydia stared, open-mouthed for a heartbeat, and then snapped her lips together.

She watched her father puff with pride as he glimpsed the men. He dropped her arm and hurried to greet them.

'Forgive the lateness, Fabius Aro.' Her father made a sketch of a bow. 'You know how these women will dawdle at Venus's temple. My daughter wanted to make one more sacrifice.'

'The wait was worth it.' His eyes held more gold flecks than ever. 'The bride brings joy to us all.'

The heat rose on Lydia's cheeks as she echoed her father's words of welcome. Her hand tingled in remembrance of the brief brush of his lips. A mutual attraction was a pleasant addition to a marriage, or so her old nurse used say with great solemnity.

The very thought acted like icy water. This was not a marriage of two hearts, the sort of marriage her parents had enjoyed. This was a political marriage, one which she had entered to save her father's dignity. One she'd stay in as long as her father deemed it necessary and not a drip on the water-clock longer. She would remain as she always had been—a dutiful daughter.

'Shall we get the ceremony started?' she asked, keeping her voice cool, and her gaze away from Aro. Emotion would have no place in this marriage. It was a simple business trans-action. A wife instead of wine. 'There is little point in delaying the ceremony if everyone has arrived. Where is the auspex?'

'He travelled with my party.' Aro indicated a tall thin man dressed in priestly robes. 'His predictions are generally con-sidered accurate.'

A murmuring of agreement rose from the assembled senators as the priest came forward. Lydia saw her father readjust his toga and stand straighter. His face took the expression he saved for consuls or people's tribunes, men he considered his equals.

'The atrium is the best place for the ceremony, away from the public view. We are beginning to gather a crowd.' Her father licked his lips. 'It has been a long time since I have welcomed such a distinguished priest into the house.'

'Lydia,' Sulpicia whispered as Lydia was escorted into the atrium, and the large gate to the compound banged shut, 'how did Fabius Aro achieve it? That man is the assistant to the Pontifax Maximus. It is almost as if you are to be married with the *conferreatio,* almost as if it were a com-pletely patrician marriage.'

'Money can buy many things, Sulpicia,' Lydia replied with

an ease she did not feel. She watched Sulpicia flush slightly, and then hurry over to the auspex.

Lydia drew a deep breath and tried to contain the war elephants that had taken up residence in her stomach. The choice of this priest and the witnesses gave the impression that this had been planned for a long time.

A pig was led in and the ritual began. Lydia watched with bated breath. Half-hoping, half-fearing the auspex would not find the entrails favourable, and all the while aware of the man standing next to her, his toga brushing her gown. His eyes were straight ahead, his face uncompromising.

As soon as the pig's entrails were revealed, the auspex proclaimed the omens favourable and the gods well pleased. The marriage could proceed with their blessings. The crowd gave a rousing cheer.

'You must be pleased, the gods have blessed this marriage,' she murmured to Aro.

'Pleased?' He lifted an eyebrow. 'It was no more than I expected. Some things are too important to be left to chance.'

Lydia's mouth framed an O and then the witnesses crowded around, preventing her from questioning Aro further.

Just as quickly the contracts were exchanged and the ten seals placed on them, signifying it had been duly witnessed. Lydia peered over her father's shoulder and saw the Quintus Fabius Aro. Three names. She glanced again at Aro, standing there, hand over his heart, looking for all the world like a senator or a people's tribune rather than the simple sea captain she knew him to be.

Had she made a mistake? Was there more to this man? Exactly what was his parentage?

All the senators Aro had brought were former sympathis-ers with Marius, the man who had fought and lost to Sulla, men her father rarely dealt with. Early on in the civil war, he had backed Sulla, and the family fortunes had grown, but her father owed Sulla a life-debt from when they had served as young tribunes. He had never asked for Sulla's favours.

A sneaking dread filled Lydia. There was more to Quintus Fabius Aro than she had first assumed. This marriage had happened fast, much too fast. She pressed the fingertips of her hands together.

'Father—'

'Child, will you not learn to be quiet? You nearly inter-rupted the auspex.'

Before she had time to question or consider further, the augur started the next and final part of the ceremony, the joining of hands. Lydia tried to ignore the growing pit in her stomach. Her father knew something, something that he wanted to hide from her until the last possible heartbeat.

Lydia shook her head, trying to keep a tight rein on her fear.

This part of the ceremony was all a formality, a vestige of long-ago times. Aro would graciously decline her father's offer of her hand. She would remain under her father's control.

It was the way things were. Her earlier fears were products of an over-active imagination. She would conduct herself with the dignity required of a woman from one of the premier families in Rome.

'I, Lucius Veratius Cornelius, do give my daughter's, Lydia Veratia's, hand to you, Quintus Fabius Aro, from this day forth.'

'I accept the honour you do me.'

Her father placed Lydia's hand in Aro's and he took it.

Lydia stared at the warm hand covering hers and back at her father. She noted the small things: the veil blowing against her mouth, the pinch of her sandal strap. Everything and nothing as Fabius Aro completed the ritual. At first she thought she had misheard her father's words. She had to have. Things like this never happened in today's Rome. But then she glanced to her left and saw Sulpicia's shocked expression and knew she hadn't.

He had done it.

Her father had done the unthinkable.

He had married her to Aro, to the Sea Wolf, *cum manu*, with hand. And the Sea Wolf had accepted it.

How could he have done such a thing? How could her father let this happen, without telling her, without giving her any opportunity to protest?

She wanted to cry out, to protest, but no sound came from her throat. Already, the auspex was wrapping the cloth around their hands, instead of placing it over her head. The deed was done. She was no longer one of the Veratii.

All her property, everything ceased to be under her father's benevolent gaze and belonged to her husband.

There was a collective intake of breath from the onlookers. Her father stood, eyes to the front, no expression on his face. Already he had taken the ritual step backwards, relinquishing control. Her father had known about the type of marriage and had avoided her questioning. He had deceived her as surely as Ulysses deceived the Cyclops.

'Father,' she whispered, halting his movement.

'I had no choice, daughter, but you must trust me and my judgement. I will do what I can.' Her father's hand squeezed her elbow before he took a step backwards. 'Make me proud.'

Aro gave no indication that he had seen anything amiss. His smooth voice recited after the auspex. 'I pledge to look after your daughter with my life. *Ubi tu Lydia Fabia, ego Quintus Fabius Aro.*'

'And now, Lydia,' the auspex said, his dark gaze piercing her. 'It is your turn. Repeat after me. *Ubi tu...*'

Lydia struggled to say the words around the lump in her throat. But she had to, she had no choice. To refuse now would be to shame her father in front of these senators and she was certain Aro would not hesitate to claim the gold they owed him, and the true state of their indebtedness would become known. Aro would be within his rights to insist everything be sold to pay the debt. None of her father's friends would lift a finger; instead, they would behave in the same manner as carrion crows. They would try to acquire as much as they could as cheaply as possible, while mouthing sympathetic pieties. She had seen the situation played out too many times in recent years.

No, she had no choice at all.

In order to save her father and his reputation, she had to give up being part of her father's family and become part of her husband's family. She would not have the right to divorce him, or to leave him. By giving her 'with hand', her father had taken away that right.

Lydia started to speak the ritual words and gave a small squeak on *'ubi'*. She stopped, closed her eyes and concentrated on not allowing her voice to tremble. She refused to

shame her family. She had to be strong and confident. She
opened her eyes and stared directly into Aro's eyes, eyes like
hard lumps of amber. No sound emerged from her mouth.

Her father's elbow nudged her in the back. She started again.

'*Ubi tu Quintus Fabius Aro, ego Lydia Fabia.*'

'You are now man and wife, *cum manu,*' the auspex pronounced. 'You may kiss the bride.'

Lydia dutifully lifted her mouth, expecting the brief brush
of lips, a repeat of yesterday's performance. Hard arms drew
her to Aro's unyielding chest and his mouth swooped down,
taking what had become his by right. His lips captured hers,
plundered and held them. Sensation filled her body. She gave
to the pressure and opened her mouth, tasting his. Everything
ceased to matter but the kiss.

As suddenly as it began, it was over. His arms fell away,
and Lydia was left gasping for breath. A knowing smile
played on his lips. Lydia's limbs trembled and she struggled
to straighten the flaming orange veil that had become skewed
during the kiss. No one, not even Titus, had kissed her like
that before. And certainly never in front of a crowd.

The cheers of 'felicitations' and 'kiss the bride', along
with other cruder remarks, rose from the assembled throng.
Her cheeks burnt as brightly as Jupiter Maximus's golden
roof at sunset and she was glad the veil provided some protection from onlookers. She cast a sideways glance at Aro.
He gave a short satisfied nod. With a start, she realised the
crowd was behaving just how he wanted them to. Instead of
focusing on the unusually old-fashioned nature of the
marriage, they were now intent on the passionate kiss.

Lydia's insides wriggled as the comments grew louder. Aro

put an arm about her waist. She saw several people speaking behind their hands. It was all too easy to guess what they would be saying with knowing nods and furious whispers.

'Why did you do that?' she asked Aro in an undertone.

His eyes twinkled and he wore an unrepentant look on his face. 'Do what? Isn't a man allowed to kiss his bride on their wedding day?'

'You made it seem like…like we were already intimate.'

'And?'

'Tomorrow at the baths, my waist will be inspected to see if I am breeding,' Lydia voiced her fears. 'Between the auspex, the senators and now the kiss, no one will believe that this marriage was hastily arranged. No doubt rumours have already reached the Forum.'

'People will say what they will. The truth hardly matters. It is what people believe. I learnt that lesson a long time ago.' He gave a little shrug, but failed to remove his hand. Lydia felt the warmth radiate outwards from where his hand touched her waist. 'We are married, legitimately, and no one can whisper there are other reasons for the marriage.'

'But it is not the truth.'

His hand abruptly dropped, leaving cold air to encircle where his palm had rested.

'Would you rather they whispered your father has money difficulties?' he asked in a harsh voice. 'That he sold his only daughter for a cargo of wine?'

Lydia looked down at the chipped mosaic floor and didn't answer.

'Would you rather he was held up to ridicule and lose his senatorial dignity? It can be arranged, I assure you.'

There was no mistaking the determination in Aro's voice. Lydia jerked her head upwards.

'No, but—'

'Let the curious and the gossipmongers inspect your waist. It is quite slender. I can almost join my two hands about it.' He demonstrated.

Lydia kept her body stiff and tried to ignore the spreading warmth. In another heartbeat, she'd beg for the touch of his lips again. She wanted the treacherous warmth to leave her. He had to understand that any good will had been lost when he had married her in that fashion.

'It is not what I expected.'

'What did you expect?'

Lydia rubbed the back of her neck. The question caused her to pause, to consider. She had to think, but her thoughts kept circling back to the kiss. 'I expected things to be as they normally are—for people to behave with proper dignity.'

'You're saying you didn't like the kiss.' He ran a thumb along the edge of her jaw. His voice lowered to a husky whisper. 'Or are you asking for another demonstration?'

He had deliberately misunderstood her!

'Another demonstration of what? Your prowess with women? I will take your word for it. I am not one of your bored women from Baiae!' She started to swish her skirt away. She found it impossible to determine if she was more annoyed at him for kissing her that way in public or at her body for responding to his touch. She ran her tongue experimentally over her full lips. 'The banquet has started. You have no idea how hard it was to find enough fattened dormice and good quality figs on such short notice…'

His fingers caught her arm, forced her to face him. His dark eyes searched hers. 'There is more to this than misplaced outrage at a kiss. I would never describe you as a woman of Baiae. You are nothing like them.'

Lydia dropped her gaze to the mosaic and concentrated on the missing tile from the dolphin's fin. She owed him some sort of explanation, but to do so here would be to invite more gossip. If someone overheard, all the good this marriage had done her father would be lost.

Already, well-wishers were advancing towards them, hands outstretched, faces wreathed in smiles. For now she'd hold her tongue, but she intended to discover why he had married her in such a fashion.

Lydia moved her elbow and he released her. A temporary reprieve. The Fates had tangled her thread very nicely. All the familiar routines and rituals of her existence ended. No longer could she look to her father, the man who had raised her and who held her best interests close to his heart as her guardian against the world. Her life now depended on a man she barely knew, a man with a reputation for a fearsome temper. A man whose intentions she could not guess.

'Guests are arriving for the feast. We will speak of this later,' she said with quiet determination.

'As you desire, but you will find that I do not intend to be cheated.' He made a bow and turned to greet a well-wisher.

## Chapter Five

Aro glanced at the blood-red sun sinking slowly over the Capitoline. The time had come to start the next part of the ceremony. Only the bones of the roast pig and three amphorae of muslum wine were left. All it remained for him to do was to collect his errant bride and take her to his house. The three boys who would lead the procession were there along with the flute players. In keeping with tradition, he had chosen three boys whose parents were alive, sons of his seamen rather than hired boys. He had no wish for anyone to say that things were not done properly. No one would have cause to challenge this marriage.

He spotted Lydia's orange veil first. She was chatting to a heavily pregnant woman underneath a faded fresco of olive trees and doves. He briefly closed his eyes, remembering another time in this city when two women had gossiped and he had played about on the mosaic floor with his toys. All too soon the peaceful idyll had ended, and his family had been driven from their house, forced to run for their very lives. And one of the men chiefly responsible, if his father's ex-slave could be believed, was his new wife's grandfather. There was a certain irony in that.

He had vowed to his mother and father as they lay dying of fever that he'd return in triumph. Today was the start of that triumph.

'Aro,' he heard Piso's low tone calling him back from his memories. He frowned, annoyed that memory should have such a strong pull on him that he had forgotten where he was and what his purpose was.

The light tinkle of laughter rose like the sweet sound of a westward wind over the company. Lydia. Her gentle laugh sounded again as her greyhound caught a bone in mid-air. She was a puzzle, his wife. He had felt the passion rise in her when they kissed, but then she berated him. He stroked his chin, watching her throw the bone a third time. Perhaps her former husband had been rough with her. Perhaps some misguided person had whispered stories in her ear. He wanted his wife to be an equal participant in his bed, not a woman who feared coupling. He did not hold with the notion that a Roman matron should be rigid in bed, or else she was a lady of the night. That would bring no pleasure for either of them. When they coupled, she would respond and experience joy.

'Fabius Aro,' Piso's voice came again, with more urgency and Aro drew his attention away from his bride.

'Yes, I know we need to depart. We need to get the ceremony finished.' Aro shook his head. 'The auspex has had his ear bent by that many people, requesting his opinion on the future. You are quite right. The time has come to start for home.'

'No, over there. Our most recent arrivals.' Piso nodded towards a group of men. 'Ofellius and his henchmen. Come specially to give a rousing send-off to the new bride and groom. Did you invite them, boss, or shall we give them the sort of welcome they gave us?'

The leader of the group stopped in the middle of the atrium, a smirk on his face and a swagger to his step. Just behind him were the two men who had attacked Aro in the wine shop, sporting bruises. Aro was pleased to see how gingerly they had to walk. The next time, they would respect his right to drink unmolested.

After he had paid his compliments to Cornelius, Ofellius turned towards Aro and flicked his fingers under his double chin. The insult was unmistakable and provocative. Piso gave a low growl in the back of his throat and started forward.

Aro caught Piso's tunic, held him in place. He forced a smile on to his lips. There would be no unprovoked attacks on his wedding day. He refused to allow it, but neither did he intend to let the insult pass. The question was where and when to strike.

'No, it is only a gesture,' Aro remarked with slow deliberation. 'I have no wish for my wedding day to be bathed in blood.'

'But you know what he did. What he is. After what his men did yesterday. He started the violence again. After you both gave your solemn pledge less than six months ago. I told you—you should have denounced him to Pompey as the slave trader he is.'

'He *attempted* to start a fight.' Aro ignored the pulling pain every time he moved his shoulder. His toga hid the worst of the purple bruising on his arm. 'I doubt Ofellius will try that again. See, the bruises they sport. It was a simple misunderstanding over the right to drink in a tavern. Do not make it into anything else. The peace holds. It is good for business, good for the Lupan House and good for Rome. It is as true now as six months ago.'

'Yes, but—'

'He didn't succeed last March and he won't succeed now,' Aro replied, his eyes following Ofellius's every move. 'This is a wedding, not the deck of a ship nor the inside of a run-down wine shop in one of the alleyways near the Forum. Ofellius does posses a small amount of intelligence.'

'But why didn't Pompey crucify him?' Piso's hand rested on the hilt of his dagger. 'His reputation is notorious. You personally freed those Roman soldiers.'

'Friends in high places, Piso.' Aro watched Ofellius take a cup of wine and toast Lydia and her father. Several senators joined in the toast. Aro derived a certain amount of satisfaction that two other senators, senators with whom he had a good working relationship, refused to join in. 'Those friends will not protect him for ever. See, already several look uncomfortable. If he makes one mistake, tries to take one thing that belongs to me that I can prove in a court of law, all previous agreements will cease. And it will be war between the houses, but not today. Today I am in a forgiving mood.'

'You're in charge.' Piso pulled away from Aro and straightened his tunic, but his eyes were mutinous.

'Good, now enjoy the wedding feast.' Aro clapped him on the shoulder. 'I understand Veratius Cornelius has access to some rather excellent wine. Make sure some of our guests are offered it. I want them to drink deeply to my marriage. Weddings are times of happiness, not for settling old scores.'

'I understand you.' Piso grasped Aro's wrist. 'But for Poseidon's sake, be careful. You mean too much to the sailors.'

'It is my wedding day, Piso. The gods of the Capitoline have blessed this marriage. I shall be safe.'

Aro clapped Piso on the back and advanced towards the late arrivals. The sea of people parted and allowed him easy passage. The room fell silent as if waiting for a signal from him. All eyes were on him. Aro knew his actions would have far more consequences beyond a simple greeting of two rival traders. It had to be correct.

'It is good of you to come, Ofellius, and partake of my wedding day feast' he said, standing in front of Ofellius with his feet apart, arms crossed. The noise in the room grew again, as people turned back to their abandoned conversations. 'It has been a long while since we last met.'

'Ah, yes, I recall.' The pirate dipped his head slightly. 'You were having a bit of difficulty with the sea. Your ship had taken on water.'

'Nothing I could not handle.' Aro permitted his smile to grow wider. 'The sea and I are brothers. My cargo of olive oil and wine was safely delivered to Corinth. A profitable voyage.'

'And now you are married. To a Veratii. Quite a rise from a sailor with barely *denarii* to his name.'

'Some are born lucky.'

Ofellius leant forward and tapped the side of his nose.

'The whisper is you were caught in her bed, and that is the only reason why her father permitted the marriage.'

'The whisper is that you are a pirate who indulges in slave trade and your powerful friends in the Senate are about to fall.' Aro paused, beginning to enjoy himself as Ofellius's nostrils flared. 'Dangerous things, rumours.'

'Quite.' Ofellius wiped his forehead with the corner of his cloak.

'Now, if you will excuse me, it is time for my bride and me to depart to our new home. Your men are welcome to join in the festivities if they come as friends.'

'You would do well to remember our agreement has proved beneficial…to both us and our men. I would hate for anything to disrupt it,' Ofellius called after him.

Aro halted, forced the air into his lungs. Once he would have acted without thinking, but not here, not with half the biggest gossips in the Senate looking on. Nothing must interfere with the good omens of the day. He had to be enrolled in the Senate when the censors next met. It was what he had worked for.

'Our agreement, such as it was, was violated when your men attacked me without warning. No more assaults, was that not what we agreed?'

'My men made a mistake. They swear to me that they did not recognise you in the darkness of that drinking hole.'

'They had best contain their excitement. They are at a wedding.'

Ofellius sucked his lips. 'They were punished. They have made a sacrifice to Mercury. You will receive your compensation from the priests.'

'I refuse to have Lydia frightened. The agreement must be extended.'

Ofellius dusted a speck off his cloak. 'Why are these bridegrooms always so hot-tempered about their wives? I was speaking of business, not of women, of cargoes, not soft sighs. As for wine shops, can I help it if my men like to drink free from the smell of the docks?'

Aro's fingers itched to draw his dagger, but to do so would be to play into his rival's hands. The whisper would reach the Forum in no time of his temper, and subtly the contracts would be withdrawn. The censors would discover a reason to deny him. Aro forced his fingers to ease. 'I noticed a distinct improvement in the stench once your followers departed.'

'The incident will not be repeated.'

'Next time, they should know who they are attacking.' Aro held his gaze steady.

'It does make me wonder if you would stoop so low as to marry to ensure trade. You have often proclaimed the need to stay unencumbered.' Ofellius leant forward. 'Tell me, Aro, how is business? I hear you are having trouble delivering some promised wine.'

'As I said, one mustn't believe rumours.'

'I have some Falerian wine, if you find yourself short. Acquired at an excellent price, I might add.' He clapped his hands. 'Here, I brought some as a wedding present. An exceptionally fine vintage.'

'So I am given to understand.' Aro turned his back on his business rival. He also ignored Piso's amused grin.

'I believe we have discovered the mysterious purchaser of the Falerian wine.' He patted his purse. 'I believe my purse should be several *denarii* heavier by this time tomorrow, old friend,' he said, referring to their bet.

Aro regarded Lydia, laughing with her friends and relations. Why had she sold the wine to that pirate whose reputation was such that no honest man would deal with him?

Aro watched Ofellius walk over and present his compliments to Lydia with a flourishing bow. Lydia said something and Aro saw the large man frown, his hand start towards his dagger.

Quickly Aro stepped forward, reaching her side before Ofellius drew his next breath. 'Is there some problem, Lydia?' he asked, keeping his eyes on Ofellius, daring him to try something.

'Not a problem,' Lydia said stiffly, but her eyes blazed. 'Merely a question about *liquamen.*'

'Your wife has the heart of a man.' Ofellius gave a hearty laugh. 'There are not many who would dare question me. And on her wedding day no less.'

'Lydia?' A muscle jumped in Aro's cheek. He placed a hand on the back of her chair. His fingers lightly touched the back of her neck. He could feel the tension in her muscles. A wave of protectiveness surged through him. Lydia was his wife and he would not have her facing Ofellius on her own. He would not expose her as her father and brother seemed to have done to such men. 'Is there something I can help you with?'

'It is nothing, merely an old settling of accounts. Something to do with my old life.' Lydia's smile brightened. 'I believe it is time we departed.'

'We will discuss this…settling of accounts later,' Aro said through gritted teeth. Nothing was going to spoil the final part of the ceremony. He would have no man or woman claiming this marriage was not blessed by the gods. He had come too far in his quest to be denied.

'There is nothing to discuss.' Her eyes blazed at him. 'As I said, it was old business, family business.'

Aro gritted his teeth until his jaw hurt. It angered him that she should cling to her old family and consort with his sworn enemy.

'You belong to my family now. Any business you had with this man is past.'

'Aro.' Ofellius leant towards him, his garlic-tinged breath near Aro's ear. 'I shall look forward to seeing the dance your lady wife will lead you.'

Aro lifted his eyebrow. 'It will be me who does the leading in my house.'


'Kiss the bride.'

Lydia attempted to ignore the singing and shouting that accompanied the procession as it wound its way from the lower slopes of the Palatine across the Circus Maximus and up into the Aventine district, past the firmly shut market stalls and shops. The crowds had been much sparser when she married Titus. But this time she had married the head of the most important trading house in Rome, and it appeared as if half the Palatine and the entire Aventine were there.

As they reached the crest of the Aventine hill, she gave one last glance over her shoulder towards the marbled villas and lush gardens of the Palatine, but her father's house had long since disappeared from view. Her father had stayed at the villa, but Sulpicia as her matron of honour followed a few steps behind her. Lydia tried to step on the uneven cobblestones with a firm tread and her head held high.

Her old life was finished and her new one had not yet

begun. She existed as a statue might, not having any real life of her own. Lydia blinked quickly and tried to tell herself that her thoughts were ridiculous.

She was the same person, no matter which family she belonged to. Veratii blood ran in her veins, not Fabii, despite the words she had been forced to utter during the marriage ceremony.

In the golden glow of the torchlight, she could see Aro rolling nuts towards the children who lined the route to ensure a fertile marriage. He smiled and joked with a few of the crowd, pausing to beckon to a shy child and place the nut in the child's hand. His only reward was a huge beaming grin before the child raced off to join others in a game of pick up the nuts. Aro gave a satisfied smile and continued on.

What sort of man was he? The Sea Wolf of Sulpicia's stories? Or a man with a generous heart?

On this procession, she saw his little kindnesses and jovial side. But when he and Ofellius had confronted each other in the atrium, she'd feared there would be bloodshed, that her wedding day would be marred. Thankfully, nothing had come of it.

She had been tempted to confide about the missing shipment of fish sauce, and Ofellius's less than useful response, but he had not given her a chance. Her lips twisted. No doubt, he would have repeated the advice he had given back in the study, and would have laughed at her for making the mistake. She did not intend to give him any opportunities to ridicule her like Titus had done.

Aro's laughter rang out as he replied to a particularly vulgar comment from one of the crowd. The chant was taken up and repeated by a number of sailors. Lydia's cheek burned and she was glad she was wearing the veil. The image the remark conjured up in her mind of bodies entwined was hard to dispel.

'At last, the house.' Aro gestured towards a townhouse, perched on the top of the Aventine hill, far away from the slum that occupied the lower slopes. A light breeze blew and the scent of pine wafted in front of Lydia. 'Not much, but it will do.'

'It is more than adequate. It's beautiful.' Lydia regarded the tastefully proportioned building with its large black oak door standing open, a pool of warm light beckoning her in.

A white cloth covered in green laurel leaves mixed with juniper was laid at the entrance. Aro's arms lifted Lydia up before she had a chance to protest. She was held close to his chest and his heart thumped in her ears as he cleared the greenery with one giant step.

His arms held her for another heartbeat, strong and warm. Her throat constricted around a sudden unexpected blockage. Against all reason, she felt safe in those arms. Then they loosened and she was set on to the black-and-white marbled floor.

Lydia made a show of straightening her robes. Her mouth and throat were parched. She could do nothing but watch Aro and try to keep her mind away from the bedding with a man she barely knew.

A long betrothal had preceded her marriage to Titus, so she had known what to expect. She had lived with Titus's mother and father for a while. Titus had been more like a younger brother or a companion. His touch had never made her feel the way Aro's touch had done.

Beyond Sulpicia's lurid stories and the brief glimpses she had seen of Aro, she knew nothing of him as a person or how he treated women. If Titus had changed so drastically, what about Aro? Would he become the snarling wolf of her dream?

'Have you caught your breath?' His low voice rumbled in her ear. 'My household wishes to welcome you with the traditional gifts.'

Lydia gazed through the orange veil, waiting for the fire and water to be presented to her. Everything about the villa exuded great wealth. She had heard of the fabulous wealth of the merchants, but had not quite believed it. She believed it now. There would be no need for strategically placed oil lamps. No charcoal brazier mark was on the marble tiles and the frescoes were of a deeper hue than she had seen before except in Crassus's villa and his wealth was legendary.

'May the fire always burn bright on the hearth and the water flow freely with you as mistress of this house.' Aro indicated the lamp and the basin of water. 'Make my house a home, Lydia.'

'That task will be my duty as well as my pleasure.' Lydia forced the words from her mouth on the third attempt. She wanted to believe he meant the words, but his eyes appeared glacial. She placed her fingertips briefly on each of the offerings, then stepped back as custom demanded.

'Behold your new mistress.' Aro drew back her veil. 'Obey her as you would me.'

The assembled servants bowed low and murmured appreciative noise, but Lydia thought she detected fear in their eyes. With a start she also realised that not one was a woman. Because she had left Beroe with Sulpicia, she would be a

woman in a house of men. She lifted her chin and stared
at them.

'I will do my best to be a good mistress, to be a Roman
matron in the tradition of the old tales.'

A softening of his eyes to warm amber showed she had
used the correct words.

'I am sure you will. And it is time we finish the public
ceremony.' His warm fingers touched her elbow and guided
her forwards towards the next part of the ceremony—the
formal putting to bed in the bridal chamber. Sulpicia and the
other guests would depart and she'd be alone with Fabius Aro.

A fake bed, with effigies of a bride and groom, had been
set up in the atrium to keep the evil spirits away from the
marital chamber. Lydia gave Aro a sideways glance as they
passed to see if he noticed it, but the flickering oil lamps
threw shadows on his face, preventing her from reading any
emotion.

What was he thinking, this husband of hers?

Exactly why had he married her? She knew her reasons
for marriage, but his?

She had to suppose he wanted to enter Roman society.
Marriage to an old established family would give him entry
to the best circles and the most select dinner tables where the
true business of Rome was conducted. She forced her arms
to stay at her sides.

Was it too much to ask for—to be wanted for herself rather
than for her family connections? She wanted to have more
of a purpose in her life than gossip.

She ignored the growing trembling in her stomach and
allowed Aro to guide her into the luxurious room with its

blazing charcoal brazier, table laden with silver fruit platters and amber goblets filled with wine. And the bed strewn with cushions and embroidered blankets.

'I bring your distaff and spindle, the symbols of your industrious nature. Use them well,' Sulpicia said, nearly treading on Lydia's gown. She made a surprised clucking noise in the back of her throat. Lydia knew she was weighing up the cost of the furnishings. 'You will have no need of your cloak here.'

This was it, the final act of the marriage ceremony. Lydia paused. Everything would be fine. She knew that. It was merely a matter of getting through tonight and hoping that she did not displease him. She became aware everyone was staring at her, expecting her to play her part.

With trembling fingers, Lydia undid her orange *palla*. It fell to the ground with a soft whoosh. Next she undid the metal choker, handing it to the waiting Sulpicia.

She turned to Aro, and held her breath. With one sharp movement of his dagger, he sliced through the Herculean-knotted belt that bound her gown beneath her breasts. The assembled throng cheered. Aro handed the severed cord to Sulpicia, who bowed and left the room, closing the door with a loud click behind her.

## *Chapter Six*

A few good-natured calls and whistles echoed through the heavy oak door, sounds of merriment and laughter, but inside the room, Lydia stood as if rooted to the spot. Aro appeared unaffected as he crossed the room and poured a cup of wine from the jug. He held it out to her, but she shook her head. How could she think about wine when the bed appeared bigger with each breath that she took?

She watched his long fingers as they curled around the cup of wine, remembered the feel of his mouth against hers and the wild fire that passed through her body.

What would it be like to be pressed against his firm chest?

He made no move towards her, but stood in the middle of the room, watching her with his tawny eyes.

'It sounds as if they will carry on all night,' she said, nodding towards the door. She needed to say something, anything to break the spell, to get her mind away from the shape of his mouth.

'Who?' His eyebrow raised in question. A smile twitched

at the corner of his mouth. 'It will quieten soon. Most are my men and their families, and the ships sail tomorrow. They will have a long voyage ahead of them if they start with sore heads.'

'Do you depart as well?' Lydia asked. His insistence on the marriage made sense if he was about to depart. Once he left, she'd be free to do what she wanted, but she had no status in this house. It was quite possible that the servants would use the excuse of waiting until the master came back. It was against her nature simply to sit, spin and gossip. She wanted to be useful. She wanted to use her mind to run this house and perhaps even to help out with his business. It was not unheard of for women to manage a family's business while her husband was away. Maybe not tomorrow, but in time... 'How long will you be gone?'

He set the cup down, the glass clinking softly against the table. His lips drew back in a curve. On some it might have passed for a smile.

'Alas, the head of a merchant house rarely sails. My days are spent chasing up missing shipments of grain. All roads lead to Rome with trade.' The words were lightly said, but his body gave the impression of a wolf about to spring. 'A dull existence, but one which ensures a rather longer life than battling against Neptune and his fury.'

'The Sea Wolf no longer puts to sea?' The name rolled off her tongue before she could stop it.

'You know the name.' The shadows in his face heightened and she found it impossible to tell if he was displeased.

'I have heard it.'

'Do not believe every story you hear.'

'I never do.' Lydia raised her head and met his gaze full on. 'In Rome, there are many with silver tongues, and a smooth manner.'

'Spoken by one who has encountered such men before? Or has your father kept you away from such things?'

'My father…' Lydia hesitated.

How much did he know about her relationship with her father, and his illness? How could she begin to explain that where he had once encouraged her to be interested in business and learning, since his illness, he seemed to have forgotten she even existed?

He had become like a different person. Her father, but not the gentle but firm man she remembered. Sometimes it was as if a Fury had touched his mind. He spoke sharply without cause, losing his temper over little things, and then later, after the temper left him, becoming quiet and almost child-like with little or no memory of his outbursts.

Would Aro understand? Or would he seek to use the knowledge to his advantage?

Her hands touched the crimson net that imprisoned her hair. Now she wished that she had stayed to hear the conversation between Aro and her father. Her father's final words echoed in her brain—keep the family's business secret. If her father had kept it a secret, she owed him her loyalty.

'My father allowed me some measure of freedom. He thought it best for me to learn what the world was like. After my mother's death, he encouraged me to take charge of the household.'

'And you think you will have to give all that up now.' A statement, not a question, but quietly said with a firm authority.

'I have no idea.' She held palms upwards, showing she had nothing to hide. 'From my father's business dealings, I have heard of the Lupan House. Stories about the Sea Wolf and his exploits swirl about the Forum, but I know little of the man. I judge people by what I know of them, not by the stories the gossips spout in the market place.'

'You will know more of the man hereafter.' A low husky laugh filled the room, a laugh that made the warmth in her belly grow and curl around her insides, reminding her of the kiss they had shared and how her body had reacted to it. 'A wife should not be ignorant of her husband or his desires.'

'Quintus…' Lydia rolled his first name around on her tongue. 'Where does that come from? Are you the fifth brother?'

'It is an old family name, and one I never use, one I dislike. It was my father's name and his before that. The last person to use it was my mother.'

'What shall I call you?' In the back of her mind a little voice kept chiming—he has no desire for you to call him by his first name. First names are for intimates. He does not intend for you to be anything but a trophy.

'Aro will suffice, Lydia Fabia. It pleases me much more. It is the name I chose.' He stretched out his arms in a welcoming gesture, but a flash of pain crossed his face.

'You're hurt.'

'It is nothing. Piso and I had a minor disagreement yesterday with some locals. I bruised my wrist and my side.' He held out his hand and in the flickering light, Lydia could see purple bruising on his arm. 'It will teach me to be a little quicker the next time. It appears I strained my shoulder again when I lifted you just now.'

'You shouldn't have carried me over the threshold. You have injured yourself far more. That was foolish of you.' Silently, she cursed for not having noticing sooner. She should have. She prided herself on noticing little things.

'It is but a small thing.' He gave a soft laugh, but one which did strange things to her insides. 'What sort of bridegroom would I have been if I had failed to carry my bride into her new house?'

'I would have understood.'

'I want all the omens to be good for this marriage.' His voice was no more than whisper, a whisper that sent shivers down her back.

'I have some salve, my own special recipe,' she said, concentrating on the purple marks, rather than on his golden gaze. 'My father finds it effective against his aches and pains. He swears by it. Or at least he used to.' Lydia found the need to be truthful.

'Sounds soothing.' His fingers captured hers, and held them next to his wrist. 'Like your hands.'

'I can get the ointment if you wish. It will be with my things.' She started towards the door, then stopped, remembering where she was. 'If you will let me know where I might find my things…'

His fingers reached out, touched her jaw with a light butterfly caress. 'Later.'

Her breath caught in her throat as his hands entangled themselves in the hair net and pulled it off, freeing her hair. One by one the pins that held the elaborate hairstyle in place fell to the ground. Her hair fell in waves, cascading about her face and upper body.

'Beautiful,' he murmured against her ear. 'Like the sea on a summer's night, rippling in the moonlight.'

'You are speaking nonsense.' Lydia shook her head, but a surge of pleasure swept through her at the compliment. 'It is hair. I can never get it to stay in place properly. Beroe despairs.'

'Finer than silk.' His hands ran through her hair, lifting it to his lips.

Lydia held her body still. She did not want to do anything wrong. She had no wish to anger him. The memory of her last wedding night and its humiliation was too raw.

His hand stroked her head and she leant back slightly, revealing her throat. His lips touched her neck just above her gown. His thumb slipped underneath the gown, touching her with a firm but insistent stroke. An involuntary shiver went through her.

Immediately, Aro stiffened. His hand withdrew and he regarded her face.

'Tell me what is wrong. All evening, something has bothered you.' Aro's voice was a warm whisper in her ear. 'Tell me what it is you fear about me. What is it about my touch that displeases you?'

'I had not expected the marriage to make you my master.' Lydia felt her throat close and forced the words out around the sudden lump. If she gave in to his touch, she would be no better than the whores and courtesans who plied their trade in the alleyways and bars around the Forum. What would he think of her? 'It is rarely done. I had thought my father would stay my guardian.'

His hand withdrew and he moved away from her. She heard the sound of wine being poured.

'I do not blow with fashions. A *cum manu* marriage was good enough for my parents. It is good enough for me. My mother never questioned the wisdom of the thing.'

'Times change,' Lydia said between gritted teeth. No doubt his mother was a paragon of virtue who spun all her family's cloth and always deferred to her husband's wishes as well. 'My parents were married *sine manu*. *Cum manu* is only for those seeking to become the high priest of Juno. Are you seeking that office?'

'I have my reasons for marrying this way, and your father agreed. Becoming Juno's priest was not one of them.' He gave an ironic laugh. 'Above all, I expect my wife to be loyal.'

'Loyalty can not be bought or sold like grain in the market place, Fabius Aro.' Lydia held her head high. 'Loyalty, true loyalty, can only be earned.'

Lydia held her breath and watched Aro's eyes darken in the golden lamp light. Her words hung between them. Something flickered in his eyes and died.

'Your father has given your hand to me. He trusts me to look after you properly. I gave my word. I always keep my word.'

'Did he tell you my husband was on board ship when that storm struck?' The words flowed from her mouth. 'You gave your word. You promised to save everyone on board ship. You broke your promise.'

'I regret that I could not save everyone.' His voice was cold and remote. A muscle jumped in his cheek. 'I lost two of my best crew to the seas that day. Neptune was in a fearsome temper. Would that it were otherwise. I only promised to try. There is a difference. Be grateful your father's life was saved.'

Lydia swallowed hard. She had made it sound like it was Aro's fault that Titus had drowned. Her father had assured her that it was no one's fault, that the mast had hit him and he had slipped over board. The man who had saved her father had risked his life, and had plucked him from the very entrance of Hades.

Lydia had always wondered what would have happened if Titus had not died. Would they have become friends again or would they have continued to drift apart? She always hated the fact that when she had first heard it had been her husband who perished and not her father, she hadn't felt despair, but relief, relief she no longer had to worry about a husband whom she had little respect for. Grief for Titus came later, but her first emotion had been one of gratitude that, if the gods had demanded someone die, it had been her husband. The guilt she felt afterwards woke her at night. She knew Titus with his shy smile had deserved a better wife.

Did Aro?

'Enough of this.' He reached for her, an intent expression on his face. 'What is done, is done. The ritual has been performed. Your father gave your hand to me. We are husband and wife. A wife owes her husband loyalty. You will put the Lupan House and me first.'

She wasn't ready, her nerves still tingled. She retreated to the other side of the room, away from the bed. She picked up a cup of wine and brought it to her lips. The sweetened liquid tasted bitter. 'I will do what I promised to do.'

He gave a slight nod, and ran his fingers through his hair, making it stand straight up.

'You know how to run a household?' he asked. 'Or have

I made a bad bargain, with your father unable to wait to get rid of you after spoiling you rotten?'

'My father has never had any complaints about the way I have run his house.' She made sure her chin was lifted and that she looked him in the eye. 'You will find me more than adequately trained. I mean to make you a good wife and to uphold the ideals of a Roman matron.'

'But you fear me. You fear my reputation. It is written in your eyes.' His eyes deepened to golden brown and his voice became more cajoling. 'Who has been filling your ears with tales? Is this why you object to me holding sway over you? Most of those tales are of wine-shop gossip from people who have never met me and are envious of the way the gods favour me and the Lupan House. You are now part of my family and I offer you my protection. I will let none harm you.'

'I never said I fear you,' Lydia said quickly, too quickly. 'I am not afraid of you.'

His expression had softened. The golden flecks in his eyes now glowed with the warmth of a hundred oil lamps.

'Your manner says differently. It has changed since you found out who I am. I know the stories that go around the docks. The Sea Wolf who is half-immortal and hunts down any who would try to steal from him. Therefore, none wish to cross me and my cargo remains safe. The sea is a harsh enough mistress without worrying about pirates. The tales serve their purpose, but they are just tales. My people, the people I have helped, know the truth.'

'Thank you.'

He took the cup from her unresisting fingers and set it down on the table. A shiver went through her. The oil lamps highlighted the scar on his cheek. The pads of her fingers itched to touch it, to see if it was silky smooth or rough. She pressed her hands together, remembering the admonitions she had been given. A Roman matron behaves like a lady at all times, not like a prostitute in the streets. She had no desire to become notorious like her distant kinswoman Clodia Metellia or Servilia Junia. She wanted to be like her mother who was beloved by all.

He rested a hand on her shoulder, smoothing away the cloth so the tops of her breasts were revealed. His eyes danced with a hidden fire and then sobered as she flinched when her brooch bit into her skin. Instantly, he withdrew his hand.

'Fear not, Lydia, I will not force you.' His lips touched her forehead. He returned her dress to the base of her neck and stepped away from her. 'Get into bed. You have had a long day.'

'If you will give me some time, I need to make the appropriate sacrifices to Venus.'

'You made the sacrifices to Venus this morning.' There was laughter in his voice. 'You do not need to make more. Gods and goddesses don't need to be bothered that often.'

There was nothing for it. The time had come. He would bed her without any wooing.

She allowed her gown to fall to the floor and then stepped away from it. Would he be gentle with her? His eyes assessed her, roamed over her body. She ran her hands up and down her arms, trying to get some warmth back into her body, cold despite her under-tunic.

'You need not look at me like that. I have never forced a woman and I never will.' He gave an exaggerated stretch. 'I find my side pains me.'

'What is that you want from me?' she whispered.

'I told you before—to make my house a home.' His eyes met hers, a long steady gaze where his eyes glowed golden in the lamplight. 'Now, get into bed; the hour is late and I wish to sleep.'

Not needing any second warning, Lydia scrambled over to the bed and pulled the coverlets up to her chin. 'Where will you sleep?'

'With you. I don't intend to sleep on the floor.'

Without waiting to hear her reply, Aro unclasped his toga and climbed into the narrow bed.

'I gave you my word, Lydia.' His breath tickled her ear. His right arm curled around her waist. 'I am not an animal to take you by force. We will consummate this marriage in our time, rather than with rowdy men outside blowing trumpets and banging drums.'

Lydia's throat closed. She had not expected kindness. She shifted her body, trying to ignore the growing warmth between her legs. His scent and nearness was doing strange things to her.

'Hold still, if you wish nothing to happen to you. Keep moving and I will forget my good intentions.'

With a gulp, Lydia stopped and held her body rigid. She waited, all senses alert until she heard his regular breathing. He had granted her a reprieve for a reason she didn't understand. She had expected him to take her, to treat her in the same unfeeling manner Titus had, taking his pleasure and giving her none, but he hadn't. He was sensitive to her nervousness. Maybe marriage to the Sea Wolf was not going to be as awful as Sulpicia had predicted. In time, perhaps they could find some measure of peace together. In the morning, when the men had gone, they could begin their marriage properly.

She found some comfort in the heavy arm about her waist, keeping her from falling off the side of the bed.

Aro forced his breathing to be steady, listening for a change in the rhythm of Lydia's breath. Her hips were tucked snugly against his, and her hair tickled his nostrils. He shifted to ease the ache in his side. Perhaps he had been hasty in dismissing her salve, but the pain would ease eventually. It always did.

Lydia moaned slightly in her sleep and sought the middle of the bed. Her dark hair tumbled against the white of the pillow. Her under-tunic had slipped, revealing her creamy skin. Aro felt his loins tighten as her warm soft scent of rose, intermingled with something indefinable, tickled his nose.

Temptation swept over him and he longed to touch his lips to hers and awake the passion he felt when they had kissed earlier, but he had given his word. Keeping his word meant that he was different from Ofellius and the other traders who plied the Mediterranean, he had honour. Aro gave a wry smile. The long years he had spent at sea, building his business, meant he had learnt the value of patience. To the one who waited and who was ready to act on opportunity came all things.

He eased his way out of bed and pulled up the coverlet. His fingers smoothed a damp curl away from her temple.

'Sleep well, Lydia, for I shall not.'

# Chapter Seven

'You should have sent for me earlier,' Aro said, pushing through the crowd of silent onlookers.

The smouldering ruins of the main Roman warehouse for the Lupan House glowed orange in the half-light before dawn. The heat from the fire burned his face. The smoke stung his eyes. Smoke invaded his mouth with every breath he drew.

'I didn't want to pull you from your marriage bed before you had the chance to accomplish anything.'

Aro made a noise at the back of his throat. He would have welcomed the distraction. Anything to keep his mind from remembering Lydia clad in her thin under-tunic and the warmth of her body against his.

'There is plenty of time for such things. You wouldn't have suffered the wrath of the Sea Wolf. The Lupan House and its business comes before any personal consideration. You know that. My marriage changes nothing.'

'I thought you could use a little more time before confronting this. The men and I were perfectly capable of handling it.' Piso swayed slightly. His ash-stained tunic bore little resemblance to the snow-white tunic of a few hours before. Lines of tiredness and worry creased his face.

'Tell me the worst—how much have we lost? Everything? Senator Appius's consignment of black cumin and cinnamon? A few amphorae of olive oil? Quickly, man. Hold nothing back. Have we saved anything?'

'My men and I handled the removal of the spices and silks. We may have lost five or six amphorae of olive oil, but nothing more.' Piso wiped a sooty hand across his brow. 'Nearly all the cargo had been loaded on the barges. Your obsession for early morning departure has worked once again in our favour. I may grumble about them, Aro, but your rules have served us well again.'

'The departure will have to be delayed.'

Aro watched the relief grow on Piso's face. There could be no doubt his captain would have put to sea if he had ordered it, but what would have been the point? Overly tired men meant mistakes, mistakes meant lost cargo and Aro did not intend to lose any more than he had to.

'For a few days only.' Piso's face looked a little less careworn. 'These men are exhausted; even with Poseidon and Hermes's grace, I would not like to put to sea. We are not all Fabius Aro.'

'You will have two days. Plans have changed. Instead of Corinth, you head up the coast and pick up a consignment of wine and be back within five days. Mergus and his crew can take the ship to Corinth. It is about time he sampled their delights again. I think the city *aediles* and the baths will have just about recovered from the last time.'

'Two days and an easy coast run is more than generous, Aro.' Piso inclined his head. 'More than I had hoped for.'

'I expect those days to be spent getting ready, not visiting Flora's wine shop.'

A wide smile broke out across Piso's face. 'Now whatever gave you that idea? I had gone off the lady a bit after our last encounter, but now you mention it, her…wine tickles the palate.'

Aro placed his hands on his hips and surveyed the smouldering ruin. After Piso returned from the voyage, they would discover if the fragile truce with Ofellius held. The last thing he wanted to do was to break the agreement without sufficient cause. But his instincts were telling him—Ofellius had a hand in this fire somewhere.

One of the roof timbers crashed to the earth, sending a stream of sparks into the sky.

'Any idea of what caused it?' Aro asked as a gang rushed forward with brooms and water to beat the new flames out. 'It seems past coincidence a fire should start now of all times. Were all the safety checks made? Did anyone leave an oil lamp burning?'

'The men obeyed your instructions like they always do. No one has the desire to cross the Sea Wolf. They value their pay too much. They all know what happens to men who do not follow your rules.'

'Good. I am glad you investigated.'

'First thing I thought about. You can't be too careful with oil lamps and charcoal braziers.'

'Then why did the fire happen?'

'Fires are always a problem in Rome, Aro. You know that. I have lost count how many dwellings have burnt since

March. And I spotted at least five other blazes in the night sky,' Piso said with a shrug. He indicated the night watchman, who was standing respectfully behind him. 'Thanks to Rufus's quick thinking, the worst failed to happen. If any of our warehouses here or in Ostia had to burn, it was as well that it was this one.'

'I don't know how it happened.' Rufus raised his soot-streaked face, tiredness and grief etched firmly on his body. He swayed slightly, but appeared determined to stand without aid. He'd make the elderly night watchman see a doctor, Aro thought and none of the usual excuses. Rufus had known him since he was a small boy, and was one of the few who felt he could speak his mind to the Sea Wolf, but this time he would be obeyed.

'I had double-checked that warehouse not an hour before and hadn't smelt no smoke.' Rufus's voice sounded close to tears. 'Still as Neptune's sea on a clear day. I'd gone to investigate a noise, but it turned out to be a stray dog. When I turned back, the thing went up like Hades on me.'

'I know you did your best, Rufus. You always do.'

Time and again Rufus had proved his usefulness with sword and sail until an accident had put an end to his sailing days. His eldest had been Aro's navigator until he was lost during the rescue of Veratius Cornelius and the misbegotten cargo of spice. Aro had ordered him back to the boat, but the lad had insisted on trying one more time, that the last amphora of garum was too precious to be lost. A large wave washed him and the young senator, Lydia's first husband, overboard. Aro had been only able to watch helplessly from the deck of his ship.

'Thank you Fabius Aro. The Fabii mean everything.'

'It was lucky as Rufus started to raise the alarm, my men and I returned.' Piso laid a hand on Rufus's shoulder. 'It had taken us a bit longer than I expected to get back here.'

'No doubt a wine shop or two is richer because of your delay.'

'No doubt, but we put our backs into it once we saw the blaze.'

Rufus cleared his throat and moved away from Piso's supporting arm.

'What is it, old friend?' Aro asked quietly. 'What else are you hiding from me?'

'You have made some powerful enemies, Aro,' Piso answered, all merriment vanishing from his face. 'Someone wants to bring you down.'

'Many have tried and failed.'

'A curse tablet was stuck on the side of the warehouse.' Rufus gestured towards the far wall. 'It was when I was tearing the thing down that I discovered the fire had taken hold.'

'The things our rivals will try.' Aro kept his voice light. He might not believe in such things, preferring to trust his own skill and hard work, but the others were superstitious. 'The gods have always been with me. They are with me still.'

'It's not the gods I'd be worried about. It's them Veratii. You should never have married one of those Veratii. Your father always said they were trouble. They couldn't be trusted and would use anything to wriggle out of an agreement. Shouldn't wonder if there was something in the marriage contract. Veratius Cornelius's father helped with your father's proscription.'

'There was never any proof of that.'

'Your father always said so.' Rufus's voice quavered. 'They'll be behind it, I shouldn't wonder. You mark my words—they'll have hired someone else to do the dirty work, but they'll be there.'

'To what purpose?' Aro knew his father had blamed Veratius Cornelius's father for engineering the proscription. It had been one of the reasons he had demanded such a high price for the rescue, but Veratius Cornelius had proved a man of his word. He had not tried to postpone the wedding at all. He had agreed to every demand. Aro had been determined there would be no loopholes for the man to wriggle through. He pressed his lips together. There was one, an annulment on the grounds of non-consummation, but Cornelius could not have guessed that would happen. No, Lydia's show of nerves had been true. 'You must have a reason for saying this, Rufus. I will not have my father-in-law's integrity questioned without proof.'

'I don't know. It's a feeling I got. Who would benefit most from the fire, I thought, but then what does the likes of an ex-slave know about the mind of a Roman senator?' Rufus's eyes blazed defiantly. Behind him, another timber crashed to the ground. 'It passes all coincidence, it does. Why tonight? You mark my words—your wife will be demanding to see her father today.'

'Do not search for connections when there are none.'

Rufus gave low moan, slid to the floor and lay still.

'A doctor, quick,' Aro barked to a nearby man. Aro knelt down beside the slumped figure, and laid his ear to the elderly man's chest. He could hear the noisy rattle of his breath.

'And not the soothsaying quack from around the corner either. I want one who knows what he is doing.'

'As you say, Fabius Aro.'

Aro regarded his captain. 'Piso, clean up your carcass, go back to the compound, wait for my wife.'

'But there are things I could do here…'

'Do as I ask, Piso.' Aro nodded towards the curse and watched the comprehension dawn in Piso's eyes. 'She must not be left alone. I want to be the one to tell her of the fire. I don't want to worry her unnecessarily.'

'What are you going to do?'

'I need to make sure this fire does not cause more damage to the Lupan House. The augurs must read the signs correctly when they arrive to bless this place.' Aro looked again at the lead tablet. Whoever had cursed him had paid more than a few *denarii*. Had they paid for the fire to be started as well? 'A fire can be the symbol of a new beginning as well as the destruction of dreams. It all depends on the priest's interpretation.'

Sunlight fell in barred slats through the half-open shutters when Lydia awoke from her confused dreams about wolves, the crashing seas and the need to rescue someone, a nameless person. A cold wet nose pushed at her hand and she heard a low whimper.

'Korina,' she said to the dog who lay by the side of the bed. 'I had the strangest dream.'

The dog gave a low woof.

Disorientated, Lydia blinked the sleep away and realised that her marriage was no dream. Her tiny bedroom at the back of the house and well-ordered life were no more. She was now the wife of Fabius Aro and in charge of one of the largest houses on the Aventine.

She had married a man she barely knew. She ought to hate him, but, after last night, she found that impossible. Most men would have insisted on their marital privileges, but he hadn't. He had considered her needs. Surely that must count for something.

The corners of her mouth tugged as she remembered the way his body felt against hers. There could be something more to this marriage if he was willing to meet her halfway. She planned on fulfilling her vows. She would make him a good wife. She intended on showing him that she could do more than simply run a house—she could help in his business and perhaps then he would start to value her as something more than a status symbol.

Rising, she went to an open door, which revealed a tiny dressing room. She spied her favourite blue gown and matching shawl hanging there. On the dressing table, someone had placed her boxes of wine dregs, powders and various jars of ointment. It appeared that this was indeed meant to be her private room. She pulled on the gown and adjusted the sleeves and neckline. Months of having to wait for Beroe to finish with Sulpicia had taught Lydia how to arrange her hair in a simple but effective style. Her make-up was equally simple, no more than a few strokes with a brush, and she would be ready, ready to meet her husband and begin her new life.

She stifled a slight of disappointment. Then she made a wry face in the bronze mirror. Had she really expected Aro to be here, holding her in his arms? He must have a thousand other things to do.

Last night she had thought he was being kind, but in reality he had probably not wanted to lie with her—any more than Titus had. Lydia pressed her hands against her thighs and ignored the sudden tightening of her throat.

'Korina, I can't sit here all day, waiting for Aro to appear.' She stood up and forced her lips to smile. 'I need to find him and tell that I must return home for a little while. Sulpicia does not have the least idea of how to look after my father.'

Lydia began to apply the wine dregs and face powder to her face. Her hand hovered over an unfamiliar jar. She opened it, and looked at the unfamiliar brown pills flecked with gold. Somehow, her father's pills had journeyed with her.

She squashed the rising sense of panic. Her father had been free from attacks since three Kalends ago and his strength was slowly returning. The gods willing, he would never have another attack, but the doctors had warned the next one would have the potential to kill. Those pills needed to be in a place where her father could get them if an attack started. She also needed to explain to Sulpicia and her father's man-servant what to do, the exact procedure of administering the pills. If they were not given at the precise time, they could do more harm than good, or so the apothecary had said with a dubious shake of his head.

It broke with tradition, but she'd have to return home.

Today.

She had no other choice.

Once she had explained, she was certain Aro would understand. Her jaw clenched. He would have to understand. Her father's life was at risk. Then, a shiver passed over her. One of her father's last words had been to keep her family secrets safe. She couldn't tell Aro without betraying her father. She gritted her teeth. He would have to understand. She'd make him understand without breaking her promise to her father and betraying his secret.

She thrust open the door, went into the atrium with its fountain and goldfish flashing in the sun, but no one was there, not even a servant. Korina tilted her head and looked at her questioningly. Lydia reached down, and gave Korina's ears a stroke.

'Something has happened. The servants are far too quiet. A house should be far noisier than this. Shall we go and find out, and then we will go h…to my father's?'

Korina gave a low bark in agreement.

Lydia, with her heart pounding in her ears, tried several doors. Each led to a frescoed room with a wide variety of statues—Greek statues, some modern, but others clearly copies of more famous works—all very tasteful and the height of fashion, but empty with no one, not even a servant, dusting the figurines.

She was about to give up in frustration and return to her room when she heard a small noise coming from behind the final door.

She cautiously opened the door and peered into the dining room. A fresco of a scene from the myth of Orpheus dominated the walls. The table was laid with plates of silver with platters of cheese, fruit and cakes occupying the centre.

A stab of disappointment ran through her. Rather than the hoped for broad shoulders and trim figure of Aro, a large man reclined on the middle couch, breaking bread. A servant stood behind him with a jug of water. Lydia frowned and attempted to draw back into the shadows of the corridor.

'You are awake. It is nearly time for lunch,' the man said conversationally, and indicated a couch on his right.

'It can't be that late. I never sleep that late.'

'I told Aro you would wake soon and want something to eat, but he assured me that you had had a long night and would sleep.' His large face broke into a huge smile. 'It is pleasing to see the bridegroom understands his bride's needs.'

'You are—?' Lydia choked back the words, asking where Aro was. She would find him soon enough. Silently she offered up a prayer that no harm would come to her father because of the delay.

'Piso, his most senior captain,' he said as if it explained everything. He filled a plate full of figs, hard cheese and brown bread. 'Eat. Tell me about yourself. Aro has said precious little. He is a sly one, that one. I had no idea he was negotiating for a bride until after the betrothal was set.'

Korina padded up to the man, sniffed and took a bite of his bread.

'Oh, Korina!' Lydia's fingers tugged at Korina's collar. She had to get Korina out of here before she did some sort of damage, like climbing on the table and eating all the cheese. All she would need was for Aro to take offence and force her to get rid of the dog.

'She has done no harm.' He leant down and offered some bread to Korina. The imp took it with a sharp bark of delight and several wags of her tail. 'There is more than enough to go around.'

'She had no cause to do that. She is normally better trained.' Lydia withdrew her hand from Korina.

'Aro sets a fine table.' Piso broke off another piece of bread and fed it to Korina. 'Hercules knows where he found his chef, but I swear his pyramid cakes are second to none. The gods on Mount Olympus do not feast as well as this. Try one.'

Piso held out a plate piled high with golden cakes. The delicious scent of warm honey wafted towards her. Lydia's stomach rumbled, reminding her that she had eaten very little yesterday. She took the cake and took a nibble. 'Very good.'

'You must have something more to eat than one cake.'

'Are you normally this free with someone else's food?' Lydia perched on a side couch, tucking her feet under the seat.

'I am part of the family.' Piso tapped the side of his nose. 'Aro allows me to reside here when my ship is in harbour.'

'He never told me.' Lydia's mind raced. She needed to leave without delay, but she had no wish to alienate this man, this senior captain. Perhaps he could prove an ally. She had to play her glass counters carefully.

'Probably had other things on his mind.' Piso's deep brown eyes roamed over her figure. 'He will return when he can.'

Lydia gave a small nod. A bridegroom who could not be bothered to wake his bride would not be bothered if his bride went to visit her family. All she needed to do was tell Piso where she was going and it would be simple. Minerva was with her.

She'd go now while she had the chance, before she had to explain. She stood up, smoothed her gown and snapped her fingers to Korina to alert her they were going. She'd give a polite half-truth, and go. With any luck, she'd be back before Aro had returned. 'The cakes and the other delicacies are tempting, but there are things I must be doing. Places I have to go. This house…'

'Don't tell me that Aro has put you to work already.' Piso made an expansive gesture. 'Come, sit. Beautify this room with your presence. A woman like you enhances the room she is in.'

'Really, I—'

'Here I discover you, Lydia, eating pyramid cakes with one of my captains.' Aro's voice washed over Lydia, stopping her planned words of departure. 'Has he devoured them all?'

Lydia closed her mouth with a snap. The bland excuse she had been about to give would no longer work. She turned towards Aro.

Dressed in a short white tunic, Aro stooped and fondled Korina's ears. His hair glistened as if it were freshly washed. Lydia's hand curled. He had been to the baths! That was what had drawn him from her side. The baths. Here, she had worried that something might be wrong, and he had been to the baths! He could have left word. When Titus had gone out on the town with his friends, he had always left word.

He reached over, plucked a pyramid cake from the pile and fed it to the dog, who had trotted over to him. The traitorous dog gobbled the cake and then lay down at his feet with a satisfied sigh.

Lydia drew her blue shawl tighter about her body. She refused to be as easily won over as Korina. She would maintain a dignified but injured silence until he explained.

His face had become sterner. There were lines that had not been there last night. The Sea Wolf was back. Last night, she had thought perhaps they had reached some sort of agreement, but now she saw she was wrong. Her stomach knotted as the tales Sulpicia whispered to her resurfaced. How he had raced the wind with shipments of Egyptian grain to be the first to arrive in Rome for three years running, how he fought sea monsters and won. A man only the brave dare cross.

'Wish you good fortune.' Piso rose and dusted his tunic down. His eyes roamed up and down her gown. A smile tugged at his cheek. 'Your wife has been keeping me company, Aro. You are a lucky man to snare such a wife. Such a wife might indeed induce me into the coils of matrimony.'

'I live to see the day.' Aro held out his arms, beckoned towards her. 'Lydia, are you going to greet your husband or have the Furies done away with your tongue in the night? You never have had trouble speaking before.'

'My voice is my own, even if little else is.' Lydia brought her head up sharply. It irritated her. Not only had he disappeared without a word, he expected her to be overjoyed at his return as if that was all she desired in the world. She did want to see him, but not like this.

'So she does have a voice this morning. Come and greet me, wife.' His eyes crinkled at the corners and he held out both his hands. The stern lines on his face vanished and his eyes took on a tender expression. 'You were fast asleep when I had to leave you.'

'You should have woken me.' Lydia inclined her head. How did he expect her to greet him? With a kiss? Despite the memory of the taste of his mouth flooding through her, Lydia rejected the idea. She was no simpering nanny goat.

He settled it for her, reached out and brushed his lips

against her cheeks. His warm scent of sandalwood, intermingled with something all his own, enveloped her and held
her, driving away all other thoughts. Then she stepped away
from him, and all the doubts crowded back in.

Lydia reached out and gave Korina a stroke. The Aro of
this morning was very different from the man who had held
her close last night. Very few men would have thought about
a wife's nerves. If she had woken when he did, maybe things
could have been said. She could have thanked him for his consideration, but not now, here in front of his captain.

Lydia straightened her spine.

Such thoughts were nonsense. She did have a purpose in life
and that was ensuring her father's well being. She had promised
Publius that she'd look after him; more importantly, she had
promised her mother on her death bed. Inadvertently, she had
put her father's life at risk. She had to act now, before it was too
late. Surely he could not refuse a request to visit her family, as
out of the ordinary as it was, not when he had visited the baths.

'I had come looking for you.' Her voice sounded high and
strained. Lydia paused, wiped her hands against her gown.
This was much harder than she thought. 'I wanted to discover
how I could obtain a litter. I wish to pay a visit to my father.'

'You bade your father farewell, yesterday. To visit him so
soon after the wedding would cause people to talk, and to
question the omens for the marriage.' Aro's eyes flashed gold.
The light-heartedness vanished. His hand rested heavy on
Lydia's shoulder, preventing her from moving away from
him. His chest that had seemed comforting last night
appeared hard and unyielding. 'You belong to this family
now. You are my responsibility now.'

# Chapter Eight

⥀⥁

Aro's words resounded in Lydia's brain. He had forbidden her to see her father!

Lydia pulled away from his hand and put some distance between them. He made no attempt to keep her there. She drew a deep breath and tried not to panic. She must have misunderstood.

'But I desire to pay my father a visit.'

'Some time, but not today. It would not be seemly.'

Lydia's mouth dropped open and then she shut it firmly, pressing her lips together. She stared at her husband with his face stern and unyielding. He was already turning to Piso to speak of something else.

How could he do such a thing? It was as if she had asked to visit the gods on Mount Olympus, instead of making a short journey to the Palatine. He had just been to the baths. He could go wherever he wished without asking her, but she was little better than a slave. She was expected to obey him and get his permission. The injustice of it all.

She forced her body to relax. Lose her temper and she'd risk losing everything.

'Nevertheless, I need to return to my father's compound today,' Lydia began and wondered how she might explain without alerting him to her father's weakness. She had to respect her father's wishes if he had not confided in his son-in-law. How could she discover how much Aro knew? Her heart pounded in her ears. 'There are things I have to do there. My father depends on me to manage his house.'

Aro stopped. His back stiffened. Piso started to say something, but Aro gave a quick shake of his head.

'Your sister-in-law lives with your father. Surely she has a duty to see to the house.' All warmth had drained out of his voice. The scar on the side of his face glowed white. 'I see no reason for you to return so quickly to your father's house. It is against tradition. We will speak no more of this. My mind is quite decided.'

Lydia forced her head to remain erect. She refused to beg, to explain about her father's illness. It had nothing to do with Aro. Standing there with his hands balled on his hips as if he expected her to meekly take his word for it, he had to understand that she intended to lead her life much as she had done before.

'There are plenty of reasons why I need to return. Sulpicia chooses not to have anything to do with the running of the house. She helps out with the spinning or the weaving if the mood strikes her, but she has no idea about the accounts or where things are stored.'

'She appears to be an intelligent woman. A naked woman soon learns the art of spinning, as my old nurse used to say.'

'This marriage was very sudden and…' Lydia tried again,

but with each word, she felt herself slipping deeper into the ooze of lies '…and I want to make sure that all the food has been properly stored, and the wool is properly marked. You have no idea how quickly household affairs can become muddled.'

'Your father's villa seemed well stocked with slaves when I was last there. In my experience, if slaves have been trained by a good mistress they know what to do, before they are asked.' He paused, his golden gaze drilling into her. He crossed his arms, the forbidding captain of a ship rather than the man who had held her in his arms last night. 'Tell me the truth, Lydia. Why is it so important that you go right today, this very hour? If I deem it appropriate, you may go.'

She'd try the truth this time, ungilded and plain. Then he would no doubt let her go.

Lydia drew herself up to her full height. He might dismiss servants and his men, but not her. She intended to fight. Her father's life was important. To save it, she would have to break her promise to him. Surely he'd understand. He had to understand.

'My father is ill.' Her voice was quiet, but assured. 'He has suffered attacks, pains in his head.'

He lifted an eyebrow, but his lips were pressed into a tight line. 'He seemed well enough yesterday, positively brimming with life, greeting all the guests. I have heard no rumours of this trouble. Before that he was in the Senate. Have you heard any rumours, Piso?'

The other man shrugged and shook his head. Lydia's heart sank. The gold she had given the doctors had worked—too well.

'You must believe me. He has been ill, seriously ill.

We…that is…Publius and I kept it quiet.' Lydia clasped her hands together. She couldn't believe this was happening to her. She had told the truth and he refused to believe her. 'There are things I have been attending to. There wasn't time—'

'If he was that ill, why did your brother go with Pompey? Why did he not remain behind to look after your father?'

Lydia traced the mosaic pattern with the toe of her sandal. There was no use in attempting to explain Publius's behaviour. She had argued with him to stay. But her father and Publius had quarrelled violently and Publius had stormed off.

'Publius did what he thought was right. He knew I would never leave my father to suffer—'

'Your brother and sister-in-law have used you.' Aro's voice cut across hers as his hands clenched at his sides. Lydia became aware of the power in his shoulders and legs. 'Pay some time getting to know this household and how it works, rather than returning to your old life, Lydia of the Fabii. Your father said as much to me last night before we left. He will not be expecting you. Do not disobey me on this, wife. Your duty is clear.'

Lydia stared at him. The full impact of her new life hit her. She had no rights. She was going to be kept a prisoner here.

'I need to see my father.'

'Will you do me the dignity of telling me the true reason?' Aro's eyes flashed. He seemed to grow in stature. Korina hid her nose under her paws and Lydia wished she might do something similar. 'Or are you going to persist in telling tales, each one more fanciful than the next, until out of sheer exhaustion I give in? In the space of a few breaths you have told me three different reasons why you wish to return to your old house. None of those reasons are urgent as far as I can discern.'

'I told you the truth. My father has been ill and I have a few matters I need to see to.'

'Other people can see to them.' His brows knit together in a black frown and the corners of his lips turned down. 'He has slaves, men of work. Now, tell me the truth.'

'Why do you persist in telling me that I am lying?'

'What is so urgent that you need to run back to your family on the morning after your wedding night? What story do you wish to tell him?'

'I have told you the truth.'

She forced her back to stay straight and still. He did not care where she went. He had not bothered to be there when she woke up. He had gone to the baths, rather than stay by her side. It was only now, in front of his friend, that he made a show of being concerned. Her throat closed around a tight hard lump of tears.

'You must respect my reasons,' she said, fighting to keep her voice calm. She had to keep her dignity. Without it, she had nothing. 'If my father chose not to inform you, his new son-in-law, of the exact nature of his illness, I must honour his wishes.'

'Very well,' he said after a long silence where the only noise was the thumping of Korina's tail. 'I must insist you stay here. You have enough to occupy you here and Veratius Cornelius and Sulpicia can fend for themselves for a short period. They will not starve.'

'If you insist.' Lydia bowed her head, resting her chin on her hands. She had to hope that her father did not have another attack and, if he did, Sulpicia would know what to do. That was all. Sulpicia could be sensible when she chose, despite wringing her hands and fainting the last time. The servants were too much in awe of her father to be much use. Someone would have to force the pills down his throat.

'I do insist.' His eyes softened then. He held out a hand towards her and gave a half-smile. 'I am not an ogre, Lydia. Give it time. Your father will not be expecting to see you today. He is not in any danger. You are a bride. He knows you will be with me. If you are seen returning to your old house, people might begin to question the omens for the marriage.'

The implication in his voice was there. A small curl of warmth wound its way around Lydia's insides. She damped it down. Aro had spent time in the baths, rather than with her.

Lydia raised her head and met his eyes, a sudden thought occurring to her. If she timed it correctly, Sulpicia should be there. She offered a small prayer of thanksgiving to Juno. Sulpicia was a creature of habit. If she hurried, Lydia would reach the baths in time. They could have a quick word and Lydia could explain. Surely Aro could not object to that. 'Will I be able to go the baths today?'

Aro's expression turned sceptical, and she struggled to keep her head held high, refusing to flinch. It was a small deception, nothing serious, forced on her by his intolerable attitude. Somehow the thought did not ease the knots in her stomach.

'There should be no reason why you should not,' he said, drawing his eyebrows together. 'The local baths are well known for their treatments. Many come from all over the city for the waters. I will take you there later. It has a small library and I understand a few new scrolls have come in.'

'I had rather thought the baths between the Circus Maximus and the Palatine.' Lydia fought to keep her voice from quavering. She had to get the pills and instructions to Sulpicia. It was a slight subterfuge, nothing wicked. She kept her entire body still, concentrated on not allowing her voice to waver. 'It is the one I always use. The people know me there.'

Then she waited.

Every muscle in Aro's body tensed.

There was a hidden meaning to Lydia's words. She intended to go to the baths for another purpose. Aro knew that as surely as he knew the sand shoals in Ostia's harbour. He made his living out of his ability to read faces.

'Let her go, Aro,' Piso called out from where he reclined. 'There is probably a hairdresser she wants to see. You know what women are like. The wrong hairstyle and they are in a vile temper for days.'

'Piso, it will take too much time.' Aro turned towards his old friend. Until he had discerned Lydia's motives, he intended to keep her away from her usual haunts. Whose aid would she try to enlist there? 'One bath house is much like another.'

As he said the words, he watched the light dim in Lydia's eyes.

Rufus's words had proved prophetic. Lydia had asked to see her father immediately when he had arrived back, not giving him a chance to explain about the fire. She had not even asked where he'd been. Instead she demanded that she return to her father's house, giving a series of reasons that might or might not be true. Now she was not content to go to the nearest baths, but wanted to visit one very close to her father's house. Why was she acting so suspiciously? He regretted he had given in to his impulse and had taken pity on her last night. She seemed determined to find a reason to end their marriage.

'I will go with her,' Piso said.

Tears appeared to shimmer in Lydia's eyes, but she glanced away before Aro had a chance to examine them more closely. 'No, no, it is fine. I can use the bath suite here.'

'If you wish.' Aro stared at the point where her hair kissed the back of her neck. He was torn between the desire to comfort her, and the need to ensure this marriage was celebrated as a success.

'Thank you,' she said and hurried away, her sandals clicking on the mosaic-tiled floor and her dog following at her heels.

'Why did you feel the need to do that, Aro?'

'Do what?' Aro asked, watching the door. It bothered him that she had not asked where he had been. How typically Veratii. Why he had expected different behaviour from her, he didn't know, but he wanted it. He had wanted to believe that this woman was different from the Veratii of his father's tales. He had seen her courage and her sense of honour that day in the study, and had been sure she was different.

'Forbid her to see her family?' Piso stood up and dusted off his tunic. 'Or is this another Roman tradition of which I remain in blissful ignorance?'

'She lies. You heard Rufus as well as I did. Lydia would demand to see her father as soon as she could.'

'I had forgotten that.' Piso's eyes widened. 'I always considered the Furies drove him mad after his son's death, and didn't pay much attention to his rambling rants.'

'He has been a good and loyal servant to my family, in particular my father for many years. He has a long memory, and he may be right to be cautious. If my father had followed his advice about Veratius's father, he might have avoided proscription.'

Piso broke off a chunk of bread. 'Lydia did seem insistent though. Women are odd, inexplicable creatures. A totally different species. They take strange notions into their heads. Funny she should say about her father being ill—wasn't he at the Senate the other day?'

'He gave no indication to me that he is ill. Far from it. He mentioned several times how glad he was that he had returned to full health. Whatever ailment he had early in the year has cleared up. Trust me, my friend, he has no fear of it returning.'

'Rufus said that Veratius might have put something in the contract.' Piso stroked his chin thoughtfully. 'By Poseidon's trident, I can't think of anything he could. You are too clever for that.'

'Annulment.'

'But surely you slept with her?' Piso's eyes widened. 'She wouldn't lie about such a thing as that. I saw how her cheeks flushed when you came into the room.'

Aro gazed at the frescoes on the dining room wall, frescoes that echoed the rooms and gardens of his childhood, avoiding the question.

'That fire was deliberately set, Piso. No other warehouse or building in the area burnt—just ours and the empty shop behind it. I discovered another curse on the side of the compound when I returned. Now against tradition, suddenly my wife wants to make a private journey to her old home.'

'It gave me no pleasure to drag you from your marriage bed. What should I have done?'

Aro didn't bother to explain that he had been standing looking out at the moonlight when Piso's summons came. He didn't know at that moment who he despised more—Lydia for accepting his marriage bargain or himself for wanting it. Whatever happened, he did not intend to be cheated out of it.

'You did the right thing, Piso.' Aro reached for a grape, tossed it in the air. 'The priests have decided that it was a good omen, a new beginning. Whoever wanted to use this fire against me gained very little.'

'Lydia came looking for you.' Piso's voice was quiet. 'She wanted to find you and discovered me instead. Mayhap she felt you did not want her.'

'Why in the name of Apollo would she think that? I married her.'

Piso gave a careless shrug. 'Women are like that, Aro. You should know better than most. Perhaps she felt piqued you were not there when she woke, or that you had stopped to wash the soot from your hair. If I understood a woman's mind, I would be a rich man.'

Aro kneaded his right shoulder. He wished he had remembered to ask for Lydia's ointment. His whole body ached from searching through the ruins and from the rituals he had helped perform. The gods willing this was the end of it, but he doubted it. He had read the curse tablets.

'Until we understand exactly who is behind the fire and

the curses, I want to keep her safe and in this compound. With me. I want to see what she does next.'

'Do you think she will do something more? What more could she do?'

'Attempt to contact her sister-in-law.'

'And what will you do if she does?'

'I will sail through that storm, if I have to, but this time the Veratii will yield to the Fabii.'

Lydia tapped the scroll against her mouth and resisted the temptation to pace the room. Normally a firm favourite, the tale of Psyche and Cupid and their star-crossed love affair did not hold its usual pleasure. She had made a mess of her recent confrontation with Aro. She knew that.

She should have told Aro the truth to begin with. She had intended on confessing the truth, but then it had seemed such a trivial thing.

Why should he care how her father fared?

And why shouldn't he allow her to visit whom she pleased, even if was against tradition? Surely someone such as Aro couldn't care about tradition. He had built his fortune from nothing. And it wouldn't be a bad omen, necessarily. Only if it was combined with something else.

Equally she did not want her father's enemies to know about his illness. She might now belong to the Fabii, but it did not stop her being Veratii. Surely Aro must understand that. Her feelings and loyalties remained the same despite the words that the auspex had spoken.

She only hoped the tablet she had sent Sulpicia would be understood and that Sulpicia would immediately come for a visit. The message was a bit cryptic, but she had to make Sulpicia hurry. It was the only way to ensure that those pills reached her father and Sulpicia knew how and when to use them.

She hated stooping to subterfuge, but what choice did she have if Aro failed to listen?

She refused to sacrifice her father, simply because her new husband on a whim demanded she not return to her family's home.

'Why have you asked for your sister-in-law to visit you, Lydia? Without delay? To discuss an urgent matter?' Aro's voice dripped ice.

Lydia set the scroll down with a trembling hand. She stood up and put her hand on Korina's collar, keeping her close. Aro's eyes glittered gold. His frame filled the doorway. The tablet she had hastily scribbled not more than an hour ago was in his hand rather than on its way to Sulpicia.

She was prepared for a rage. She had dealt with her father's rages all the time. Rages were over quickly. But this was a cold deliberate way of speaking, something not easily handled or controlled.

'Is there any reason why she shouldn't?' she asked, striving to keep her voice steady and her breathing even. She would be serene, the very picture of a Roman matron. Above all she would not lose her temper. 'She is a friend of mine. As you would not let me go to my father's house or to my usual baths, I felt that it might be pleasant to have someone from my family visit me.'

'On the day after your wedding?'

'Surely you do not intend to cut me off from all my friends?' she asked with her gaze demurely on the tiled floor.

'I will not dignify that remark with an answer. If that is your only contribution…'

Lydia shifted in her sandals. Juno, she sounded worse than Sulpicia when Publius had told her to return the two silk gowns she had just purchased. She had to apologise, to take back the words.

'I'm sorry. You have never said anything of the sort.' She pressed her hands together to keep them still. 'My family is very important to me. I fail to see how inviting Sulpicia to take a cup of mint tea with me will break any protocol. And what gives you the right to read my personal correspondence?'

She waited for his answer, but he stood there, in silence, tapping the tablet against his arm. His face betrayed no emotion. Here was no softening of his features, nothing to say that he had accepted her apology. She wanted to go back to last night's fleeting bit of closeness. Surely the man who had been sympathetic to her then would understand now.

'My servants tell me everything that is happening in this house. When my wife attempts to send a tablet out, begging for her sister-in-law to visit her after I have told her she can't go to her father's house, I become concerned.'

'There is an innocent explanation.'

He tossed the tablet back into Lydia's lap. Lydia stared at it. 'Why do you need to see her so urgently? What has happened that you need to confide in her?'

Lydia stared back at him. His eyes glittered with an ice-cold fury. It was easy to see why he was called the Sea Wolf, why people would be terrified of crossing him. She refused to be—for her father's sake.

'As you refused to let me go to my father, getting Sulpicia to come to me seemed to be the easiest solution. I wanted to tell her exactly what she needs to do, if he should ever have an attack again.'

He lifted an eyebrow. 'Why didn't you ask me to send a note?'

His hand reached out. Lydia evaded his fingers by standing and crossing the room to look out of the window at the fountain in the atrium.

'You refused to listen,' she said. 'I have no idea what you think I want to do, but my father has been ill. Somehow, the pills he needs in case of another attack became mixed up with my jars and ointments.'

His expression showed he refused to believe her. He simply stood there, stony faced, disapproving. 'Veratius Cornelius made no mention of it when we last spoke. He appeared to be well and hearty. I understand he was defending in court this morning. Hardly the actions of a man on his deathbed. Why should I believe you?'

'I am telling the truth.' She held up her palms. He had to believe her. 'He was ill before. It was why I sold the wine— to pay the doctors and buy their silence. You asked before and I couldn't give you an answer. Now I am. I sold the wine to save my father's life and I am proud of it.'

'And the pills, where are they?'

'They are on my dressing table.'

'If you give them to me, I will see that he gets them.' He held his hand.

Lydia acted. This was perhaps her only chance to get the pills to her father. It was also her chance to prove to Aro that she was trustworthy and that she told the truth about her father's ill heath. Once he saw the pills, he'd realise how wrong he had been. She looked forward to seeing his face, hearing his grovelling apology.

'Here you are.' She thrust the jar of pills at him, struggling slightly to catch her breath. 'If you give me a little time, I will write down the instructions. They are very precise.'

Without waiting for an answer, she reached for her stylus and a blank wooden tablet and began scribbling.

'Your father doesn't know how to take them?' His tone held a disbelieving note as he examined the pills. 'Why didn't you simply send the pills to him and avoid this mystery?'

'I wanted to be sure that Sulpicia knew exactly what to do in case of another attack.' Lydia glanced up from her writing and directly into his gold-flecked eyes. He had lifted an eyebrow, but this time there was no mockery in his glance. She swallowed hard and tried to concentrate on her writing. 'As far as I can tell, he remembers very little of the first attack. The doctors fought long and hard to save his life. Sulpicia never pays any attention to what other people do.'

'And what makes you think she will this time?'

'She will have to,' Lydia answered. 'She is the mistress of the house now. She will have to do more than arrange flowers, a bit of light spinning and gossiping with her friends.'

Aro felt the packet grow heavy in his hand. His mouth twisted as he watched Lydia writing away. Her tongue just poked out from her lips. She tucked a stray lock of hair behind her ear. She looked earnest and determined. Exactly how much had she been responsible for?

After she finished writing, he read it over. She wrote in a

fair, precise hand. The tablet seemed innocent enough, a list of instructions. There was always the chance that Piso was correct. Rufus was overwrought from the fire. His mind wandered some days. Had he risked his marriage for nothing?

He clapped his hands and one of the servants appeared, bowing low. Aro ordered the pills to be taken to the Veratii compound. After the servant left, Aro waited and watched Lydia like the falcon watches a mouse to see if she betrayed any sign of nervousness, but she stood in the middle of the room, her eyes accusing him. Many women he knew would have dissolved in tears or hysterics by now. But Lydia was different, fearless. She had argued with him.

'There, you see, all is solved. There was no need for this subterfuge.' He held out his arms and smiled, but Lydia remained where she was, watching him with wary eyes. 'Next time, you have but to ask and the thing will be done.'

'May I ask a question?'

Aro smiled down at her. 'If your request is reasonable, I will grant it.'

She pursed her lips, started to say something and then stopped. When at last she spoke, her question was unexpected. 'Why are there no women?'

'I am not sure I understand.' Aro was taken back. He'd expected her to demand a new gown or even bracelet for her wrist, as the widows in Baiae did.

'Why no women, here, in this house?' Lydia gestured about her. 'There is not so much as a loom or a spindle. The servants I have seen are all male.'

'Does that pose a problem?' Aro leant forward, watching her. He had not thought about it, but Lydia had brought no slaves of her own, only her dog. She needed someone to look after her, female company. 'All my servants are retired seamen. They are used to my ways. They strew the sawdust in the mornings to clean the floors, polish the columns, and scrub the cornices with a minimum of fuss. Women can be distracting.'

Lydia longed to ask if she was a distraction. She pressed her lips together. It was obvious from the way he had behaved today that he did not intend her to be. He intended to lead his life as he had always done, while disrupting hers.

'You needn't fear,' he continued, not noticing her annoyance. 'They will obey you. Or by Neptune's trident, they will answer to me.'

'None has given me trouble,' Lydia hastened to reassure him. She touched the knot of hair at the back of her head. Her curls were already escaping. 'I would like to have a tire-woman, someone to help do my hair and look after my gowns. I left my old tire-woman with Sulpicia.'

He stared at her and made a little gesture for her to continue. Lydia closed her eyes. She knew how it must look to Aro, how it would look to any Roman. A senator's daughter who had to share a tire-woman. Her only consolation was that he did know something of their financial circumstances.

'You left your tire-woman with your sister-in-law, the one who spends her time gossiping.'

'Beroe and Sulpicia get along. I saw no reason to bring Beroe here with me.' She kept her head high. He did not need to know her reasons. 'I had hoped you would have had a woman I could use.'

'Forgive me, it was not something I had considered.'

'I was able to manage on my own for today.'

'It is very pleasing.' His hand moved a curl off her forehead. 'I like it better than the hairstyle you wore yesterday or to the betrothal.'

A flush of pleasure coursed through her—he liked her simple hairstyle. Ruthlessly she pushed it away. She was not ready to forgive him. Too often Publius or Sulpicia thought they could get around her with honeyed words. If she had followed her inclinations, rather than Sulpicia's blandishments, she might never have married Aro.

'I will need to obtain the services of a tire-woman as soon as possible. This hairstyle may do for around the house, but I will be expected to go out and meet my friends. You will want your wife to be thought a leader of fashion.'

Aro regarded her with a steady eye. She needed a tire-woman and he knew of the woman he would choose. It would be a way to help Rufus's family and break down the barriers that had arisen between Lydia and him.

'I will see what I can do. It won't be today, but there is no hurry. No one will expect newlyweds to entertain or dine out.'

Her face became closed. All the warmth vanished as if it had never been. What had he done wrong now? He was trying to make it easier for her. To ease her worries.

'Am I expected to remain here, then, alone and without a tire-woman?'

'Yes, for a little while.' Aro ran his hand through his hair as her expression turned thunderous. 'Only until I can arrange it. I think I know the girl for you.'

'How long is a little while? A day? Two? And why can't I chose the woman I want?'

'We need to discuss a few things.' Aro crossed his arms and prepared to explain about the danger to her. He needed to discover who was behind the curse tablets, before he could allow her to wander freely about the city, visiting her friends. If Ofellius had been prepared to burn his warehouse, there was no telling what lengths he might go to. He refused to risk Lydia simply because a pirate could not behave himself and respect an agreement. The question was how to put it. He had no wish for her becoming scared of her own shadow. He had to choose his words carefully. 'I want to explain—'

'I thought you wanted a wife, not a slave.'

Lydia turned on her heel and Aro was left staring at a vacant doorway before he had a chance to explain further.

Lydia staggered a few steps down the hall and then put her face against the smooth marble that lined the walls.

What had she done to deserve this?

What did he think she would do if she went to visit her father? Or if she had a tire-woman of her own choosing?

It made absolutely no sense. She wasn't asking for much, simply a reason. And until she received one, she was determined to act like a prisoner, and seek a chance to escape.

# Chapter Nine

Later that afternoon, the porter brought Aro the reply from Sulpicia along with several other notes from the woman begging for Lydia's advice on things such as where the amphorae of olive oil should be stored to how to make sure she was not cheated by the silk merchant, and a short tablet for Aro from Veratius Cornelius, thanking him for the tablets and expressing a hope that he found his new wife satisfactory. If Lydia had planned to escape back to her father's, she was acting on her own. He frowned.

Had he really expected anything else? He had allowed an old man's embittered fears to twist his judgement.

Aro tapped the sheaf of tablets against the table. He was tempted to keep back the tablets from Sulpicia demanding help with the house and give Lydia a brief respite, but she would probably want to see them. He had no wish to play her gaoler.

Lydia was where he had expected, sitting in the bedroom, staring out of the window, where she had been since their quarrel.

He placed the tablets on the table and stood awkwardly beside it. 'Sulpicia sent you seven tablets, Lydia. It seems you were correct, she does need your advice.'

She inclined her head and gave a polite smile that did not reach her eyes, the very picture of the haughty Roman matron. 'Thank you. It is such a trifling matter I wonder you brought them yourself.'

'No matter is too trifling where my wife is concerned.'

'No doubt you have a thousand other things to do.' She nodded towards the door.

She was intent on dismissing him. He might deserve it, but Aro tightened his jaw. He refused to be dictated to. Lydia bore some responsibility for the argument they had had.

'If you had come straight to me, all this unpleasantness would have been avoided.' Aro gave a stiff bow. 'I'm sorry for the unpleasantness earlier.'

She bent her head and Aro saw the cream of her neck, the curl of hair artfully placed on her shoulder so it pointed towards the swell of her breasts. A surge of desire throbbed through him as he remembered the feel of her warm body next to his last night, their wedding night. He had tasted passion on her mouth when they shared their marriage kiss.

'I did try,' she whispered, bottom lip trembling. 'You refused to listen.'

'I am listening now.' He covered her delicate hand with his. Even after months of being on shore, it still bore calluses from the sea, so very different from her soft skin.

She removed her hand from his and picked up a scroll. 'I told you the reasons. There is no need to go over and over them. I had no other thought but my father's welfare.'

'You put your father's welfare above our marriage, above what people might think about the omens and entrails. Such whispers could do much damage to my business, to my hopes for becoming a senator. I could not risk it on a whim, Lydia.'

'The confidence was not mine to share.' Her voice was low, without a hint of tremor. 'I am sorry, but I did my duty as I saw it. If you do not wish such a woman for a wife, I understand. Give me time and I will sell my dowry and pay you back.'

'We are married and that is the end to it. It remains for me to discover if I have made a poor bargain.'

'I understand.' She released a long breath, and he saw she did not.

'Your father is lucky to have such a daughter. Do you ever consider yourself, Lydia?'

'I am no paragon of virtue. I made a promise to Publius that I would look after things while he was away. Someone had to do it and Sulpicia can have feathers for brains.'

'And now you have made a promise to me.'

'Yes,' she breathed, looking up at him with large eyes.

His hand smoothed the top of her head, feeling the silk of her curls under the pads of his fingers. Sparks leapt through him. He wanted her, wanted to make her his and ignite the passion that he knew simmered under the surface. He needed to banish the lingering doubts.

She did not draw away, but sat there, still as still could be, head tilted to one side, curls escaping from the bun at the back of her neck.

'There was a fire at one of my warehouses last night,' he said at last, breaking the silence and removing his hand. 'It is why I was not there to greet you this morning. I intended telling you sooner, but our misunderstanding got in the way.'

'You should have said something before. It explains so much. A fire.' Her hand covered her mouth and her hazel eyes widened, becoming a deep green. 'Was anyone hurt? How bad was it? Is there anything I can do to help?'

'The watchman had a few burns, but we lost very little. Most of the cargo had already been loaded.'

'The ointment I told you about works wonders on burns. I will go and…'

She started to rise, but Aro moved his hand and kept her where she was.

'He is under the care of the best surgeon in Rome. When he is better, I will take you to him. He would enjoy meeting you.'

He wanted her here with him, not off administering to the sick and injured. He refused to give her another excuse to postpone their consummation. If she was truly frightened by the thought of coupling, delays would only make the fear grow more, not less. Or if his suspicious were correct, he was not going to give her another opportunity. The time had come.

'It might ease his injuries.' She held out a stone jar. 'If you will take me to him…'

'One of the servants will take it.'

Lydia sank back down, her body hunched. All the light had gone out of her eyes. Aro's heart twisted, but he reminded himself why he was here. He wouldn't force her. He had never forced a woman before and he refused to begin with his wife. But they had to consummate the marriage. In the end she'd want him as much as he wanted her.

'But why?' she asked with a catch in her voice. 'Why are you trying to keep me here? What have I done wrong?'

'You have done nothing wrong. By the side of my night watchman is not your proper place. I want you here with me, where you are safe.'

'Is there some reason I should not be safe?' She gave a hollow laugh. 'I am nearly twenty. I have lived in Rome all my life.'

Aro walked over to the window. In the courtyard, the servants were busy cleaning the atrium's pool, continuing on with their tasks and duties. Simple everyday tasks he had watched a thousand times before, but it was easier to watch them than to face his wife.

'The fire was deliberately set.'

'But fires happen all the time in Rome. Only last week, a large part of Subura caught fire. We could see the glow from the house.'

'Curse tablets were found.' He turned and stared directly at her. 'One named my wife and threatened harm. I want to make sure you have some protection.'

Her small white teeth caught her bottom lip. A line appeared between her brows. Aro released a breath. She had not tried to argue with him and find yet another excuse to immediately depart.

'Sulpicia once had her litter attacked. Her brother was in a dispute about an election. I had not considered it in that way.' She reached out. 'Forgive me, but if you had told me where you had gone, I would have understood. I thought you had gone to see clients at the baths. That you had left me as soon as you could. That you regretted your choice in a wife.'

'I had gone to the baths to wash the soot and ash from my body before I joined my wife. I had no wish to disturb her thoughts.'

'I worry more when I don't know. I thought I had displeased you.'

Her hand touched his arm. Her warm scent held him and he was reminded of roses on a summer day. His fingers closed over her hand, holding it there. Her eyelashes fluttered and a small sigh escaped from her throat. Her tongue darted out between her lips, moistening them, making them as red as cherries in the summertime.

Aro gathered her in his arms, bent his head and tasted her lips. Her body strained against his arms at first, but he increased the pressure and she melted against him, her curves moulding to his body. Her mouth parted, inviting him to drink long and deep. Desire throbbed through him. The memory of her body against his last night surged through him and he struggled to hold on to his self-control. He refused to use force if she was unwilling, but he felt that here, here without the revellers of last night, she would succumb.

He cupped the back of her head, tangling his fingers in her hair. He felt her slight shudder, and knew this time it was not fear, but the awakening of passion. He had guessed correctly. Aro resisted the temptation to crow.

Her body arched towards and she tilted her head back slightly. The golden sunlight lit the column of her throat, making a path his lips ached to follow. The neckline of her gown showed where the two mounds of her breasts started.

Aro's breath quickened. This was his wife, the woman who would bear his children. It no longer mattered that she had attempted to play games, or that she might now be playing a game.

His hands cupped her breasts, and his thumbs rubbed against her nipples. They hardened to points at the merest touch. She moaned in the back of her throat and her back arched towards him. Then she pressed her hands against his chest and spun out of his grasp.

'Lydia,' he whispered, his breathing ragged, 'what are you playing at now? You don't start something like this unless you mean to finish it.'

Lydia swallowed hard. She knew what he meant, what they were about to do, but she couldn't help remembering the time with Titus. How she had made mistakes and how Titus had turned against her. She didn't want that to happen with Aro. Too much was at stake, not only for her father, but also for her future. This man was the guardian of her future as well her husband.

She forced herself to step backwards. The heavy wooden shutter pressed into her back. Her body protested at the sudden rush of cold air.

She hated the way he seemed to see through her, and read her soul. It unnerved her. But by all the gods on the Capitoline, she wanted to feel his mouth against hers.

'I had no intention of starting anything,' she whispered. Her tongue tentatively touched her bottom lip.

'But you have.'

His fingers reached out and captured her chin, holding her there. Her lips quivered, aching for his touch. A whisper of a moan passed through them.

He bent his head and recaptured her lips. This time his tongue licked them, demanding entrance. She parted her mouth and tasted him. Everything ceased to exist except the fresh clean sensation of his tongue teasing hers, overcoming her fears.

Her hands reached up and buried themselves in his thick black hair, pulling his face closer.

She felt the strength in his arms as they came around her waist and held her steady. A shudder went through her.

'Please.' The word was torn from her throat.

He raised his head and his eyes were golden-flecked pools.

'Please what? Please stop or please continue?'

'Please don't stop.'

His mouth nibbled down the side of her throat, sending little pulses of warmth through her. They had started small but now they had become hotter than a charcoal brazier on a cold winter's day.

Her body arched towards him, her breasts brushed his chest, her tightly puckered nipples seeking some sort of relief.

'You see what you are doing to me,' he growled in her ear.

The hardness of him pressed into her, demanding a response. A response her body wanted to give. It no longer mattered what had happened in the past or what might happen in the future, all that mattered, all she desired, was the taste of his mouth and the touch of his body.

Her shawl fell from her shoulders with a soft whoosh. His hands undid the belt just under her breasts, unclasped the brooches that held her gown and that too fell to the ground with a whisper.

She stood, clad in her thin under-tunic, not daring to move a muscle, waiting to see what he would do next. She risked a glance upwards. His face had an intent look.

'There can be no turning back.'

Lydia brought her fingers to her lips and gave the slightest of nods.

His arms came around and crushed her to his chest. His mouth returned to hers with hard urgency. This time their tongues tangled, touched and twisted. Her body became molten wax and she struggled to stay upright. Gently Aro eased her down against the cushions on the bed, the heavy silk coverlet cool against her feverish skin.

His hands cupped her breasts and his thumbs drew small rings over the top of her under-tunic. The coolness of the fabric contrasted with the hotness of his mouth as he captured the nipple through the fabric and slightly tugged. She moaned softly in the back of her throat.

She wanted him to continue. She needed him to continue. This was nothing like she'd expected. His hands and mouth were playing her body as if she were a harp.

His fingers pushed the linen down, revealing her breasts. Then, much as a cat laps milk, his tongue touched a hardened point and curled around it. A bolt of lightening shot through her, driving all thoughts from her mind.

Dimly she registered he had shed his tunic and she was now staring up at his smooth chest with a dusting of fine black hair. A narrow gold chain with a signet ring hung about his neck. His wide shoulders tapered down to a narrow waist, all smooth and sculpted like a marble statue of Apollo. She reached out a tentative hand. Not cold marble, but living flesh. Instantly his nipples contracted, mirroring hers.

Her hands ran over his warm skin. Here and there were

small indentations, scars from past battles, she supposed. Her tongue darted forward and tasted his skin.

A groan escaped from his throat, but he didn't move. Emboldened, she touched him again, drawing circles on his chest as he had done to her.

When her hand wandered lower, his fingers captured hers and brought them to his lips. 'Shall we take it slow, Lydia? Savour our time together? If you keep touching me like that, this will be over before it has properly begun.'

Her hand stilled. She had done something wrong yet again. Misery washed over her. She wanted to curl into a ball. But as his lips travelled slowly down the length of her arm, she forgot to think and began to feel.

She gasped when his hand moved down her belly to become entangled in her curls. Her body bucked, wanting something more. She felt him ease her thighs apart. Then he slipped a finger inside her. All her muscles contracted. Warmth spurted from her. And she groaned in the back of her throat. Her hands pulled at his shoulders. She needed something more, her body demanded something. He seemed to understand.

He moved upwards, and placed his mouth on hers. His tongue entered her mouth at the same time as she felt his shaft enter her, mirroring, echoing the movement. Her body opened and allowed him to fill her.

He stopped, kissed her neck and began to move backward and forward. She followed his rhythm, the speed increasing, bringing her to a crest.

This was it, she thought. This was what it is supposed to be like, why poets sing and women sigh.

\* \* \*

Aro raised himself on his elbow. The dying embers of the sun lit his wife's skin to a rose gold. Her eyelashes made black smudges on her cheeks. He listened to her steady breathing. There was a passion between them, something more than the dutiful coupling of man and wife, something to build their relationship on. The world made new.

Her eyes fluttered open and her hand reached out to touch his father's ring.

'Whose ring?'

'My father's.' Aro swallowed hard. He had worn it for such a long time it had become part of him. 'I never take it off.'

'Why not wear it on your finger?' Lydia's brows knit together.

'I wear it there because I am not yet fit to wear it on my finger. I made a vow to my father that remains unfulfilled.'

'I hope you fulfil the vow soon then.' She withdrew her hand and dipped her head.

'Our marriage has been consummated, Lydia,' he said softly, testing her feelings, as he drew a finger down her neck. 'There will be no annulment.'

Her eyes flew open and she levered herself out of his arms. Within a heartbeat, she pulled on her under-tunic and was struggling into her gown. 'How dare you!'

Aro stared at her and cursed his wayward tongue. Her reaction revealed his words were very close to the mark. She had thought about it, maybe even a vague idea had formed in her brain. The knowledge tasted bitter.

'How dare I?' He raised his body up.

'I have never sought such a thing. How could I? When… when I know the amount my family owes you!' Her hands fumbled with her belt. 'For me a bargain is a bargain. I never ask more than my fair share or attempt to cheat, once it has been struck. It was not the way in which I raised.'

'And the Falerian wine?'

'I have paid for my mistake with my body.'

Her eyes flashed and the implication hung in the air as if she had directly accused him. Aro flinched.

He hadn't wanted to hurt her, but it appeared he had. He wanted to draw her into his arms and kiss the hurt away.

'I have no idea what sort of game you are playing, Fabius Aro, but you won't win.' She spun away from his outstretched arm. Her lips trembled. 'Why do you want me to renege on our bargain? I will not be the instrument that ruins my father. You made a vow to your father. Please believe me, I hold my father in the same esteem. I would never knowingly try to break an agreement he entered into.'

'Game?' Aro stood up and advanced towards her. 'I assure you, Lydia, it is no game. I am deadly serious.'

Lydia brought her hand back as if to strike, but then appeared to think better of it. Her hand dropped to her side. Instead she caught up her shawl and headed towards the door, wrenched it open and hurried off down the hall.

Aro cursed under his breath. He refused to go after her and haul her back. Whatever peace had been between them had been destroyed. He had listened to the ramblings of an old man instead of trusting his instincts. The ring around his neck grew heavier.

Lydia did not pause to see if Aro followed or not. All she knew was that she had to put the maximum amount of space between her and Aro. The walls in the room had closed in as if to suffocate her and she wanted to breathe fresh clean air away from the place where she had given her body and he had cynically taken.

The difficulties of her situation pressed in on her, making her struggle for each breath. What sort of man was Quintus Fabius Aro?

She had thought he had made love to her because he wanted to, not because he wanted to seal the marriage contract, because he thought she was trying to cheat him. It was a direct attack on her integrity, on all that she stood for. She had given her word.

The door to the outside stood before her, beckoning. All she had to do was confront the porter and she'd be gone. She'd be able to breathe again and find some sort of peace in the steady rhythm of the city.

'Exactly where do you think you are headed?' A hand caught her elbow and pulled her back against the wall.

'Out.'

'In bare feet?'

Lydia gritted her teeth and glanced downwards. Her toes peeped out from under her gown. She cursed under breath.

Why hadn't she grabbed her sandals?

She lifted her chin, dared Aro to laugh. 'If that is what I want, yes.'

'You will cut your feet. A terrible thing to happen to such pretty feet.' His face looked lean and determined. 'Why do you need to leave in such hurry, I wonder?'

Lydia fought against the hard grip, pulling first one way and then the other. 'Let me go, Fabius Aro. Or I will…'

'You will what?'

He spun her around so she faced him. He had pulled his tunic on, but had not bothered to belt it. He exuded a raw masculinity and she could see the place at the base of his throat where she had willingly laid her head.

'You don't answer me.' His voice was but a rasp in her ear. 'Answer me, Lydia.'

'What is it to do with you, where I go?' She opted for a careless shrug to show that she was indifferent to him, that his nearness was not doing strange things to her insides. 'Perhaps I will go to my father's, as you said—there can be no annulment now. There is no reason for you to pretend concern for my safety.'

'He will send you back.' An amused smile tugged at the corner of his mouth.

'You are very sure of that.'

'He sent me his assurances along with the tablet from Sulpicia.'

Lydia stood. Her feet seemed to be turned to marble. In the background she heard the trickle of the atrium's fountain. He had known everything was fine and yet had played with her emotions. Was there no end to the perfidy of the man! He had written to her father, received assurances and still he had felt the need to question her motives. He had cold-bloodedly seduced her.

'If you know my father would return me here, why should I not go out and visit him?' She placed her hands on her hip.

'It is not safe, especially for women who go out without their sandals on. I explained before.' He put his face close to hers. 'You must trust me on this. I am doing it for your own good.'

Lydia gave her head a little shake. She had had enough of these bland statements. She was the daughter of a senator. She deserved the truth. Unlike a Greek woman, she could walk in her city with her face uncovered. She did not have to hide her face. 'Why should I believe you? Sulla forbade the carrying of arms in the city. I have often wandered the streets on my own. My father has allowed me some measure of freedom.'

'Your father neglected his duty. He should have taken better care of you.'

Lydia ducked her head. Her last statement was a slight bending of the truth. When she went anywhere, she did tend to take several of her father's retainers for protection, but Aro did not need to know that. All that mattered now was that she regain something of her old life.

If she gave in to his autocratic demand, where would it stop?

The marriage was *cum manu*. She couldn't change that, but she wanted to keep some sort of freedom. She had seen how, when her parents quarrelled, her mother had won the arguments because her father did not have complete control and all she had to do was to threaten to leave. And Sulpicia's dowry had remained out of Publius's creditors' reach as her guardian had refused him access. She wanted no more than the protections her mother and sister-in-law enjoyed.

'Lydia.' Aro's eyes looked sorrowful, but a muscle in his jaw jumped. 'Why should I lie to you? What purpose would that serve? Why would I want to poison our marriage?'

'If I knew your purpose, this conversation would never have started!'

Aro ran his hand through his hair, making it stand up on

end. Lydia noted with a pang that the action only made him better looking. Why was it that men became better looking with mussed-up hair and women only looked like they needed a tire-woman? It wasn't fair. She wanted him to be unattractive, but her body remembered the touch of his hands on her skin, the taste of his mouth. She glared at him, trying to detail all the reasons why she should hate him. Then he smiled, and it was like the sun coming out after a rainstorm.

'Come with me to the warehouse. I will show you the burnt-out shell and the curse tablets.'

Lydia blinked. He was actually offering to show her something rather than simply stating that it was so. She had anticipated other reactions, but not this, this willingness to demonstrate. If she met him halfway, then she'd show him that she was capable of doing things, not simply being some inanimate object to be wheeled out for dinner parties, much as one might show off a pet monkey. She had seen it happen to Murcia Albina. Murcia might say that she preferred it that way, but Lydia could remember the vivacious girl who won all the games at the baths and who had challenged men to foot races.

'I would welcome the chance,' she said quietly, making sure her gaze was demurely down. When she was there, she intended to show him that she was more than trustworthy, and that she was more use than an ornament in the home. She might not know everything there was to know about being a merchant, but when her father was ill, she had learnt a great deal about negotiating and the general demands of business.

'I have no desire to fight you, Lydia.' His fingers caught her chin. She jerked her head away.

'Keep your fingers away from me!'

Aro made no reply. His eyes assessed her, following her curves. Her body felt the pull of his gaze as surely as if it been stroked by his fingers and remembered the pleasure. Lydia drew her shawl more tightly about her. She refused to think about such things.

His mouth turned up into a pleased smile at the telling gesture.

'Very well, we will not couple again until you have asked for the touch of my lips three times.'

'Something I intend never to do.' She drew herself up to her full height. 'I will never plead for the touch of your lips. The whole thing was…was abhorrent to me.'

She turned her face away so he couldn't see the lie that must be surely etched on her face.

'Within seven days, you will have asked for my mouth three times.' He gave a very masculine smile. His eyes once again slowly travelled down her body and then back up to her face. His smile widened. 'I guarantee it.'

'And if that does not come about?' Lydia regarded him with narrowed eyes. 'There has to be something in it for me.'

'I have always given my partners pleasure. I heard your moans earlier. Do not try to tell me or your body any false-hoods. You will come to me.'

Lydia waited. There had to be a way to turn this to her advantage, and to ensure his arrogance did not go unpunished. She leant forward slightly. 'If you don't succeed, you can give me my freedom. If you don't succeed, you will allow me to lead my own life away from here and away from you.'

'Are you speaking of divorce?' His voice cooled dangerously and his eyes glittered like hardened points of amber. 'There will be no divorce between us.'

'Not divorce—I told you I never cheat on a bargain.' She allowed her shawl to slip. To show how confident she was of winning. 'I want to be able to visit whom I please and when I please. Just as it would be if you had married me *sine manu* and I had stayed under my father's guardianship. I want you to transfer my hand back to my father.'

'We will discuss that after the seven days are up.'

'Are you afraid of losing?' Lydia asked, pressing her advantage. 'Why, then you have already lost.'

'Are you?'

'Of course not.' She met his hooded gaze directly. 'I am convinced of winning.'

'As am I. Remember, Lydia *Fabia*, never wager something you cannot afford to lose.'

Lydia gave a brief nod, but a slight unease passed over her.

Even if he did not give her freedom, she would not have to couple again with him. How hard would it be to resist him? She removed from her mind all thoughts of their earlier coupling, how his lips had made her feel. That was before she had realised how unprincipled he was.

'You will find you are sadly mistaken,' Lydia said and looked forwarded to wiping the smug expression off his face. She refused to drop like a ripe plum into his lap. She was not like those women who inhabited the coast of Naples and Baiae, who no doubt came running at the crook of his finger. She was immune to him now.

A wolfish smile crossed his face, and he made an elaborate bow. 'You take the wager, then.'

Lydia paused. She could do this, couldn't she?

'Remember, Lydia, when I wager, I wager to win.' His silken voice tumbled down her spine.

'And you think I don't?' She lifted her chin and stared directly into his eyes. 'I take your wager! Veratii never beg.'

His eyes twinkled.

'If you want to put on your sandals, my nymph, I will take you to the Aventine baths. As charming as your feet are, I expect even at the Aventine, if my wife were to enter without her footwear, there would be comment in the Forum.'

'I thought you offered to take me to the ruined warehouse.'

'I have changed my mind. The warehouse can wait until tomorrow morning when my men are about. Most will have gone home for the day.' Aro gestured towards the sun, whose rays had turned the clay tiles to a deep rich red. 'See, already Helios drives his chariot towards the edge of the sky. Now is the time for relaxation. We shall take a litter, I think. Unless you have other ideas of how we can pleasantly pass the time'

Lydia was torn between wanting to go out, and a desire to win her wager. She should sweep past him, make straight for her room and refuse to come out. Stay there for seven days. However, if she retreated to her room with its tangled coverlets and rumpled pillows, she'd be reminded of the passion they had just shared. The touch of his hand against her skin, the feel of his mouth against hers. No, she refused to think about that.

And, given the determined glint in his eye, Aro might enter her room again. An enclosed private place might not work to her advantage after all. Somewhere in public would be better. Somewhere she could be certain of remembering she was supposed to resist him. She turned her head to one side.

'Is there a need for a litter?'

He looked at her from under hooded lids.

'Who is it that you don't trust, Lydia? Me or yourself?'

# Chapter Ten

Lydia hugged one of the wooden supports in the swaying litter, determined that Aro would not use the movement as an excuse to say that she had invited his advances.

When he said nothing, she risked a glance at the man lounging opposite her. His legs stretched nearly the entire length of the litter and his tunic was rather shorter than strictly necessary. She could see the powerful muscles in his legs and arms, muscles that had come from years of working on board his ships. The memory of how his limbs had so recently entangled with her swept over her, filling her with a sweet languor.

Lydia leant forward, and tucked the skirt of her gown more firmly about her body.

'You don't look the sort who normally takes a litter,' she said to fill the silence and to keep her mind off his legs and the curve of his calves.

'Whenever there is a beautiful lady involved—' there was a hint of amusement in his voice as if he knew his pose disturbed her '—it is the only time I would consider it.'

Lydia regarded her husband, lying back amongst the cushions with a nonchalant air. It was all too easy to imagine him seducing women in this litter. With its green gauze curtains and matching cushions, it breathed sensuality and Aro knew it. He had anticipated her reaction and thought she would slide into his arms.

Lydia stiffened her backbone and resolutely turned her face away. Less than an hour into their wager and she was already thinking of being seduced.

'And I expect it is a regular occurrence.' She forced herself to think about the tales Sulpicia had whispered about the Sea Wolf and his women. How many had he coupled with here in this litter? No doubt it was a tried and tested method with him. 'This litter positively cries out for such behaviour.'

'Not in recent memory,' Aro said with a frown. He raked his hand through his hair, making the black curls spring up. His eyes danced. 'But for you, I am prepared to make an exception.'

Lydia examined her hands, unable to think of a suitable scathing retort and unable to keep her heart from skipping a beat and a warm curl rising from deep within her.

She could fight against this attraction. She would show him that she was made of sterner fibre than he thought, than the women he was used to.

She turned her gaze resolutely away from his gold-flecked eyes and towards the swirl of humanity that crowded around the litter. The sixth hour had not sounded yet and the carts vied with the market stalls for space. Several times, the litter had to stop and wait for the road to clear. In the distance, Lydia could see the temple of Janus as well the temple of Hercules at the edge of the cattle market. She felt herself sliding closer towards Aro and struggled not to fall into his lap. Her sandalled foot touched his thigh. She jerked it back.

'It appears the way is blocked.' Lydia twitched the cushion from behind her back and carefully put it between her and Aro.

'Is it truly?'

Aro drew on all his training as a negotiator to keep his face a blank. He did not know whether to be flattered that Lydia felt the need to have a barrier between them or annoyed at her determination to avoid all physical contact with him. It was an uncomfortable thought.

'The baths are around this corner. It won't be long now.'

'Are the baths any good? What sort of treatments do they have? The ones at the Palatine had very good masseuses and hairdressers.'

Aro drew the curtains of the litter back a bit further so Lydia could peep out better. 'They may not be as new as the baths on the Palatine, but the treatments are good. Try any you like.'

'Don't worry. I plan to.'

The litter came to a stop and was lowered to the ground. Before Aro had time to say anything more, Lydia had stepped from it and started towards the baths without a backward glance. Aro put his hands on his hips and stared at the way her hips swayed. His body hardened. He gave a wry smile. Perhaps this was not going to prove as easy as he had thought.

Lydia had spent time scraping her skin with the *strigil* until it glowed with a pink healthy tinge. With each pass of the blade she thought about how she was scraping away the remains of the passion she had shared with Aro. When she emerged from the hot room, all things seemed possible. She knew she was clean and the time she had spent entangled with Aro a memory. She could concentrate on winning the wager, rather than remembering the feel of his skin against hers.

She tapped her finger against her mouth. Aro was correct about the bath's treatments—they ranged from the traditional hot bath to a variety of massages. The hairdressing and make-up area had seemed particularly promising. Her hair now was much more in keeping with the elaborate curls and braids that Beroe had favoured than her own simple efforts.

She took another look in the bronze mirror. More than presentable. With a few twists, the woman had managed to tame her curls and was now busy applying gold gilt to the hair.

Lydia bit her lip. She probably would have to apologise to Aro. She had made such a fuss about going to the Palatine baths, when in truth these baths had proved more than adequate for her needs. The new hairstyle made her eyes seem bigger, her mouth more inviting. She thought the shade of wine dregs the tire-woman used suited her colouring far more than the harsher reds that Beroe had used.

'The lady likes?' the tire-woman asked in her faint Gallic accent.

'Very much.'

'Is good. Your man will like as well.' There was a knowing look in the woman's eyes. 'All the ladies, they come back and tell me—my man likes this.'

'My man…' Thoughts of Aro and his expression when he saw her danced through her head. Lydia placed the mirror down and stood up. Privately she thought the tire-woman had been overly generous with the kohl about her eyes and the wine-dregs on her cheeks, but the results were impressive. 'It doesn't matter if Fabius Aro likes it or not.'

The room went silent. All the other hairdressers and women stared at her. Lydia wondered what she had done wrong. Was the Sea Wolf so disliked here?

'Your man is the Sea Wolf?'

'My husband.' Lydia lifted her chin and dared them to tell her their tales.

'He is a good man, that one.' The tire-woman clapped her hands together. 'He paid for this bath to be refurbished and for the grain dole last month. I know my man plans on voting for him in the next elections.'

The other women murmured their agreement.

Lydia tapped her finger against her mouth. The appreciation of Aro seemed genuine enough. Perhaps some of Sulpicia's stories had been exaggerated. 'Has he done much for the district?'

The women started detailing all the building projects he had sponsored, small ones that were designed to help the people rather than the large ones favoured by men on the make. The list was impressive.

Lydia stood up and asked for the bill, but the woman waved her hand. 'For the wife of the Sea Wolf, it is nothing. He has already done me a great favour. Any time you like, I will do your hair. The Sea Wolf is a great and generous man.'

Lydia hurried through the courtyard, where a variety of games and contests were played, towards the entrance. As she rounded a corner, she caught sight of Aro deep in conversation with another man, a senator from the broad purple stripe on his toga, but one Lydia was not familiar with. Lydia stood to one side and waited. But Aro showed no sign of noticing her. She tapped her sandal impatiently.

She cleared her throat. The pair turned. Lydia inclined her head. She made an effort to keep her expression serene.

'What a pretty piece that one is,' the senator drawled. 'I know you are renowned for your…art collection and she makes an admirable addition.'

'My wife.' Lydia heard the anger in Aro's voice, and wondered if she should have waited. Publius was always upset when she interrupted his business meetings.

'Indeed. I must apologise, Fabius Aro, for not attending the ceremony. I was…unavoidably detained in Ostia.'

'The entrails were good,' Lydia began, wondering where this line was leading.

'Yes, yes, the entrails—' the senator waved a dismissive hand '—but the Lupan House's main warehouse burnt that very night. Augurs have made mistakes before.'

'It depends on how one looks at it,' Lydia replied in a rush. The last thing she needed was someone saying the marriage was ill founded. She needed this marriage. 'Fire can be good or bad. The warehouse is rising again like a phoenix from the ashes. I understand the augurs decided it was a favourable omen.'

'A phoenix.' A sudden gleam appeared in the senator's eye. 'I do like that. Your wife is an intelligent woman, Aro. I regret that you no longer find it necessary to pay for my services in ensuring your place in the Senate when the censors next meet. No doubt your wife would love to be a senator's wife.'

'My father, Veratius Cornelius, has enough influence with the censors to enable Aro to be enrolled without paying for a *fixer.*' Lydia spat out the last word with distaste. 'Not that the enrolment of my husband would be in any doubt. You only have to look at what my husband has accomplished in this district, from the refurbishment of these baths to the employment of the men in rebuilding the warehouse. It is the people who matter. Some day he will be a magistrate and perhaps even a people's tribune.'

There was a silence. Lydia shifted slightly, wondering if she had gone too far.

'Your wife is right.' The senator inclined his head. 'You will not need to give me a gift, Fabius Aro. You have already done much for the people of Rome. You may count on my vote when you decide to stand in the elections for magistrates.'

'This is indeed an honour.' Aro gave a bow, but his face remained inscrutable. 'I had not considered asking for such a boon.'

Lydia forced a smile on her face. At the very least, he could be polite. Her quick thinking had saved the situation. She had no wish to see his business suffer from an unavoidable accident.

'Nonsense, Fabius Aro, I knew your father. A good man and an honest one. The proscription was a pity, but the water has flowed for a long time under that particular bridge.'

Lydia stared at Aro, unable to quite take in what she had heard. Things started to make sense. The augur at the wedding, the few bits of very old statuary in the garden, the death mask on the wall. She had thought he was playing at having an ancestry, but obviously not. It was also a clue as to why he wore his father's signet ring around his neck. She had a very good idea what sort of vow he must have made.

'Are you saying that Aro is the son of one of the proscribed?' Lydia asked.

The senator paid no attention to her question. 'Of course, there is no question of compensation. Such things were in the past. Sulla was a wise and generous ruler while he lasted.'

'I believe we understand each other.' Aro gave a smooth bow. 'Now I must attend to my bride.'

'You must bring her to dinner.' The senator raised Lydia's hand to his lips. 'It has been a long time since someone so lovely and with such intelligence has graced my table. I look forward to learning more about you, much more.'

'Another time.' Aro's voice was nearly a snarl.

The senator made his farewells and left. Lydia turned towards Aro. She placed a hand on her hip.

'Are you going to tell me what that was all about?'

'Ask me no questions.' Aro's face looked thunderous.

'But you are offering yourself up as a senator when the censors next meet.'

'I plan to.' Aro gave another bow. 'I made a vow and I intend to keep it.'

'Then why didn't you accept his dinner offer?' Lydia decided she would quiz Aro later about his father, but not here and not in front of so many people. People were starting to stare at them even now.

'Because I disliked him staring down my wife's cleavage.' Aro's eyes glittered dangerously. 'He is noted for his exotic tastes in women.'

Lydia rearranged her shawl to make sure her chest was more fully covered and concentrated on the fresco of Greek goddesses cavorting in a glade while Pan played his pipes. 'Where his eyes went had nothing to do me.'

Aro shrugged. 'His patronage does not matter now, in any case.'

'Yes, you will have the support of my father and his friends.'

'You changed your hairstyle.'

Lydia put a hand to the tumble of curls that now adorned the top of her head. 'Do you like it? The tire-woman assured me that it is the latest fashion. She wouldn't let me pay for it either, said she owed you something.'

'I preferred your hair the way you had it before.' His eyes raked over her and, if anything, his expression became harder. 'Your make-up is a little overdone.'

'How I choose to wear my hair has very little to do with you. I happen to like it.' She glared at him, daring him to say another word. If he dared say that she had made cow eyes at the overgrown senator… 'You were the one who brought me here and told me to use this woman. You can hardly complain if the results are not what you desire.'

Aro raised his eyebrow. 'I never said that. I said I objected to an ageing roué looking down my wife's cleavage. Another matter entirely.'

Aro signalled to one of the servants. Lydia caught her tongue between her teeth. He would go and she'd be sent home in disgrace. Lydia started, dismayed to discover she wanted to spend time with him. She wanted to tease out his secrets and learn more about the man who was her husband.

'What are you going to do?' she asked.

'I thought to enjoy the evening with a stroll up the Aventine past the temple of Diana. A much better proposition than listening to a fat senator and his cronies gossiping, don't you think?'

Lydia looked at her husband and knew the sensible course would to be go home in the litter—alone. It would mean she would not have to battle her growing attraction to this man, but after her experience with the women, she wanted to learn more about him. She wanted to learn what he hoped to accomplish in the senate and why.

'Can I join you?' She gave in to an impulse and touched his arm, then jerked her hand back as if his arm might have burnt her. 'The temple of Diana is one of my favourites. My mother and I used to go when the midsummer's moon was at its height.'

A dimple appeared in his cheek, making him look rather roguish. 'Very well, I won't make you beg.'

'I had no intention of begging. I merely asked,' she said, twisting her necklace with her hand.

'I was teasing you.' The corners of his eyes crinkled. 'You respond so well to teasing. Your company will be most welcome, my lady wife.'

The crowds and market stalls had thinned. Only a few wine shops remained open. Here and there in the dusk of the evening were pools of light beckoning from doorways where scantily clad women lounged and workmen sauntered.

Lydia enjoyed speaking with Aro about the latest plays, and prospects for the upcoming races at the Circus Maximus. She was a bit disconcerted to discover that they supported different factions. Lydia had been a passionate supporter of the

Greens for as long as she could remember. The last conversation she had had with Titus had been a disagreement over the races. He had wanted her to support the Green's great rivals, the Whites, while he was away and had become petulant and angry when she refused, telling her that she had no idea about horses or racing. Aro, despite his support of the Blues, did not try to change her allegiance and they discussed the relative merits of the horses and the charioteers.

'And what will you wager if the Blues win and the Whites lose on the day?' he asked softly.

'A ribbon for my hair.' Lydia wet her suddenly dry lips. She was almost tempted to say a kiss and see what he would do. Her mouth tingled at the thought. 'Nothing more and nothing less.'

'Are you sure?' His gaze was fastened on her lips. 'I can't tempt you to wager something else? Something more stimulating, shall we say?'

'A ribbon.' Lydia nodded her head decisively. 'I have no intention of losing. The Whites' team is very strong.'

'Neither do I. There again, I rarely do.' His eyes held hers in a steady gaze. Lydia looked down at her sandals. 'May the best team win!'

Before Lydia could reply, two men hailed Aro and asked for work as they had heard of the building project. Aro indicated both should appear at the warehouse at first light when their request would be considered.

'And what is your opinion of the men?' Aro asked after the pair had departed.

Lydia hesitated. This was her chance to show Aro she was more than an accessory, that she could be of some use in his business. 'It seems odd two men are desperate enough for work that they approach you on the street, rather than going to see your stewards at the warehouse.'

'Times are hard. The numbers receiving the grain dole have increased this year.'

'That makes no difference. They know the way the system works.' Lydia stared after the pair. 'Something strikes me as not quite right about them. I think I have seen the larger one somewhere before, but can't remember where. Perhaps they came with Ofellius when Publius and he signed the deal about the garum. I have a good memory for faces.'

'You may be right.' In the shadowy light, Aro stroked his chin and stared after the men. 'I will question them closely when I see them at the warehouse tomorrow.'

'If they are Ofellius's men, they will only lie. It is probably better to set them to work on some unimportant project where a discreet eye can be kept on them.'

Lydia fancied that he looked at her with a bit more respect as they climbed narrow and twisting streets towards the top of the Aventine.

'What did you vow to your father?' she asked quietly.

'That I would restore my family's name and fortune.' Aro's hand went under her elbow, guiding her away from an uneven stone. 'It happened a long time ago.'

'Is that why you want to be in the Senate?' Lydia asked. She could well understand the pressures. Every Roman patrician male was brought up to believe that his rightful place was in the senate, governing.

'I want to be in the Senate to do some good. The people of the Aventine need just laws to protect them from men like

Ofellius. I have no desire to have what happened to my family happen to anyone else.'

'And the money you would have had from the Falerian wine? It would have gone to pay for that fixer, to ensure you reached the Senate?'

'As you said to the good senator, your father and the people of Rome will be for me, I have no need of fixers.' He smiled down at her. 'Shall we visit the temple?'

Lydia concentrated on climbing the hill. Her words had been more in bravery than certainty. She had no illusions about the fickleness of the Roman populace. Their memories were very short. The elections were not a long time away and surely her father could deliver more than enough votes. She would speak to him about it after she had won the wager and had returned to her father's guardianship. She would show that she could be a gracious winner.

'Always when my mother brought me here, she'd make me look for the columns,' Lydia remarked as they came to the square where the ancient temple of Diana stood. 'We'd play a game about who would be the first to spot them.'

'You must have been a pretty child.' There was soft laughter in his voice.

'No, I was a horrid thing. My hair would not stay smooth and my nose was too big for my face.' She made a face. 'And I was skinny, far too skinny.'

'I must say none of those defects are noticeable now.'

'No, I grew up.'

'And I am very glad you did.' The low huskiness of his voice washed over her, warming her in the coolness of the evening. 'You filled out in all the right places.'

Rather than risk a reply, Lydia looked at the little circular temple that stood on its own in the middle of a square, bathed in the golden glow of the setting sun. Further down the hill, a child cried and was softly hushed. Carts, which clogged the streets nearer to the market, were a distant rumble. Above her in one of the pines, a bird opened its beak and a trilling song issued forth.

She had thought to return here for a quiet visit after her mother died, but something else always needed to be done—Publius wanted more money, or there was a problem with the servants, or her father needed someone to sort out the tablets—and the journey kept being put off for another day. Eventually she had forgotten about it, forgotten the peace.

Now, she was here with Aro by her side. If she wasn't careful, she'd end up in his arms. Gods, her lips tingled in anticipation. Lydia dug her nails into her palm. She would win this wager, and then she'd see about kisses.

'Thank you,' she said, 'for bringing me to this place, for giving me back a memory.'

'You can go in and make an offering if you wish. We are in no rush.'

She shook her head. 'There is no need.'

'If you are sure…'

'Quite sure. It is enough to be here and remember. I find I am remembering things I had forgotten.'

'A good thing?'

'For the most part. Some memories are bittersweet, but I have no desire to forget.'

'The house is not far from here. You may return when you like, but you must take one of the servants with you.'

A spring of happiness bubbled up within Lydia. She was to have some freedom after all. She would be trusted to go places on her own.

'I see no problem with that.'

Aro's face turned grave. 'You must promise to take someone with you at all times.'

'I understand.' The insistence grated. Who did he think she was? She had no intention of wandering around Rome on her own. It was far too easy to get lost in the myriad of streets and temples. Far too dangerous as well. She was under no illusion that the two workmen they had met would not have been so civil if Aro had not been there.

A single white daisy shone in the cracks of the temple steps. Lydia reached down to pluck it. She'd take it home and press the flower, and then keep it in the same cupboard where she kept her scrolls and other personal belongings. As her hand touched the delicate petals, she heard a low growl. Lifting her gaze, she saw two fiery eyes staring back at her through the gloom.

'Lydia, keep still! Don't panic,' came Aro's low voice.

'I have no intention of panicking,' Lydia said. Slowly she lowered her hand and started to inch back towards Aro, never taking her eyes off the dog. 'I know what dogs are like. Korina is never like this.'

'It probably guards the temple. Take it slowly.'

Lydia felt for one step. Made it. The dog had emerged from the shadows. Its lips were drawn back in a snarl and a low growl came from its throat. She took in a breath. Her foot felt for the next step.

'Call off your dog,' she heard Aro say to someone behind her.

The reply was inaudible.

'I said call the dog off. We mean no harm. We will go one way, and you the other.'

The last step. Lydia's foot touched it and then she felt her body tumble. The dog started towards her. She could imagine the jaws gripping around her leg. But suddenly Aro was there.

'Please,' she said.

He scooped her up, carried her a few steps and put her down. 'It will be fine. The dog didn't want to hurt you.'

A low whistle rent the air. Lydia looked up and saw a burly man standing on the steps, the human equivalent of the dog who now cowered at his feet, whimpering.

'Why didn't you call your dog off?' Aro asked.

'I tried, but he didn't listen.' The man gave a shrug. He held out his hand and seemed to grow taller with passing breath. 'I'll take your purse for calling him off now, though.'

Lydia felt her throat constrict and gave a low moan. She should never have tried to pick that flower. She had distracted Aro's attention. This was all her fault.

'I don't think you will,' Aro answered. He sounded as calm as if he were discussing the weather. He paused and straightened his cloak. 'Be grateful and go. The woman is un-injured.'

'Then I shall just have to take it.'

The man advanced forward, bristling menace. Lydia wanted to scream, but no sound came from her mouth. She could see the scar on his cheek and the glint of a knife in his hand, wicked and evil. She wanted to tell Aro to be careful.

Before she could draw a second breath, Aro had launched himself forward, grabbed the man and pinned both arms behind him. The knife fell to the ground with a clatter. The dog gave a low whine.

'Who is going to take my purse?' Aro demanded with one arm around the man's neck, the other holding the man's arm behind him.

'Not I.' The man's voice sounded high and unnatural. 'Who would have ever thought such a thing? To try to get a purse from you. A man would have to be a fool.'

'I trust you are no fool.'

'No.'

Aro released him and the man fell to his knees. He looked up at Aro and seemed to see him for the first time. All colour drained from the man's face. He threw himself in the dirt.

'Do you know who I am?' Aro demanded. The sunset made his eyes seem like oil lamps. Lydia swallowed hard. No doubt the tale would be around the Aventine tomorrow, lavishly embroidered.

'Everyone in the Aventine knows who you are, Sea Wolf.' The man cowered with his hands over his head. 'In the fading light…I thought…perhaps…I made a mistake.'

'This woman is my wife.' Aro gestured towards Lydia. 'I trust you and your fellows will show her every courtesy or you will answer to me. The agreement remains…for now.'

'Every courtesy, certainly, whatever you say.'

'Good, you may go now.'

The man picked himself up and ran off. Aro like some avenging god stared after him, eyes blazing and hands on hips. Lydia wanted to go to him and rest her head against his chest, but that was impossible. She'd never do that, not after what had happened earlier. There was too much between them. Instead she looked about her for the dog.

It still lay there, but its whimpers were coming faster and it kept trying to lick its paw. Behind it, a faint trail of blood oozed in the dimming light. Lydia hurried towards the injured animal.

'Lydia, we need to be going.'

'Aro,' Lydia breathed, trying not to frighten the dog. Her earlier fear was forgotten as she tried to discover the true reason for the dog's behaviour.

'Shall we go, Lydia?' He held out his hand. 'I have no wish for the man to return with his friends.'

Lydia knelt down beside the dog, trying to get a better look at the paw. The dog looked up her with pleading eyes and whimpered. 'Give me some time.'

'You are not injured?'

Lydia shook her head. She held out a trembling hand. 'Shaken, but nothing damaged.'

'Come away from the dog.'

'He's injured his paw. I simply want to take a look at him. I don't think he belonged to that man.'

Aro made a noise at the back of his throat, but before she could say anything more he was kneeling by her side.

'I have a hand on his collar. He won't attack.' Aro looked up at her. A lock of black hair fell over his forehead and his tunic no longer fell in crisp folds, but those were the only outward signs he had been in a fight.

'I don't believe he would have attacked me now. Maybe he was frightened of the man.'

The dog twisted and lay on his back, exposing his belly

as Korina did when she wanted affection. Gingerly, Lydia made her way around to the far side of the dog. All the while, Aro kept his hand on the dog's head, speaking in a low calm voice.

A large shard of glass stuck out of the right paw. She knelt down and plucked it out. The dog gave a low whimper. She removed her shawl and wrapped it around the paw.

'We can't leave him here,' she said, sitting back on her heels. 'He can't go back with that man. It would be too cruel. I hate people who mistreat animals.'

Aro took his belt off and fastened it about the dog's collar as a makeshift lead. Lydia regarded him, with his tunic now falling loose about his body. Most men would not have taken the risk of appearing unbelted in public, particularly when an election loomed. The only times that could happen were during the festival of Saturnalia or attending a funeral of a close relative. To appear that way at other times was to invite censure.

'That will have to do.' He smiled. 'Not the most conventional of solutions, but it should keep him with us. You, I presume, are able to walk on your own.'

Lydia ignored the offered arm. She knew if she so much as touched him, she would want the feel of his lips against hers.

'Where are you taking him?'

'Back to the house.' He looked surprised that Lydia should question him. 'With a warm meal and a watchful eye, he should mend. The porter lost his dog a few weeks ago to old age. It will be a good match for the both of them.'

The dog nuzzled Aro's hand. Lydia wondered what the

gossips would say if they saw that. They would probably call it some supernatural power over dogs because he was the Sea Wolf, but Lydia knew it was kindness. The dog had seen the goodness in him and had responded.

'And the man?'

'He means nothing to me.' Aro's voice held a note of finality as he walked away with the injured dog. 'He won't come, demanding his dog back. If he knows what is good for his health, he will leave the Aventine and never return. I do not intend people should be threatened so near their houses.'

Lydia bent down and picked up the discarded knife. Her breath caught in her throat. Her fingers traced the etching on the handle. She looked over Aro's shoulder towards the Palatine. A shiver passed though her. 'How did this get here?'

'Is something wrong, Lydia?' Aro stopped and looked back at her. 'Now is not the time to linger.'

'I have found our attacker's knife.' She held it aloft. 'It belongs to my father. It has the Veratii symbol on it. My father has a knife very like it in his study. It belonged to his father and his father before him. There used to be another one, but Publius lost it three years ago.'

Aro crossed the square in three steps and took the knife from her. 'Then this knife most likely is the missing one. No doubt it has been in many hands since it left Publius's. What cause would your father have to attack his daughter?'

'You're right.' She forced a smile to her lips. 'It just seemed strange.'

'Did you recognise the man?' There was an urgency in Aro's voice.

'No, but I would if I ever saw him again.'

'I pray to the gods you never do.' Aro's face had the same icy hardness she had seen when he had confronted her about her note to Sulpicia. 'It is time to return home, Lydia.'

'Yes, it is time we went back to the villa.'

The gods were not with him today, Aro reflected as he settled himself in his study with a cup of wine and a variety of tablets and scrolls. Something to keep his mind off the woman who was his wife.

The litter had been a mistake, compounded by his suggestion to stroll to the temple of Diana. He had thought it would be easy to kiss her and instead had ended up rescuing a dog. Unlike most women of his acquaintance, she had singularly failed to give way to hysterics after the attack.

Aro frowned and reached for another pile of tablets. Anything to keep his mind from returning to this afternoon.

He pressed his fingertips together. There was no mistaking the identity of the attacker. He needed to be dealt with very carefully, a measured response, but one which sent a signal. Aro's eyes lighted on a tablet about olive oil. That would provide the perfect excuse. He was a patient man.

A soft knock at the door made him glance up.

Lydia stood there, the soft light from the oil lamps giving a golden glow to her skin. Her hazel eyes were luminous and her lips tinged red. Her hair had escaped from the confines of the tire-woman's style, and now loose curls framed her face. His body leapt at the sight, but he forced himself to stay seated.

'Come in,' he said and gestured towards a low stool.

She sank gracefully down on it.

'I wanted to thank you,' she said in a low tone.

Aro put down his scrolls and tablets and leant back in his chair. 'Thank me for what?'

'For saving the dog, for everything.' She made a little gesture with her hand and her gown slipped very slightly to reveal more of the line of her neck.

It took all of Aro's strength not to draw her into his arms and bury his face in her hair. Unfortunately, he had made that foolish promise to her. She had to come to him and offer him her lips. If he followed his natural inclinations, she would never trust him again, and he found much to his surprise that he wanted her to trust him.

'It was nothing. Anyone would have done the same.'

'No, most would have walked on by. Neither my father nor brother would have sacrificed their belt for a mere dog.'

'You must not think me a hero from the old tales…' Aro permitted a smile to cross his features '…because I am anything but. You will find me an ordinary man with simple tastes. You see—Clodius has returned my belt to me. He is very happy with his new dog.'

Her gaze lowered. Her mouth turned up into a sweet smile. 'I have not thought you were anything but. Will you be dining with me?'

'I regret—no.' Aro stood up and wiped his hands against his tunic. If he dined with her, he would probably give in to temptation. And seduction was not on the menu. Then they would be no further forward than earlier today. He would distract himself with his plans of retribution.

'Yes, I understand,' she said in a much more subdued voice

as the light went out of her eyes, all passion hidden, the perfectly composed matron. 'Where are you going?'

'Out.'

'No doubt you expect me to beg you to stay.'

'The thought had crossed my mind,' Aro said carefully. He had to depart before he started to beg. He had made the wager and it suited him to play by the rules—for now. 'If you wish me to, I will.'

She hesitated, a pause no longer than it took a drip to fall from the water clock. Her tongue flicked over her lips, wetting them, making them more inviting than ever.

'I warn you, Fabius Aro, you will not win this wager.'

'It is my deep regret to inform you I always keep my promises, even when they prove on the face of it—seemingly impossible.' Aro gave a bow and quit the room.

## Chapter Eleven

'My dearest sister, I came as soon as I could,' Sulpicia said as she entered the *tablinum* the next morning with a jangle of bracelets and the scent of expensive perfume. 'Cornelius absolutely refused to let me come any earlier. He thought it would not be the done thing. But why? I argued. Why should I not see my very dearest sister-in-law? I still consider her sister, even if she has been married *cum manu*. Although why he allowed it—it is so unfashionable—I have no idea. He relented this morning and sends you his regards.'

Korina gave a joyful bark and attempted to jump at Sulpicia, who looked slightly aggravated at the faint streaks of dirt on her rose-pink gown. Lydia put the scroll she had been reading down, stood up and advanced towards her sister-in-law. She had missed Sulpicia. 'It is very kind of you to visit, Sulpicia. I look forward to hearing all the news. Other than the butcher or the wine-shop owner, who has Gallus the porter managed to annoy lately?'

'Who hasn't he? You have no idea what that man's temper is like.' Sulpicia gave one of her tinkling laughs.

They chatted for a while about Gallus and his impossible behaviour and then Lydia remembered the knife. It was probably as Aro had said—the one that had gone missing long ago.

'Has my grandfather's dagger gone missing?'

Sulpicia put her hand to her mouth. 'Which dagger would that be?'

'The one in the study.'

'Oh, that dagger.' Sulpicia gave another laugh. 'You had me worried. I would not know anything about that dagger. I never go into Cornelius's study, if I can help it. Why?'

'I had wondered. I recently saw a dagger that made me think of it.' Lydia kept her voice casual, but every nerve waited for Sulpicia's response.

'Wasn't one lost a long time ago? I seem to recall Publius saying something about it. You know how Publius is, always talking about something.'

'I know what Publius is like.'

'Oh, look.' Sulpicia clapped her hands together. 'I had heard rumours of the Sea Wolf's fabulous art collection. Is that an original Greek Pan or a copy?'

'It is an original, I believe.' Lydia allowed the conversation to drift away from the knife, but she could not help feeling that Sulpicia knew something, something she wanted to keep from Lydia. 'Perhaps you are in need of refreshment. The day is quite warm for this time of year.'

'You always know what is wrong with me!' Sulpicia gave a tinkling little laugh. 'My feet ache dreadfully. And I miss Publius. The house isn't the same without you. You do remember you promised to come to me when my time came.'

'I do remember and I will.' Lydia reached over and touched Sulpicia's hand.

Sulpicia's fingers reached out and curled around hers in a tight grip. 'Thank you.'

She signalled to a servant and within a very short space of time, he had returned with a tray with cooled mint tea and sweet wine cakes. Korina gave a faint whine and Lydia slipped a cake to her.

After taking a few sips of the tea, Sulpicia appeared to recover. She started to stalk about the room, examining the décor and making one or two remarks about the frescoes. Her eyes narrowed and she pointed to a particularly nice piece of Greek sculpture. 'Is that an original too?'

'I believe so.' Lydia took a small sip of the mint tea, determined not to show her annoyance.

'It is quite an expensive piece, but then I suppose the Sea Wolf must stuff his house with those bits and pieces he picks up on his travels. Gods knows how he gets them.' Sulpicia dropped her voice. 'I heard tell that—'

'Aro is well known for his eye in art. A noted collector, a senator said the other day.' Lydia spoke, cutting across the story. Sulpicia's continue reference to Aro as the Sea Wolf annoyed her. She longed to show Sulpicia the good Aro had done on the Aventine. 'He has a vast and varied collection. I can show it to you.'

'Some other time.' Sulpicia sat down and carefully arranged the folds of her gown. 'We have more important things to discuss.'

'Such as?'

Sulpicia signalled to one of her servants, who produced a

stylus and a scroll. She leant forward with an eager expression on her face. 'You haven't answered my tablets. Not a single one. How can you be so cruel? I sent you six this morning.'

'I answered the one about Father and his eating habits.' Lydia set down her cup of mint tea and looked at Sulpicia in disbelief. She had so wanted to see Sulpicia as a reminder of home, but Sulpicia had not even bothered to ask her how she was. Perhaps Aro was correct. Sulpicia needed to take responsibility for her own life. Lydia dismissed the thought as disloyal. Sulpicia had a hard time. All she needed was a helping hand. However, Lydia knew she could not manage two houses at the same time.

'Cornelius is in such a bad temper these days, Lydia. When everything I try to do goes wrong he shouts at me. It makes my head pain so to remember everything.'

'It is not difficult. And Father does like his dinners on time.'

'Do not let us quarrel.' Sulpicia gathered Lydia's hands and pressed them to her cheek. 'You are Publius's sister and my dear friend. It is why I feel lost without you in the house. I can do some things like spin, but I don't have the same knack of managing that you do. Just help me a little. I will try to do better. Honest, I will.'

They talked for a while about the routines of the servants and which merchants to use. Lydia began to despair that Sulpicia would ever get any routine correct. She hated to think what her father would say if the supplies ran low or, worse, out. Then she reminded herself that it was no longer her responsibility. She tried her best to answer all the questions without showing how upset it made her.

'The *liquamen* problem is solved,' Sulpicia announced, a little smile playing on her face. She stretched and waggled her purple-and-gold slippers back and forth. 'That was something I could do.'

'There is plenty of fish sauce,' Lydia answered, mentally going through the store cupboard. Honey and olive oil were in ample supply and the dried herbs should last. She could see the amphora of fish sauce as if it were standing before her. 'An amphora was delivered two days before last Kalends.'

'Not that *liquamen,* my darling sister.' Sulpicia gave her tinkling laugh, the one she gave when she was particularly pleased about something she had achieved over someone else. 'The fish sauce you sent to Corinth. The one destined for Publius and the one you promised to sort out the day you became betrothed. I wanted to tell you that there was no need to worry because it is all fixed.'

Lydia thought how strange the Fates were. A few days earlier and she would never have been in her father's study, would never have met Aro. 'Has the fish sauce arrived in Corinth?'

'The problem with the shipment is solved. Honestly, I wonder why people treat me as if I cannot do anything. I found out my answer very quickly, when you failed.'

'As long as it is settled, then.'

Sulpicia gave a mysterious smile and turned the subject towards who was divorcing whom, and who had been the cause of the latest scandal sweeping the Forum. Lydia struggled to keep her face interested. She would have rather talked about the latest play, the races or even the next gladiatorial bout, but Sulpicia was intent on relaying all the gossip.

'Now, do say you will come to the baths with me,' Sulpicia cried when Lydia tried to move the subject on to the games planned for the Festival of the Shepherds in a month's time. 'You can learn all you need to know there. Besides, everyone wants to know about the Sea Wolf. Tell me, is he as horrid as you feared? You can trust me.'

Lydia toyed with her cup. Here was her chance to explain to Sulpicia that she was wrong about Aro and tell her about all the good he had done in the Aventine. It would probably not change Sulpicia's view of Aro, but it would make Lydia feel better. 'You must not believe all the tales you hear, Sulpicia.'

'There is always a truth in rumour.'

A faint noise caused Korina to lift her head from where she was lying at Lydia's feet. Lydia put her hand on Korina's collar and glanced up. Aro stood in the doorway, his tunic immaculate but barely containing his chest and an unreadable expression on his face. Lydia swallowed. How long had he been there? How much had he heard?

He gave her a slight nod, and then he moved away down the corridor, his sandals striking the stone floor with firm unyielding steps. Sulpicia looked at her with an expectant air.

'And?' She leant forward. 'You must have something to say, Lydia.'

'I am sorry, Sulpicia, but I have other things to do.' Lydia stood up and walked to the window and pushed aside the shutter. The sun shone down on the garden. A servant raked the gravel. Even if she wanted to tell Sulpicia about Aro, where would she begin?

'I understand all. Your actions speak all too loudly, my sweet sister. The Sea Wolf has returned to his lair and now you wish to be rid of me.' Sulpicia's tone became more arched. 'If you would be so good as to call my litter, I will take my leave. I have promised Prosca and Marciana I would meet them at the baths for the fifth hour. You are welcome to come with me.'

Lydia stood up and adjusted the folds in her gown. Prosca and Marciana were two of the most notorious gossips in Rome. She had had very little time for them before she married, and she saw no reason to start now. She had so wanted a visit from Sulpicia and now she could not wait until her sister-in-law left. 'There are things I have to do…this house does not run itself.'

'As you wish…' Sulpicia's lips turned up into a thin smile.

Lydia rapidly made her farewells and then went in search of Aro. She discovered him in the garden, sitting on a bench surrounded by fragrant bushes of lavender, rosemary and thyme. His dark head was bent and Lydia could see the line of his neck, straight and firm.

The stylus scratched against a tablet. He glanced up when she appeared and pointedly laid the tablet aside.

Lydia put a hand on Korina's collar, holding her back. He had overheard, and beyond doubt it had sounded worse than it was. What could have possessed Sulpicia to make those remarks? And the Fates would have Aro appear at the same time. She had to do something.

He indicated a seat beside him and Lydia sat down. She kept her gown carefully away from the long line of his leg.

'Sulpicia has left,' she said in a faltering voice. The apology was harder than she had hoped. From the set of his body and the line of his mouth, he was not going to make it any easier.

She pressed her fingertips together and made another effort to explain. 'She came to visit. She wanted to know more about running my father's house.'

'Was that who was here?' he lifted an eyebrow, and picked up another scroll. 'I heard voices and knew you had company. I had no wish to disturb you. I hope she did not leave on my account.'

'You should have come in. Shared a cup of mint tea or muslum wine with us. Sulpicia is quite a pleasant person when you get to know her. She is not as empty-headed as she might first appear.'

'I had no wish to disturb you as you appeared to be engrossed in conversation.' He tilted his head and his eyes assessed her as if trying to decide something. 'Your friends may visit here, Lydia. I am not a demon, intent on cutting you off from your former life.'

'I never thought you intended that.'

'It is my mistake, then.' He inclined his head briefly.

'Yes, it is,' Lydia said quietly.

He made no reply, but started to work on his scroll again, giving every indication that she had been dismissed.

Lydia knew she should rise and leave, go back to her scrolls; instead she concentrated on the lavender plant. Its purple spires were just beginning to break into bloom. Soon they would have to be collected and dried. They would serve to keep the sheets and blankets smelling sweet throughout the year. But if she collected them too early, the smell would not be as strong.

After a while he glanced up and ran a hand through his hair.

'I have made enquiries,' he said in a tone that would allow for no dissent. 'Rufus's eldest granddaughter will act as your tire-woman. She is young, but eager and willing to be trained. She desires to make her own way in the world. I trust it will meet with your approval.'

'When does she start?' Lydia struggled to keep her voice steady. She was pleased to be getting a tire-woman, but she had wanted some say in the matter.

Aro clapped his hands and a servant appeared. He held up one finger. The servant bowed and disappeared back into the house.

'Tuccia arrived this morning,' Aro said. 'She's been waiting in the kitchen to be introduced to you.'

'I would have liked to have been consulted.' Lydia met his gaze with a direct gaze of her own. It was churlish of her to refuse this girl's services. She did need a tire-woman, but for it to be presented as if she had no say in the matter annoyed her. What if she disliked her or the ways she dressed hair?

'What was there to consult about? You need a tire-woman and I have found you one.' Aro crossed his arms over his chest, leaning back slightly on the bench. 'If you don't like her, you may send her away.'

The slight dark-haired girl appeared. Instantly when she saw Lydia, she darted forward, grabbed her hand and kissed it. Lydia gently withdrew her hand. The girl was clean and her hair neatly dressed. She looked to be the sort of girl Lydia would have chosen for her own tire-woman. She wanted to dislike her, find a fault, but she couldn't. 'Hello, Tuccia. Do you think you would like working here?' she asked the young girl.

'My grandmother says if you are Aro's wife, I will be in good hands.' The girl clasped her hands under her chin and looked up at Lydia with large brown eyes. 'You will find me a quick learner. I am stronger than I look. I used to do my grandmother's hair and my mother taught me a bit about what a fine lady expects. Some day I hope to run my own hairdressing booth.'

Exactly what game was Aro playing here? A small flush of pleasure swept through Lydia at the thought of her own tire-woman, one she would not have to share. But she couldn't rid herself of the thought that Aro wanted someone he trusted as her tire-woman, someone who would be loyal to him.

'And your verdict is?' Aro asked, his face inscrutable. 'Will Tuccia suit?'

Tuccia turned towards her, unable to conceal the pleading expression. The young woman wore a tidy but thin tunic, and her arms looked slender.

Lydia swallowed hard. She could hardly accuse him of seeking to spy on her, here in front of the girl. And he was right, she did need someone to help her with her clothes and hair. She had to trust him. It surprised her that she wanted to trust him.

'I am sure Tuccia will prove adequate. My needs are simple.'

'Splendid.' Aro put his hands behind his head, and his tunic tightened across his chest. He stretched his legs out, re-vealing their full muscular length. Lydia made sure her eyes were fixed on a spot somewhere behind him, but she couldn't resist taking another glance at the firm strength of his thighs.

'Is that all you wanted from me?'

'For now.' Aro's smile increased as if he knew how hard she found it to keep her attention away from the way his chest rose and fell against his tunic.

Lydia cursed under her breath. This wager was supposed to be easy. She shouldn't be thinking about the shape of his legs or any other part of him.

He lifted an eyebrow and then picked up his discarded stylus and scroll. He gave a nod towards where Tuccia stood. 'I suspect you will want to take your new tire-woman off to get better acquainted. No doubt you will have much to talk about and discuss. And, Tuccia, tell her to wear red. The colour suits her.'

'What are you going to do?' Lydia stared at her sandals, determined not to let the flush of pleasure she felt show.

'Laze here in the sun, unless you can suggest something better?' He gave her a hooded look and his voice dropped to a husky note.

'I wondered, that was all.' Lydia raised her chin a notch and stared directly into his gold-flecked eyes. 'Tuccia, if you will follow me, I will show you how I like my things kept.'

The girl nodded.

Lydia spent some time explaining how she wanted her clothes kept and cared for, and was pleased to find that Tuccia appeared to be well versed in the matter. She also confessed to a liking for spinning, a task Lydia was more than willing to relinquish to her.

'How long have your family served Fabius Aro?'

'Before Fabius Aro's father freed him, my grandfather

was a slave. We are proud to work for the Lupan House. My father was one of Fabius Aro's captains, until his death.'

'Then why are you working?'

'There is little money in the house.' Tuccia gave a small shrug. 'Now with his injuries, my grandfather won't be able to work. We don't take handouts, we work. Grandfather didn't want me coming here. He hates everything to do with the Veratii. He considers them dishonest. My grandmother was most disappointed, but Fabius Aro came to the apartment and asked for me especially.'

Lydia frowned. She wanted to question Tuccia about her grandfather, but the news that Aro had gone to the grandfather's apartment surprised her. 'He asked for you?'

'Yes, can you believe it? Quintus Fabius Aro, the Sea Wolf himself, actually climbed all the way up to our apartment and told my grandfather that no other girl would do for his wife's tire-woman.'

'Did he say why?'

'He said that I was the right sort of girl to do this job and asked Grandfather out of respect for their long friendship to allow me to come to serve you.' Tuccia's cheeks glowed with pride and her chest puffed out.

'And what did your grandfather say?'

'He wasn't happy. Your family…that is, your old family caused no end of trouble for Fabius Aro's father, and Grandfather has never trusted the Veratii since. Said you were more trouble than you were worth. But Fabius Aro was having none of it. He argued with Grandfather, Grandmother joined in, and finally Grandfather gave in. I knew he would. Grandfather trusts Fabius Aro.'

Lydia listened somewhat uncomfortably to this little recital. She had had no idea that the Veratii had any part in Aro's family's proscription. A cold shiver ran down her back. He could have exposed them when he discovered she had sold the wine, but he hadn't.

'What about your mother? Did she object? Aren't you a bit young?'

'I turned twelve in January.' Tuccia stood up straighter. 'My mother married another man last Quincillus and my grandfather looks after me and my two brothers.'

Lydia nodded. That was how it should be. Children stayed with the father's family in cases of remarriage or divorce. She didn't want to think about what might happen should she have children. How could she ever consider leaving her children? An ice-cold shiver ran down Lydia's back. She might even be pregnant now. Not an unwelcome thought, she discovered.

'Are your brothers too young to work?' she asked quickly as Tuccia gave her a searching look.

'My brothers have found jobs at the docks, taking messages. But I want something more from my life than marrying a workman. Some day I want women to come to my house and have their hair done, their faces painted.'

Tuccia started to redo Lydia's hair, brushing it smooth and then twisting it up in a simple but effective knot.

'Has your family been with the Fabii for a long time?' Lydia asked as she watched Tuccia in the bronze mirror. 'Was your grandfather with them when the family were proscribed and exiled?'

'Yes, my lady. He refused to leave even though most of

the other servants were sold. He and my grandmother accompanied them to Hispania.'

'Was there a reason for the proscription?'

'None whatsoever!' Tuccia declared hotly. 'The Fabii were always loyal to Rome. Aulus Veratius Neptus betrayed them to save his own skin.'

Lydia placed the mirror down. Tuccia's words confirmed one of her fears. There was more to Aro's desire for marriage than a simple readdressing of accounts and his need to marry a patrician. She had been so eager to undo her mistake that she had not questioned his motives. Was it possible that she had thrown herself headlong into the brazier?

His father had been her grandfather's enemy. She was sure of that. It didn't surprise her. Her grandfather had been a bitter and twisted man. Her mother had never liked him and had always thanked Juno her father had not taken after him.

But where did that leave her? Where did it leave their marriage? Would he be prepared to forget what her grandfather had done? He must be, otherwise he would never have married her. She had been so sure that day that he was going to walk out and denounce them all.

What had stopped him?

'Is there something wrong, my lady?' Tuccia asked in a worried tone. 'I have not done anything wrong, have I? You are staring at the mirror as if you had just seen the Medusa with all her snakes. We need the money, my lady. Don't send me away.'

'You have not done anything wrong. Your styling pleases me. Simple but effective.' Lydia reached back and grabbed Tuccia's cold hand. 'I am delighted to have you as my tire-woman.'

'Truly?'

'Yes, truly.' Lydia stood up and adjusted her shawl more tightly about her. 'Please will you take Korina to the kitchen and see if there is a free ham bone for her? She looks like she could use one.'

'That is the sort of job I like.' Tuccia gave a huge grin.

Lydia watched her go and then started off to find Aro. She wanted to hear the whole story from his lips. However, the garden was empty. A sparrow peeped out from a laurel bush, but that was all. A servant came out and started to brush the paths with a broom.

'Have you seen Fabius Aro?'

The servant bowed. 'He has left, my lady.'

'Left? Gone where? Do you know when he will be back?'

'There is trouble at the docks, my lady.'

'Is it anything serious?'

'Trouble is always serious, my lady. But our men will give a good accounting of themselves.'

Lydia sat down on the bench and had lunch there while she waited, but the shadows grew long and Aro did not return.

When Tuccia found her, she explained and Tuccia's eye grew big.

'My brothers,' she whispered, turning white. 'The last time there was trouble at the docks, a man was killed. Please let them be all right.'

'I am sure they will be fine.' Lydia patted the girl's hand. 'Fabius Aro is there.'

'If he is there, everything will be well.' Tuccia scrubbed her face. 'He will look after them. He has done so much for my family, since my father died.'

Lydia wished she had the same confidence that Tuccia had. 'I expect Clodius the porter will know something more.'

'I'm sorry, my lady,' Clodius said when Lydia had found him in his small room with his new dog by his side. 'I know nothing except Fabius Aro has left. He asked that you remain here, and not to let you out.'

'Not even with an escort?' Lydia cocked her head, trying to determine how bad Aro thought the situation was.

'Fabius Aro did not feel that it was safe.' The elderly man sucked his teeth and rocked back and forth. 'The compound is well-guarded, of course. But anything can happen out there. These little disturbances have a way of growing.'

'I understand.' Lydia pressed her lips together. The porter's words were designed to comfort, but they did the exact opposite.

She spent the late afternoon in the atrium, one eye trained on the door and the other on a scroll of poetry. Despite the comings and goings of several servants, Aro failed to return, and no one would say when he was expected back. Their eyes would slide away from Lydia, and they would mutter soon, but that he was safe.

Eventually Lydia spent a quiet supper dining on figs, bread and cheese and lentil soup. Korina lay at her feet with an ever-hopeful expression on her muzzle.

She was grateful for Tuccia's chatter as she brushed her hair, telling her about her father and the adventures he had shared with Aro, each more fantastical than the rest. Sea monsters and goddesses indeed. Stories for winter nights. Tuccia went off to her alcove, and Lydia settled down with several scrolls and

Korina at her feet. When she could finally no longer hold her eyelids open, she crawled into bed and slept fitfully.

A slight noise woke her. She sat up, and Korina padded over to the door. Lydia crossed to the door and peeped out. The corridor was lit by moonlight streaming through a window.

Aro stood, his face shadowed, his hand on the door to his room. At the sound of her door opening he turned.

'You weren't at dinner,' Lydia said at his questioning glance.

'I had to go out.'

'You did not bother to tell me where you were going or even to send word. All anyone would tell me was that there had been trouble at the docks and you were safe.'

'I did what I thought was right.' Aro's voice held a firm note. 'I had no wish to unduly disturb you.'

'Well, you did.'

His eyes traced the line of her figure up and down. Lydia wished she wore more than her thinnest under-tunic. Her dark hair flowed over her shoulders. She wished she had thought to grab her shawl. She forced her eyes to remain straight ahead and her head held high.

'Is this the correct time for a conversation like this?' he asked. 'It is late. We can speak of my neglect in the morning.'

Lydia bit her lip. The time didn't matter. She wanted to know. She had to know. If she didn't ask now, she'd never know. His hand was on the door handle, pushing it. In another instant, he would be gone.

'Was anyone hurt?' she asked rapidly. 'There was a fight

at the docks, wasn't there? That is what the servant meant. It is why all the servants have been speaking in hushed tones.'

He stopped, and looked at her. 'There was a scuffle at the docks, but none was seriously hurt. Does it matter?''

'Tuccia said her brothers have started working at the docks, carrying messages. I wanted to know if either of them were involved.'

'Her brothers were out of the way. I saw to that. I have a promise to keep to their late father.'

'Tuccia said he had been a captain of one of your ships.'

'What else did Tuccia tell you?' His eyes were hard.

Lydia knew now was the moment she should ask about his reasons for marrying her, but what seemed an ideal solution in the sunlit garden appeared reckless in the moonlit hallway, confronted with his bulk and uncompromising tone.

'This and that. She is talkative. Quite amusing.'

'You like your new tire-woman.'

'She is very amiable. She gets on well with Korina. Somehow she convinced the cook to give her the biggest ham bone I have ever seen.'

'That sounds like Tuccia. Always happy and chatting.' Aro gave a short laugh, but could not disguise his sharp intake of breath.

Lydia looked at him more closely. He was carrying his right arm awkwardly and there was a faint reddening of his jaw. 'You may have kept Tuccia's brothers away from the trouble, but you were in the centre of it.'

'Yes.'

'Let me get you some salve.'

Without waiting for an answer, she darted back to her

room and picked the jar out of her cupboard. Its distinctive dolphin top made it easy to find in the dark. She cursed under her breath as another jar rolled on the floor.

She came back out into the corridor. Aro was still standing there. The moonlight made his face look silver. He could almost be a statue of Apollo.

'Ah, the salve that works wonders.' His mouth twisted up into a smile. He moved his arm and it immediately turned into a grimace. 'How do you use it?'

'You spread it over your sore muscles.'

'Both my arms are sore.' He gave a little shrug. 'Can you demonstrate?'

Lydia made a little clucking noise in the back of her throat. Men, they were like children at times. Imagine not knowing how to put on a salve. She scooped some of the ointment on to her fingers and spread it on the top on his arm. Sparks shot through her, but she ignored them, concentrating instead on rubbing the ointment in, feeling the knots of muscles relax.

'It hurts higher up.'

His voice was a husky whisper and sent shivers down her spine. She should back away now, but her feet refused to move. She pushed aside the tunic and continued to rub the ointment in. His flesh was warm living marble under her palms. The sparks had lit a small curl of warmth in her middle. Her fingers trembled and she tried to concentrate on her task. His hand stopped hers, held it there.

'I can do the rest.'

'It will make everything better.' Her voice was no more than a breath.

'It already has.'

Suddenly she became aware that she was standing very close to him. She could feel the heat from his body, see the shadowy stubble on his cheek. She allowed her hand to fall to her side. In another breath, it would be curling around his neck and she'd be demanding his lips. She wanted his kiss. She barely held back the words asking for his kiss. 'I ought to leave.'

She made no move to go, found it impossible. Her body swayed slightly towards him, seeking his heat.

His hand touched hers. His eyes were deep unfathomable pools. 'Thank you. I am sorry if I caused you worry.'

She looked up at him, intending to say something, but all words vanished when she saw the intent look on his face. Her lips parted. He had to kiss her. She wanted him to kiss her. She needed to feel his mouth against hers. He bent his head.

'Is this what you want, Lydia?' he demanded against her lips. 'Say it then.'

'Kiss me…please,' she breathed.

Her arms curled round his neck and held him tight. His tongue found the small parting and entered her mouth. Their tongues touched for a heart-shuddering instant and then re-treated. Her body brushed his firm chest, causing her nipples to harden to tight points. His arms held her close. Their tongues met again, tangled, tormented and teased.

Then she realised what she was doing, and stepped back. His arms let her go. She struggled to control her breathing. It was coming fast as if she had run too many times around the courtyard at the baths.

'You said you weren't going to kiss me until I begged.'

'I apologise if the kiss was distasteful.'

'Far from it.' Lydia was compelled to be honest. 'But I wanted to let you know I never begged. I asked.'

'It was my mistake then,' he said thickly. A half-smile appeared on his lips. 'It is time you went to bed…alone.'

He gave a small bow and departed. Lydia stared after him. Her fingers traced the outline of her mouth, feeling the imprint of his kiss.

# Chapter Twelve

The first faint clatter of buckets and brooms as the servants started their daily routine woke Lydia the next morning. Korina raised her head from where she lay at the foot of the bed and padded over to the door.

Despite the early hour, Tuccia had already prepared a simple meal and then she waited to help Lydia dress. She quickly chose a dark green gown with a light green *stola* to complement it and, instead of a belt, a gold ivy-leaf *catena*. Tuccia carefully wrapped the heavy chain around Lydia's waist, crossing it over her breasts, around her neck and back around her waist.

'It is very old, this,' Tuccia said as she fastened the clasp with neat fingers.

'It was my mother's and her mother's before her.'

Tuccia gave a nod as if she was satisfied. She carefully arranged a shawl of green netting over Lydia's arms.

'There now, Fabius Aro will be unable to take his eyes off his bride.'

'I doubt I will even see him. He has many other things to do, particularly after yesterday's disturbance. He has probably already left for the docks or the warehouse.'

'You will see him.' Tuccia tapped the side of her nose.

Rather than replying, Lydia concentrated on getting the folds of her gown right. The encounter last night in the corridor had unsettled her. She had not planned on the kiss. It had just happened.

She wanted to explain he had misconstrued her actions. It was only her relief that he was not severely injured. He had to understand that. Their wager still stood. And she intended winning. Last night had been an aberration, an effect of the moonlight.

Lydia adjusted the folds of her *stola*. If she explained now, it would mean less awkwardness later. Once she had confronted him during the day, he would see her reaction had been down to the moonlight.

With Korina by her side, she strode over to the bedroom opposite and knocked. No answer. She made a face. If she entered without leave, Aro would say she had come in search of his embrace, begging for his lips, when all she wanted to do was make sure he understood what had happened.

Korina nudged the door and it swung open.

Empty.

Lydia tiptoed in and looked about her. Everything about the room, from the wolf mosaics to the carved wooden chest, proclaimed Aro. Other than the slight crumpling of the embroidered cover on the large wooden bed, the room was undisturbed. The faint scent of sandalwood tickled Lydia's nose, held her. It reminded her forcibly of Aro and the way she had felt in his arms last night and how her breasts had ached when she had stumbled back to bed after the kiss.

She shut the door with a firm click.

'Shall we go to breakfast?' she asked Korina, who tilted her head and gave a sharp bark.

She had started down the corridor to the dinning room, past the statue of Pan with his pipes, when Aro appeared, carrying a toga over his arm. Korina gave a joyful bark and ran to greet him, barking and jumping up at him. Lydia braced herself, waiting to hear the barely suppressed sigh. Korina was notorious for her pawmarks. She hated to think of the number of times her father had complained when he was dressed for the Senate in his snow-white toga. Thank Juno, Aro wore a dark blue tunic and any pawmarks wouldn't show.

'Korina,' Lydia said firmly. 'Come back here. You mustn't jump up. You'll spoil Aro's tunic.'

'She is fine. I had forgotten the joys of having a dog around. And, of course, her mistress as well.'

'Joyful?' Lydia gave an uneasy smile. To see him this way, so suddenly and unexpectedly, made it all the worse. He did not say anything about last night, nor did he make any movement towards her. She released a breath. 'Muddy paw prints over your clothes is not something I would call joyful.'

'Then perhaps we speak of different meanings.'

'Perhaps.' Lydia tilted her head. There was something about Aro this morning, a certain watchfulness, that had not been there last night.

Aro stroked Korina under the chin. His movements were slightly stiff, but if she hadn't known about the injury she'd never have noticed. The dog's tail wagged furiously. He then regarded her with intensity and Lydia wished she had chosen the deep red gown instead. She should move on and go to breakfast, but her eyes were drawn to the way his fingers fondled Korina's ears.

'You slept well, I trust,' he said, breaking the spell.

'Very well.' Lydia dipped her head and tried to collect her thoughts. She had intended on being calm and unperturbed when she next met him, not flustered by the way his tunic hung from his shoulders and moulded to his chest. She hated to think what he would have said if he had found her in his bedroom.

How could she have thought it would be the best place for a talk?

If she kept the conversation on his injuries, she might keep a piece of her dignity. She refused to give in to this attraction. 'Your arm is better this morning.'

'Much improved…' Aro paused and Lydia wondered if he had been about to say more, but instead he brushed his hand against his tunic. 'Tuccia can look after Korina this morning.'

'Korina? Korina can stay with me. I thought to take her to see my father.'

'He is expecting you?' Aro raised an eyebrow.

'No,' Lydia admitted slowly. 'It was an idea I had. I wanted to see how he and Sulpicia were managing.'

'Your visit will have to wait until later.' Aro's expression hardened. 'I have plans for you. You are coming with me to the warehouse. If there is time later, we will both go to visit your father.'

Lydia stared at Aro, torn. She wanted to see the warehouse, but to have it presented to her as something she had to do… 'Why? Why today? I am not dressed for such things.'

'Your dress is more than appropriate.' His lips twitched. 'Last evening you complained about not being kept informed and so I have rearranged my day to take you to the warehouse where you can see what is happening in the Lupan House with your own eyes. When I first met you, you said you were more interested in the daily rounds of shipping than in spinning.'

'I am.' Lydia's hand curled around the *catena*. He had remembered her comment. A warm glow filled her, but she was determined not to show how tempting the treat was. She needed to be sure she was in control of her body before she ventured into a litter with him. Last night's kiss had affected her far more than she had first thought. It was a madness of her blood.

'Is there a problem with that? Besides, a visit your father has no knowledge of—what else do you have planned? A pile of spinning, perhaps?' His eyes sparkled.

'Nothing is planned.' Lydia listened to the sound of the water in the fountain. She had to go with him or admit the true reason for her reluctance.

'If you are ready…' The corners of Aro's mouth twitched as if he was struggling to keep a straight face. As if he knew exactly what was in her mind. 'If you want to admit defeat, that I have won my wager, you only have to say. There is honour in surrender.'

'I have no plans to surrender. One kiss means nothing.' Lydia snapped her fingers in the air. 'I blame it on the moonlight. Today, I am immune.'

'As you wish…' A gleam appeared in his eyes. 'But you do seem to deny it quite loudly.'

'It is only because you provoke me so.' Lydia took a step

backwards. Already she could feel a curl of warmth in her belly in the anticipation of tasting his lips again.

'Provocation can be fun, but alas, I have little time this morning. We must leave now. We are late as it is.'

'You are still taking me to the warehouse?' Lydia asked quickly, wondering if the promised trip was about to be taken away.

'I positively insist.' Aro gave her a hooded look. 'I want you with me this morning.'

'And I have accepted your invitation. I want to understand the Lupan House better. My father and brother relied on my judgement.'

'Perhaps they relied a little too much. You should have time to enjoy life, Lydia.'

'But the business of shipping is intriguing. A puzzle for my mind,' she said and pushed aside the times she had longed to do anything but deal with long dull lists of figures. 'It needed to be done.'

'Poor nymph.' His eyes were hooded.

Lydia longed to ask more, but the water-clock in the dining room let out a loud whistle signalling the top of the hour and his expression changed.

'Shall we go in the litter?' he asked in a silken voice. 'You appeared to enjoy it the other evening.'

'No!' Lydia put her hand to her throat. 'What I mean is that I would like to see the neighbourhood, and the market stalls. When my father was ill, I had very little chance to go out and savour the sights.'

'We will not be going through the Forum. The warehouse is down near the Tiber. You might find it a long walk.'

'I am prepared for that.' Lydia thought quickly. 'Besides, the streets are sure to be jammed with carts and people going about their wares. The Senate keeps talking about a law to ban deliveries during the day, but nothing has happened yet.'

'If they start delivering during the night, none will be able to sleep.'

'I had not thought of that.'

'However, I do understand your reluctance to use a litter. We would not want to get caught again…in a crowd.'

Aro gave a slight bow. His eyes indicated he knew the reason why she did not want the litter and was prepared to humour her. It bothered Lydia that he could read her so easily. She tossed the end of her shawl over her shoulder and stared back, daring him to say a word.

Despite the last rays of the dawn being visible in the sky, the streets already teemed with life. Carters vied with market traders and shopkeepers for a space on the narrow pavement. Several times, Lydia nearly lost Aro in the crowd. Twice she had to duck around bakers carrying trays of bread and once a cart and oxen passed between her and Aro. But his height and his dark blue tunic made it easy for her to spot him where he waited for her.

'As promised, the Lupan House's main offices and the burnt warehouse,' Aro gestured towards an empty shell of a building. To one side a pile of charred timber lay and another of stone. To the other side was a series of offices. In the distance she could hear the steady rhythm of the river and the shouts of the docks. 'I had hoped to take you here yesterday afternoon, but unfortunately urgent matters commanded my attention.'

'I understand.' Lydia regarded the hard-packed dirt. Looking at the size of the operation, it was easy to see why he had not wanted a riot to get out of hand, and why he might be concerned for her safety. 'You did the right thing. Even if I didn't think so yesterday afternoon.'

'Thank you for that.' He caught her hand and lifted it to his lips. The soft touch sent sparks shooting up her arm.

'Impressive,' Lydia said, withdrawing her hand and looking at the men swarming around the blackened building. 'The coals have barely cooled and already you have stone and wood to rebuild. It normally takes days to get a building crew.'

'If you know where to look and are willing to pay an honest wage, you can find the right people.'

Aro's eyes crinkled at the corners and he put an impersonal hand on her back, guiding her towards a small stone building on the other side of the courtyard. Lydia forced her body to stay upright despite the temptation to lean into him and rest her head against his chest. When he removed his hand, the air was distinctly chillier.

'How does the loss of the warehouse affect the Lupan House?' she asked to cover her confusion.

'The augurs have deemed it to be a piece of good fortune.' Aro wore an unsmiling face. He gestured towards the piles of building stone, neatly stacked in one area. Several workmen were unloading yet another cart. 'The fire cleansed the site of demons and their curses.'

'Spare me what the priests have said.' Lydia tilted her head to get a better view. 'Please tell me the truth.'

Aro opened his mouth and closed it again. Lydia waited,

hearing the shouts of the workmen behind her. How was he going to answer the question? Every muscle tensed, waiting. Would he trust her?

'At this time of year, I need every nook and cranny of storage space,' Aro began in a different tone, serious but with a note of respect. 'In the winter months, mainly we can only trade up and down the coast, but we need to be ready for when the winds change and we can sail for Cyrene and Alexandria. Once the grain is ready, the ships will race back here. The first one to arrive will make his fortune.'

'Is Alexandria as exotic as they say?' Lydia asked, unable to keep a wistful note from her voice. Egypt was one place she had always wanted to see, ever since she had first heard tales about the ancient land with its fabled pyramids and long history.

'The lighthouse with its beacon shining far out to sea is one of the wonders of the world. You must see it. I can take you there one day. Have you travelled much?'

Lydia ducked her head and concentrated on rearranging her shawl. 'I have not been that far, only up to northern Italy. They say it is a different world.'

'Egypt is indeed another world, a civilisation mired in the past, with officials who demand their share.'

'But you enjoy the city?'

'Yes, I enjoy the city.' Aro smiled down at her. 'In the sunrise, with the low moan of the trumpets, there is nothing quite like it. Then, of course, there is the grain race, the race across the sea to Rome to be the first boat to unload this year's harvest.'

'I heard you have won it.'

'The last three years the gods have favoured the Lupan

House. Last year, we arrived a full hour before any of Ofellius's fleet appeared on the horizon.'

Lydia tilted her head and looked at Aro from under her eyelashes. His eyes held a faraway look. 'Do you miss the travel?'

'The sea is a harsh and unforgiving mistress.' His eyes held a brief tinge of sadness. 'Too many of my friends and fellow sailors have gone to meet Neptune and his court.'

'They went doing what they loved.' Inadequate words, Lydia knew, but she wanted to say something, to show she understood.

He reached out and his hand touched her cheek. His lips were no more than a breath away. Her insides became alight with a growing warmth. How was she going to remain aloof when the merest touch of his hand lit a fire? When she desired his lips?

'How long will it take to replace the warehouse?' she asked, going towards the smouldering pile of charred timber. She needed to bring the conversation away from the personal. Anything to get away from his touch and her longing for it to continue.

'Slightly less than two months. I want it finished and ready for when the wind changes and the time comes for the grain from Egypt to arrive.' His eyes danced as if he knew why she had moved away from him.

Lydia asked a few more questions about the warehouse and listened as he explained. Her mind kept returning to his touch and her body's reaction to it. She had wanted more. She had nearly asked for more. The kiss they had shared last night meant she had only two more kisses, and then she'd lose. She'd remain a Fabii and no longer a Veratii.

Lydia watched in silence as the men cleared another bit of rubble from the ruined building. She was very aware of the man standing next to her. He did not touch her again, but every movement he made, or breath he took, she seemed to feel a heightened awareness deep inside her.

Workmen came running up to him from all directions, chattering in Greek and Aramaic and several other languages that Lydia vaguely knew as well as Latin. Aro answered each in turn in the language they had spoken to him.

'I had no idea that you could speak so many different tongues,' she said when the last one had departed.

'Sailors come from all over the Mediterranean and sea voyages are long. It helps pass the time.'

'I hadn't thought of it in that way.' She saw her smile reflected in his, and felt a delicious warmth wash over her.

'The ability to speak many tongues helps in the negotiations. I can understand what is being said, not just what is being translated. It means I can get the price I want for my cargo. It is something I require of all captains.'

'Ah, now I know why you charge such high prices.'

'As long as Neptune is willing, any cargo entrusted to my house gets to its intended destination and is sold to the highest bidder. Which is more than I can say for some.'

'Sulpicia told me Publius's *liquamen* has been delivered to Corinth.'

'Your brother was one of the lucky ones, then. Not all of Ofellius's consignments find their destination so easily.'

'I realise that, but now Sulpicia's mind is at rest. I didn't want anything to disturb her as she is so pregnant. She lost their first child.'

'I didn't know.'

'It is why Publius ran up so many gambling debts.' Lydia clenched her hands and took a deep breath. Now was the time for an explanation. 'It is why I had to sell the wine. I had to find a way to save him. Father was ill and the shock of Publius's debts would have killed him.'

'You sold the wine for your brother.' A note of incredulity crept into Aro's voice. He ran his hand through his hair.

'And for my father. Remember he lay just on this side of Hades. What else could I do?' Lydia held her hands out. 'I had to keep the family's honour. It would have killed my father to lose his Senate seat. What would you have done?'

'I understand why you thought you had to do it.'

His gaze caught and held hers. Lydia was the first to look away. She ran the toe of her sandal in the dust like a child, saying nothing. She found herself dangerously close to liking Aro. She had to remember that he was no better than Ofellius or a hundred other merchants. He had forced her into this marriage, and would keep her there.

'Have you discovered the identity of the man who accosted us the other night?'

'It has been taken care of. Why?' He fixed her with his eye.

'I wondered.'

'You need not worry. He won't trouble you again.' There was a cold finality in his voice. He put a hand on her elbow, guiding her away from the workmen. 'Allow me to show you my favourite place in Rome.'

Aro led her into a small office at one side of the warehouse. Scrolls and tablets were stacked neatly against one wall and the whole room smelled of dusty spices as well as the all-pervading smell of smoke. It was the sort of room Lydia knew she could happily spend hours in—a place to write, read and to think. A small altar with figurines of Mercury, Neptune and Minerva stood in one corner.

'It's absolutely lovely. No wonder you like it.' She peeped out of the small window, catching a glimpse of the Tiber and barges making their way along it. In the distance, she could hear the shouts and calls of the men.

'Thankfully, we were able to stop the fire before it spread here. Otherwise, a great deal more than a few amphorae of oil and a building would have been lost.'

'You have a lot of scrolls and tablets here.' Lydia nodded towards the towering piles of tablets propped against the back wall. 'But everything is in such order.'

'Order saves time.' Aro hooked his thumbs through his belt. 'Knowing where things are and putting them back saves time in the long run. By your right hand are shipping lists for last summer's consignments to Egypt.'

Lydia picked up a few of the tablets, shipping lists, all carefully written in the same neat hand. Aro's.

'Impressive. And over here?' She gestured towards a dustier stack.

'Shipments from Ostia to Hispania from three years ago.'

Lydia blew the dust off the top tablet and smiled. Same neat writing and he was correct. She compared the order to the chaos that was her father's study, and how long it had taken her to find anything. 'You do know where everything in this room is.'

'Yes, but there again, I'm a good guesser.' Aro smiled and the sunshine broke over his face. 'It helps to be lucky in my line of business.'

'Are you lucky?'

'I like to think so.' His voice was low and held hidden meaning.

The room had contracted. If either of them took very many steps, they would end up touching each other. Lydia turned towards the small altar and started rearranging the figurines.

'Why do you keep this number of tablets and scrolls here?'

'This is where I prefer to work when I am in Rome.'

'I would have thought you'd do most of your work at the house, having clients come and visit you.'

'It is easier to be here where I am easily accessible in case of problems. Wind and water wait for no man.' He lounged against the table, sandalled foot dangling in the air. A smile played on his lips as if he knew exactly why she had picked up the small figurine of Mercury for the third time. 'My house is for those who need to be impressed, but the heart of the business remains on these docks and warehouses.'

Lydia hurriedly placed the figurine down. She had no need of soothsayers or augurs to interpret his words. Aro was telling her that he intended to keep his two lives separate. The villa where she belonged would always be second place to where his true life lay, where his true happiness was. He needed no help here. Everything was perfectly organised, unlike her father's study. She could never imagine Aro turning to her for help and advice.

She hated the confirmation of her fears. She had no more value to him than an expensive statue, an addition to his fabled art collection as the senator from the baths had said. And like a statue, she was going to be kept under lock and key, exhibited when the time was right. She had seen it happen to other women, but had never considered it would happen to her.

'Yes, I understand.'

Aro did not reply, but his body became alert. Gone was the easy relaxed manner, and in its place a watchful stillness. He glanced over to the water-clock and gave a satisfied nod. Lydia parted her lips to ask what was going on, but Aro held up one finger, silencing her.

'He will see me,' came a strident voice. 'I will have words with him.'

The door was flung open and Ofellius, red-faced but resplendent in a deep purple cloak and matching tunic, marched in. Two of his men stood behind him. Lydia gave a small gasp when she saw the man on the right side, the man who had menaced her and Aro two nights earlier. She recognised the jagged scar running down his face, although now one of his eyes was closed and bruised. She started to cry out, but Aro's warning look silenced her.

'Do come in, old friend. If you had but knocked…' Aro strode over to greet Ofellius. He was pleased Lydia had remained near the window. He extended his hand and gripped Ofellius's forearm in the traditional manner. No hidden daggers. Behind Ofellius and his entourage, one of Rufus's grandsons held up two fingers to make a V sign. Five men. There again, he had possibly stationed his other men down an alleyway waiting for the signal to strike.

Aro inclined his head sideways, but Rufus's grandson shook his head. No more men. Aro permitted a tight smile to cross his lips. Everything was going as planned.

Ofellius would not find what he sought here. The visit was expected, but he had not known if Ofellius intended an all-out attack. Only five meant he knew as Aro did that the Ofellian House had no legal right to that cargo. This visit was for bluster, to keep face with his men. A show of force in hopes of intimidation. Other men had tried and failed. Ofellius would get nothing.

'I had expected to find you at your house.' Ofellius made a tiny noise in the back of his throat.

'It is far too late for that.' Aro indicated Lydia. 'I have been showing my wife the splendours of the Lupan House in Rome.'

Ofellius turned with a start. His eyes narrowed and he gave a stiff bow. Lydia inclined her head slightly, betraying no surprise at the encounter. Aro was proud of her demeanour. Many women would be in hysterics if a door had suddenly crashed in. The potential for hysterics or vapours was one of the reasons he had brought her with him today. He had to be here, but he had not wanted to leave her on her own, guarded by only a few slaves and servants, in case Ofellius had tried to wreak his revenge on the house.

'Your men interfered with a cargo of olive oil yesterday.' Ofellius drew back his lips in a snarl. 'They took it off one of my ships. Boarded the ship without my permission.'

'Did they, indeed?' Aro arched an eyebrow. 'How very remiss of them.'

'They behaved like pirates.'

Behind him, he heard Lydia's sudden intake of breath. Aro regretted alarming Lydia, but he had little choice. He dare not take the risk that she was disloyal.

'There are no pirates in Rome, my friend. General Pompey

saw to that.' He made a slight bow. 'My wife is fond of informing me of this fact.'

Ofellius blanched and Aro wondered again exactly who protected this man. He should have been crucified, but somehow the Fates had smiled on him, Pompey had forgiven him and he still continued his operations of intimidation and theft.

'I want it back. Every last drop.' Ofellius slammed his fist into his open hand. 'You had no right to board one of my ships.'

'To retrieve my own cargo? I suspect the dock workers were in error. They confused one ship for another in the very early morning light. There was a meeting about this problem last Ides. The other trading houses and I thought we had come to an agreement.'

Ofellius pursed his lips. 'It has been known to happen, but I want compensation.'

'I am very sorry, but that is impossible,' Aro replied through clenched teeth.

'Why?'

'Because the cargo had my seal on it.' Aro crossed the room and stood, facing Ofellius, his arms behind his back. 'The seals on the amphorae are mine. When my captain sent word, I hurried down to the docks and found the error. It took several hours to put right.'

'My senior captain respectfully disagrees.'

Aro glanced at the man who now sported a black eye and swelling jaw.

'You have hidden our amphorae here,' the man growled. 'You took them without authority.'

*And your man attacked my wife.* Aro managed to hang on to his temper by the thinnest of threads. He refused to allow Lydia to become worried or upset. Until he knew the exact reason for Ofellius's campaign of disruption, he did not want to worry her. After he had won his seat in the Senate and fulfilled his vow to his father, then he'd tell her. He'd take her to Alexandria and show her the sights, but for now, he had to keep her safe.

He risked a glance at Lydia's tight-lipped face. It had given him great pleasure to land the punch on the man's face last evening. Unfortunately, he was one of Ofellius's senior captains and protected under the agreement as he had not physically harmed Lydia. Aro had to weigh the danger to his own captains with the satisfaction a quiet dumping of the body in the Tiber would bring. It was a matter of some regret that the man was able to walk. He had to be losing his touch.

Aro blew on his nails and waited for Ofellius to make the formal inspection request.

'Of course you may check over the site,' Lydia exploded, her eyes blazing with fury. 'Fabius Aro does not hide things. If he says there was a mistake, then that is what happened. Search away.'

'Do you agree?' Ofellius asked, a look of incredulity passing over his face.

Aro resisted the temptation to kiss Lydia. Her intervention was exactly what was required. He contented himself with a nod.

'As my wife says, we have nothing to hide. My men will show your captain any place he might require to look. He may look until he is satisfied.'

Ofellius shrugged. 'Very well.'

Aro signalled to the porter and explained the situation. The porter bowed low and took the men away. Aro signalled to another servant who brought in a platter of bread and figs as well as honeyed wine and cool mint tea.

'I trust you will join me in a cup of something while we wait,' Aro said. This was Ofellius's chance to declare war, and openly insult his house.

'When one is in the presence of a lady, one must of course drink to your lady's health.' Ofellius reached his beringed fingers towards a goblet.

'And to yours.' Lydia raised her goblet, but her eyes were full of questions.

Aro released a breath. The time for open warfare between the houses was not yet. The conversation then turned towards the price of fish sauce, the conditions of the docks at Ostia and the necessity of bribes in Alexandria. To Aro's pleasure, Lydia made several knowledgeable comments about trade routes and potential problems.

'Your wife appears to know more than is good for her about the shipping business.'

'The counsel of a faithful wife is worth more than silk or gold,' Aro returned smoothly.

Lydia swirled the dregs of her honeyed wine in the goblet, listening to the banter between the two men. There was much more here than the surface chatter about trade routes. She could not rid herself of the suspicion that Aro had expected Ofellius to make an appearance and that he had brought her here for a specific purpose. Just as the conversation was starting to turn dangerously toward olive oil, Ofellius's men reappeared. One grabbed Ofellius's arm and murmured in his ear. Ofellius pursed his lips as if the wine had become very bitter indeed. The colour drained from his face.

'It does appear you were correct after all, Fabius Aro, forgive me for detaining you.'

Lydia's fingers became nerveless and she struggled to keep the cup from crashing out of her hand.

'You do seem to have a problem with mislaying your cargo, Ofellius—first Publius's fish sauce and now this olive oil,' Lydia said and enjoyed watching the merchant squirm. 'May you have as much luck finding your missing olive oil as you did with the fish sauce. My sister-in-law informs that it has all been resolved. Amazing what can be discovered when you put your mind to it.'

Ofellius's demeanour changed. 'Yes, it was a small over-sight of a clerk who regrettably is no longer with us. I do hope that the olive oil proves as easy to solve.'

'Should my men or I happen upon any of your amphorae, we shall send them to you, as I would expect you to do for me.' Aro gave a tight smile.

'As I would do for you.'

'One other thing before you depart, Ofellius—the next time you send your men on a shopping expedition, do tell them to avoid my ships and merchandise, it makes it much simpler all around.'

Ofellius glared at him, but turned on his heel and left. Lydia released a breath and set her cup down. She wanted to run to Aro and bury her face against his shoulder, but the wager was between them. She had to draw comfort from him being in the same room.

'Do you have the olive oil?' Lydia asked after Aro shut the door.

'It is my oil.' Aro held out his hands, palms upwards, the very picture of offended innocence. 'His men raided my ship at Ostia under cover of darkness and relieved it of several amphorae. Thankfully, a guard had sharp eyes. Last night, we merely took back what was ours by right. Nothing else.'

'Did you see the man who accompanied Ofellius, his captain no less?' she asked. 'He is the man who attacked us the other night. I am sure of it. The one who dropped the knife. You said nothing, did nothing.'

Aro walked over the window and looked out. His knuckles were white against the window frame. A chill passed over Lydia. Had she said something wrong?

'I had hoped you hadn't seen.' His voice was low. 'Or had perhaps forgotten.'

'You knew.'

'I knew who he was when we met the other evening.' Aro turned back, his face grim. 'I don't forget faces, Lydia. Payment has been exacted. That man will not bother you again.'

Lydia remembered the bruises on the man's face and saw Aro's intent look. Aro's injuries last night had not happened by chance. Had he gone to find this man and discovered the amphorae only later? Instantly Lydia dismissed the thought. Aro did not care for her. He would never have done such a thing. Or if he had, it would only be because his honour had been slighted.

'Why didn't you tell me?'

'What would it have served?' Aro turned back to the

window, hiding his face. 'You would have been upset over nothing, fearful. And the man in question now knows what happens if someone dares tangle with the Sea Wolf. No doubt it will spawn another of the Forum tales, embroidered beyond all recognition.'

'Why are you called the Sea Wolf?'

'It is a name I chose when I started my business. I wanted to honour my ancestor Romulus, who was suckled by a she-wolf and who founded Rome. It served to remind me of what my family had lost.'

'Nothing to do with piracy, then.'

Aro gave a wide smile, making him look years younger.

'Never, I pride myself on being a man of integrity. I follow my code. The one thing Sulla could not take away from my family was our integrity. I trust anyone could play a game of *micatio* with me in the dark.'

*To play* micatio *in the dark.* Lydia gave a small nod. *Micatio,* or odds and evens, was one of the few gambling games that Romans could play openly on the street corners. It required speed, wit and ability to read one's opponent's body language as the player tried to guess the total numbers of fingers that were going to be held out. One would only consider doing that in the dark with a man of utmost integrity as most wanted to verify the total with their eyes.

Lydia placed her goblet down and went to stand near Aro. She could see a barge loaded with amphorae slowly making its way down the river. Out of the corner of her eye she could see the tension in Aro's neck muscles and wished he had trusted her enough to confide in her.

'It seems strange. I had understood Ofellius's reputation was that of an honest man,' Lydia said.

'I would not play *micatio* with him at any time, let alone in the dark.' Aro gave a crooked smile. 'I find it incredible your father does business with him. His reputation is unsavoury. He has built his reputation on the backs of ruined men.'

'Publius's fish sauce has arrived in Corinth.' Lydia concentrated on the small altar to Mercury and its half-burnt candle. 'Sulpicia told me yesterday.'

'You do amaze me.' Aro lifted his eyebrow. 'Every last amphorae of *liquamen?*'

'It is the truth. You were wrong to make me fear for its safety. Publius must not go back into debt. It would kill my father.'

The corners of Aro's mouth twitched. 'When did I do that? When did I make you fear for Publius's fish sauce?'

'When we first met, you told me Ofellius wouldn't deliver the fish sauce, because of the seal on the tablet, and that it was *denarii* upfront but he has. Sulpicia told me.'

Aro leant forward and captured her chin with his fingers, tilting it upwards. His eyes sparkled with some emotion. 'For some reason, Ofellius has seen fit to deliver the fish sauce to Corinth, but there will be more to it than that. Much more.'

'How much?' Lydia asked, aware that her voice had become husky.

She looked into his eyes with their flecks of gold. His hair curled softly at his temples. The white scar on his cheek gave him a raffish appearance. She should move, but couldn't.

'I was very proud of you,' he said and his breath kissed

her cheek. 'I had expected our friend from the temple to be unable to walk. Last seen he was writhing on the ground, calling for his mother. Perhaps I should have warned you, but I did not want to worry you. I wanted to protect you.'

Lydia bit her lip. She wanted to be angry with him, but discovered a small piece of her was pleased. It had been a long time since anyone had cared enough to look after her. 'Thank you.'

He lifted her hand to his mouth. His lips brushed her palm, a featherlight touch. Lydia tried to think about something other than the shape of his mouth and the warmth spreading through out her body. There was a question in his eyes.

'Aro,' she whispered, but did not draw her hand away. 'Please.'

He bent his head and his mouth touched hers, softly at first with no more pressure than a butterfly visiting a flower. She opened her mouth, allowed him entrance. Their tongues entangled and she pressed her body against his, unable to resist the urge to give herself fully to the kiss.

Then, as suddenly as a summer storm passes, it was over. Lydia ran her tongue experimentally over her lips. She should be angry, but she found she was breathing as if she had run a race. She became aware of the little things, the creases in his tunic, the way his hair curled at the nape of his neck, the sound of the Tiber.

Aro reluctantly raised his mouth and regarded Lydia. Her eyes were partly shut, her mouth full and red. It had tasted of honey and mint, opening sweetly for him, making him long to plunge himself deep within her and make her his again. Except he had given his word and he was a man of honour.

The damnable wager lay between them. He had to let her come to him. She had to start trusting him. She would surrender and then she would begin to understand what he offered her.

He touched her cheek, and her head turned away from him. She wrapped her arms about her waist, then started to rearrange her shawl, covering and hiding her body.

'If the danger is over, I would like to visit my father.' Her voice was small and thin. 'I have neglected him and Sulpicia long enough. The number of tablets Sulpicia sends me, you would think it would be easier for her to do the jobs herself, rather than asking for my advice.'

Aro regarded her face for a long time. He wanted to tell her that she did not need to be running after her spoilt sister-in-law, that it was time she allowed her family to stand or fall on their own, but she wouldn't listen. She had spent her whole life looking after them.

'Would you like me to accompany you?' Aro asked and carefully kept the emotion from his voice. 'Or shall I send several of my men?'

'I have no desire to pull you away from your work,' she replied and drew the shawl over her face.

'As you wish.'

# Chapter Thirteen

'Veratius Cornelius and the lady Sulpicia are not in.'

Lydia bit her lip and stared with frustration at Gallus, her father's porter. Beyond him, she could glimpse a bit of the atrium, and the goldfish pool and her mother's portrait bust. They seemed much smaller, and slightly shabbier, but no less beloved for it. She had failed to realise how much she had missed this house. It was home in a way that the villa on the Aventine could never be. 'Not in?'

'The senator and his daughter-in-law have gone to dine.' Gallus ran his hands through his hair, making it stand on end. 'I regret, Lydia Ver…Fabia, I have no idea when they will return.'

'Tell them I called.' Lydia gave one last wistful glimpse at the garden denied her and turned resolutely back towards the Aventine.

'My lady, it was good to see you. We all miss you.' Gallus's voice floated after her.

Lydia gave a small gasp and forced her sandals to increase their speed.

On the way back, her mind kept returning to the two kisses she had shared with Aro. If she wanted to keep any sort of self-respect or freedom, she had to refrain from kissing him a third time for at least four more days.

When she reached the villa, Tuccia took one look at her and started fussing over her, insisting she bathe and redo her hair, chatting away all the time about what mischief Korina and Hortus, Clodius the porter's dog, had got into. Lydia tried to be stern when she heard about the way the dogs had managed to get a ham bone, but failed.

After Lydia had applied fresh wine dregs to her lips and Tuccia pronounced herself satisfied with the result, she went out to the garden and sat down on the stone bench. Korina promptly lay down with her nose resting on Lydia's sandals and began to snore, a contented expression on her face.

Resting her cheek on her hand in the late afternoon sunshine, Lydia reflected how very different everything was here, so pristine and perfect, how she could never feel comfortable here. Everything was too...Aro. Everywhere she looked, she saw signs of him and his hand; as pleasant as the surroundings were, they were still a gilded cage. It could never be a home, not in the sense she thought of her home.

She twisted the *arra* ring about on her finger. She had almost grown used to its weight. Legend had it that it connected the hearts, twining them into one. She gave a sad smile at the thought. There could never be the love between Aro and her as there had once been between her parents. It was fruitless to wish for something like that. He had made it subtly clear before Ofellius appeared that he intended to keep his two lives separate and which life he preferred.

Korina pricked up one ear and gave a joyful bark. Lydia turned her head towards the entrance to the garden. Aro stood in the doorway, his skin glowing and his dark green tunic spotless. She fancied she saw a flash of joy, but it was so fleeting that Lydia became convinced she had imagined it.

'I thought you were visiting your father.' Aro crossed the garden in a few steps with Korina running joyful circles around him. He stopped and gave the dog a piece of cheese. At once Korina turned over and wriggled on her back, squirming with pleasure when Aro's long fingers reached out and stroked her belly. Lydia tried not to think about the way his hands had felt when they had stroked her hair earlier, and the sensations they evoked.

'He was dining out.' Lydia plucked at her skirt, smoothing the folds. She wanted to go to him, and bury her face in his shoulder. She wanted the comfort of his arms and it frightened her. 'I left a message and will see him later.'

Aro nodded and, without waiting for an invitation, sat down next to her, closer than strictly necessary. Lydia felt warmth start to curl in her midriff. She scooted several inches away from him. She was not going to give in to these feelings again. If she touched him, it would be far too easy to end up in his arms again. Her cushion of two kisses had vanished. She was able to control her impulses and urges. She had to control them. To give in would mean she would have to give up her family for ever.

Aro raised an eyebrow as if he knew why she had moved.

His hand reached out and plucked a blossom from her hair. 'The tree is trying to decorate you.'

'Tuccia will have something to say about that. She has already complained I dressed too quickly this morning.' Lydia laughed, and then the laughter died on her lips as she saw his intent expression. Rapidly she stood up and crossed to the pool. The fish turned in the sunlight, making bright darts in the water.

'You are already a slave to your tire-woman?'

'Hardly that, but she does have an excellent eye.' Lydia resisted the urge to pat her hair.

'My sister used to say the same thing about Tuccia's mother.' Aro gave a brief laugh and his eyes became misty as if remembering through the years.

Lydia stilled. Every nerve was alert. She wanted to learn more, to hear about Aro's past, and perhaps discover if it had any bearing on their marriage.

'I didn't realise you had a sister. Do you have any brothers?'

'She's dead. And she was my only sibling, since you ask.' His words were flatly spoken and no encouragement.

'How did she die?' Lydia asked, keeping one hand on Korina's collar to steady her nerves. She had to find out. All sorts of possibilities raced through her brain.

'She was carried off by a fever, the same fever that killed my parents. In good health one day, and suffering from a high fever and stomach pains the next. She had been unhappy in her marriage for a time and had returned for an extended visit.'

Lydia tightened her fingers about Korina's collar. 'Were you there when it happened?'

'I had made my goodbyes the morning before and was travelling towards the port.' He ran his hand through his hair and stood up, pacing about the courtyard. 'My father delayed calling the doctor until it was too late. By the time he sent word to me, he too was waiting for the boatman to cross the River Styx.'

'There was nothing you could have done.'

'How do you know?'

'My mother, she died of a fever. She had taken some food to one of my father's clients. There was no need for her to do it. She could have sent one of the servants.' Lydia swallowed hard, forcing her memory away from that awful day. 'By the time they had sent for me, it was too late. And I had seen her only that morning…'

'What happened happened. A long time ago and far away. Nothing you or I do will bring the dead back.'

The words seemed to resound off the walls. Lydia felt the shutters going up, blocking her out from that part of his life. It was as if the past was a forbidden place for her.

'And yet you never married,' she said quietly. 'Never tried for a new family.'

'I married you.' He turned back, his voice fierce.

Lydia kept her head bent, examining Korina's multi-coloured fur, plucking out a stray hair, anything but directly gazing into his eyes.

'You needed a wife.' She forced her voice to sound carefree and unconcerned. 'You are about to make a try for the greasy pole that is the Senate. You needed my father's support.'

Aro regarded her with glittering gold eyes. Lydia was

reminded more than ever of a wolf, sitting, waiting, watching. She wanted him to say something, to deny her reasoning. She wanted him to say that he had married her because he wanted her. That he had married her in spite of his misgivings about their family's past.

'As you say.' He made a sketch of a bow. His voice was heavy with irony. 'I had my reasons.'

'As you say, you had your reasons.' Lydia stood up and straightened the folds of her gown. 'If you will forgive me, it is nearly time for dinner.'

'You do not speak of your dead husband.' His voice stopped her. 'He has been gone for eighteen months. Time enough for you to remarry. Why hadn't you done so?'

Lydia regarded the pool of water sparkling in the sunshine. It was hard to explain. Titus belonged to another life, when she had been someone else. She had been so much younger then. She hadn't wanted to marry out of guilt for all the wrong reasons.

'It was never the right time,' she said. 'My father became ill, Sulpicia lost her baby and all my concerns had to be put to one side. I had to fight for my family's survival.'

'As you say, things happen.' He turned and walked towards the precipice where Rome was laid out at his feet. The last rays of the sun hit the gold-roofed temples of Jupiter and Saturn on the Capitoline. A faint mist hung in the marshland across the Tiber.

Lydia was torn. If she hurried after him, she'd end up in his arms again, and she didn't want to be there. Or did she?

'We ought to go into dinner. The servants will be waiting to wash our feet and hands,' Lydia called after him.

'If that is what you want…'

* * *

Over the next few days, Lydia argued with herself that she should have said or done something more. Somehow after their talk, there had been a slight shift in the air. Nothing spoken, but Aro was far more distant and reserved. He made no attempt to kiss her or even place her in a situation where that might happen. She could not help feeling that she had lost something or made a mistake somewhere.

Aro also made no mention of keeping her at the villa. It was as if he had lost interest in the wager. Lydia wondered if for some reason he had changed his mind.

On the last day of the wager, Lydia went out to the baths and discovered that an old friend of her mother's lived quite close by. She went and passed a pleasant hour, discussing her mother and childhood memories. Yet all the time in the back of her mind was a certain amount of sadness. She was going to win, not because she was not attracted to Aro, but because he had lost interest in the chase. The victory tasted hollow.

When she arrived back from Livia's house, she discovered Tuccia in her room, weeping as she straightened the jars and ointments.

'Tell me, what is the problem?' Lydia went over and put an arm around her tire-woman. Tuccia gave a great sob and buried her face in Lydia's *stola*. 'Are you unhappy here? Surely life can't be that awful.'

Tuccia stepped back, wiped her eyes with the corner of her gown and gave a great hiccup.

'No, not that, my lady. I beg your pardon, my lady. I have

dripped all over your *stola*.' She picked up a cloth and started to dab at the damp patch.

'Something is wrong, Tuccia. Tell me.' Lydia put her hand over Tuccia's. 'Did you break a jar or spill some of my perfume? You need not fear, I am not in the habit of abusing my tire-woman.'

'My grandfather sent word my grandmother is ill, seriously ill.' Tuccia dissolved into another bout of hiccups. 'There is no one left to look after them. Both my brothers have gone off to Ostia. And my mother…well…she does not want to have anything to do with them. They never got on and now she is far too busy with her husband and new baby. I'm terrified something will happen. Who will fetch the bread and wine? They live on the fourth floor.'

'You shall go to them and stay until they are well enough to look after themselves.' Lydia raised Tuccia's face and looked directly into her red-rimmed eyes. 'I can manage well enough on my own.'

'But my lady, I couldn't.' Tuccia wiped the tears from her eyes.

'Why ever not?' Lydia asked. 'It is clear you will be of no use to me here, worrying about your grandparents. I'd far rather have you know your grandparents are safe. Your grandfather did a great service to the Lupan House when he raised the alarm about the fire and then fought it by himself. It would be a dreadful shame if he wasn't looked after properly.'

Tuccia's face broke out into a wreath of smiles, sunshine after a storm. If only her own problems were that easily solved, Lydia thought.

'Thank you, my lady. May Juno bless you and this house.'

Tuccia's hand knocked the alabaster jar of ointment, sending it rolling along the cupboard shelf.

Lydia reached out and caught it before it crashed to the floor. Her special salve. She started to put it back and then hesitated, a plan forming. She would be dignified in winning and show Aro that she fully intended to take an interest in the Lupan House and all those connected with it.

'I should like to meet your grandfather and give him this jar of ointment as thanks for all he did in the fire.'

'You are too kind, my lady.'

'Nonsense, I should have done so earlier when I first heard about the fire.' Lydia cringed slightly when she thought of what her mother would have done. She'd have gone the first day she learnt of the man's plight. She'd never seen her mother shy away from visiting any of her father's sick clients, declaring it was her duty.

'You don't need to do that, my lady. He was pleased to do what he did. The Fabii mean much to him. He owes them his life and his freedom.'

'It is not a matter of having to, Tuccia. It is a matter of wanting to. You are not to return to my care until your grandmother is quite well. I can look after my own hair and make-up for a short time.'

Tuccia looked doubtful. 'Are you sure, my lady?'

'I mean that. It won't be to your standard, of course, but I can do it.'

The servants were occupied with cleaning the atrium's pool, and therefore Lydia decided that she could make do with one escort instead of the usual two that Aro had insisted on. With a massive scar running down the side of his face and tree-trunk arms, Strabo could surely cope with anything that they might meet. Besides, it was broad daylight and she'd be back long before the seventh hour.

Not that Aro would care or be here to meet her, she thought with a pang.

Strabo and Tuccia led the way up and down a complex maze of back streets and alleyways. Unlike the Palatine where she had lived before or even the top of the Aventine, the streets near the waterfront were filled with narrow multi-storeyed dwellings, rising high and shutting out the sun. Lydia shivered slightly and pulled her shawl tighter. Here and there were little sunlit squares where merchants and traders spread their wares, and women filled their earthenware jars with water from fountains, chatting and gossiping as children and dogs tumbled about in the dust.

Tuccia stopped outside one of these dwellings. On the ground a baker's jostled for space with a wine shop. A flight of stairs disappeared up into darkness. A smell of stale oil and sour wine permeated the area.

'My grandparents live on the fourth floor,' Tuccia said and raced up the stone steps.

'Shall I wait for you here?' Strabo offered. 'There ain't much room up there. Unless you'd like me to take it up for you, my lady, and bring you word that Tuccia is safely with her grandparents? Or maybe they will come down?'

'No, I'll do it myself.' Lydia glanced over her shoulders at the men stumbling from the wine shop. She readjusted her shawl. It was not a place to linger. 'I have not come all this way to wait outside. I am not such a grand person that I cannot climb a few steps.'

After the first flight of wide stone steps, the stairs became steep, narrow and wooden. Lydia had to pause on the third-floor landing to allow a heavyset man and his wife to descend. Tuccia waited for her, eyes gleaming. 'My grandmother will be pleased to see you. It is a great honour you are doing our family.'

The door swung open, revealing a grizzled man with arms swathed in bandages. 'Tuccia! What are you doing here? You have not run away, child, have you?'

'She received word this morning of your wife's illness,' Lydia said quickly. She was pleased she had decided to accompany Tuccia or otherwise she might have been sent back in disgrace.

'This is Fabius Aro's wife.' Tuccia tugged at Lydia's hand, propelling her forward.

The man's face instantly changed, became less welcoming. 'Does Fabius Aro know you are here?

'In a manner of speaking, yes, he does.' Lydia wished Aro was standing beside her. It would make everything much easier. As it was, she had to hope she was doing the correct thing.

'Who is it, Rufus?' a voice called from within.

'Fabius Aro's new wife. Come to visit.' He nodded towards the room. 'You had best come in. It wouldn't do to have the boss's wife standing out on the landing like a fishwife, now would it?'

The apartment was average size with a couch in one corner. Shabby but clean. On the table food was set out—a loaf of bread, several figs and a piece of hard cheese. Tuccia's grandmother lay in the one bed with a cloth over her eyes. Tuccia rushed over to her, making soothing noises.

The woman reached out her hand when Lydia went over to meet her. 'You and Fabius Aro have already been so good to Rufus and me and now you visit. See what he sent the other day—fish sauce. He remembered that Rufus is partial to the vile stuff.'

An amphora of fish sauce was propped up against the back wall, next to the tiny charcoal brazier. Lydia's mouth went dry and she longed to examine it more closely, as the markings looked familiar. No wonder Publius had complained of his fish sauce's non-arrival. It had never left Rome. Aro had known that day in her father's study. He had to have, but when they were at the warehouse, he had let her think all was right and correct. Exactly how had he come by the *garum?* Had he bought it from Ofellius and was that why Sulpicia had said that everything had been taken care of?

'Tell me, are you displeased with our Tuccia's work?' the grandmother asked.

'Hush now, woman. You don't demand things of Fabius Aro's wife. She's a grand lady.' Rufus made an exaggerated bow, and indicated the one chair in the room.

Lydia ignored his sarcasm and answered the old lady's question. 'Tuccia has real skill in her fingers. I have never known my hair so easily tamed.' Lydia held out the jar of ointment. 'When I heard of your difficulty, I thought to bring you some of my salve. It works wonders for burns. My cook…that is, my father's cook swears by it. It was my mother's recipe.'

Rufus's face broke into a wreath of smiles. 'Now that is really kind of Aro. Never forgets those who are loyal to him. There were others who said otherwise, but I never thought any different.'

Lydia put the jar down on the tiny table. 'Aro is a good man. He does the right thing by those in his employ.'

'We thank you kindly for the ointment, my lady, 'Rufus said. 'I'm sure it will be of great use. Tuccia, it was good of you to call.'

'I…that is…Fabius Aro wishes Tuccia to stay here and look after you both.' A white lie, but a necessary one. Lydia felt positive that Aro would agree with her decision, once she informed him of it. From the way Rufus had struggled to open the door, and Tuccia's grandmother's attempts at raising her head off the sleeping couch, they needed someone. Unless they thought the order had come from Aro, Rufus was sure to insist Tuccia return with her. 'Tuccia may return when you are both well. Fabius Aro told me so.'

The elderly lady had tears in her eyes. 'May the gods bless you, my lady. I know this is your doing. See, Rufus, I told you it was the right thing to send word through our neigh- bour. Fabius Aro would never marry someone horrible, not like you said the Veratii were. He is too intelligent for that. You are an old fool.'

Rufus hung his head and shuffled his feet.

'If you don't mind me saying, my lady, I was afeared when I first heard Fabius Aro was marrying a Veratii. No good has ever come of them, says I. But he went ahead, and right glad I am that you have taken Tuccia under your wing. You're a real lady. May the gods bless you and your marriage.'

Back on the street, Lydia looked for her guide, but he had vanished. She pinched the skin between her eyebrows, unde- cided. She took a half-step into the road and glanced at the

wine shop where a large crowd of working men had gathered.
Where was Strabo?

Rough hands caught her shoulders.

'My, my, my, look at what we have found.'

## Chapter Fourteen

The house felt different the instant Aro entered it. He swiftly made his way to the *tablinum,* but the sole occupant was Korina. The dog lifted her nose from her paws and softly padded over to him, tail wagging. She gave him a questioning look.

'Your mistress is not here?' he asked, giving the dog a pat.

It annoyed him that Lydia had seen fit to leave the villa without sending word of her whereabouts. When he returned to the villa, Clodius the porter informed him that Lydia, Tuccia and Strabo had departed several hours ago, and none had come back. Clodius had neglected to enquire about their destination. He had had vague hopes Lydia had slipped in unnoticed.

Aro cursed under his breath.

He had come back early with the intention of spending the afternoon with her, and she had gone out. The seven days were nearly up and she had not turned to him as he had planned. The curse tablets kept arriving and the low-level disruption continued, taking him away from her more than he wished. The whispers had started that the augurs were wrong and the gods did not favour his marriage to Lydia.

He was left with no option as the water dripped away in the water-clock—he would have to seduce her. He would win their wager, and she would find it enjoyable. He could not risk her leaving him, tearing his heart out as she did. She had become more important to him than he had thought possible.

Why hadn't she left a note?

'I suspect she plans on coming back.' Aro gave Korina another pat. 'She would have hardly left you if she hadn't.'

Korina gave a sharp bark in agreement and then settled at his feet, her head resting against his sandal.

Aro reviewed his options. Lydia had neatly boxed him in with her demure smiles and ready agreement to his plan. He could hardly go to her father's house, seeking his missing wife. The scene was all too easy to imagine—Lydia coolly sipping her cup of mint tea, calmly rising to greet him, point proved. He'd give her another hour to return and then he'd send his men in search of her.

He thanked the gods that she had seen sense to take one of his men with her. Wherever she was, she would be safe. But when she returned, he would demand a full explanation. He would not be taken in by fluttering eyelashes or soft sighs. He needed to know why she had decided to ignore him and his advice.

Lydia fought against the rough hands that held her in place. She aimed a well-timed kick at her captor's shin, followed by a knee. She heard the low groan and felt the hands loosen. She took a step backwards. Her sandal slipped slightly on the stone pavement. She started to run, but other hands grabbed her, holding her fast. Lydia tried struggling, but found it impossible to free herself.

'Lydia Fabia, what a delight it is to see you! And looking so well too. Doesn't she look well, boys? A real treat for the eyes.'

Lydia froze. She could hear the mockery in Ofellius's high-pitched voice. The hands keeping her captive released her without warning and she stumbled forward, nearly falling to the ground. Before turning towards the voice, she took a deep breath and straightened her shawl.

Dignity, she thought. It was necessary to show Ofellius that she was not in the slightest bit afraid or perturbed by this rough treatment. She was above all things a Roman, and conducted herself with a certain amount of decorum. She only wished someone had remembered to tell her knees as they threatened to give way.

'What exactly is going on here, Ofellius? Why do you seek to hold me captive?'

'Captivity is a harsh word, my lady.' His thin lips revealed his yellowed teeth. 'I prefer protective custody.'

'It is the same thing. Let me go about my business.' Lydia fought against the hands that held her again.

'A Roman matron of your standing discovered in a back alley without any protection. Somebody had to act for the sake of…decorum.'

'I became separated from my bodyguard.' Lydia drew herself up to her full height and wished she was a bit taller and more intimidating. She had to get away. If she ran, she might be able to make it back to Tuccia. Somehow, they could send word to Aro and he would rescue her. She should have gone back the instant she realised Strabo had disappeared. 'He is looking for me. Let me go back to Rufus's apartment and wait for him there.'

'Tsk, tsk, how unfortunate. And careless of you.'

A cold prickling went down the back of her neck. She was tempted to push her way around him, but three of his men stood behind him. One she noticed was the same man who had nearly pushed her down the stairs earlier.

'I will be going now.' Her voice sounded high and thin to her ears.

'Aro must be very foolish to misplace his woman like this,' Ofellius continued as if she had not spoken.

'I am not Aro's woman,' Lydia said. 'I am his wife.'

Ofellius lifted an eyebrow. 'Is there a difference?'

'Most assuredly, yes. A wife is for political purposes only.'

'Don't sell yourself short, my lady. There are no half-measures about you.' Ofellius ran a long finger down the side of her cheek. Lydia forced her body to remain still, not to flinch. 'I am sure Aro will be very glad to know you are in safe hands.'

An ominous foreboding filled Lydia. Ofellius did not intend to return her to Aro. He was going to use her as bait, but when he discovered that she meant very little to Aro—what then? Her stomach churned. The worst part was that she had trusted this…this pirate with Publius's fish sauce.

'Are you offering to see me home, Ofellius?' Lydia crossed her arms to prevent their trembling and stared hard at the man. 'It is very kind of you to take such an interest in my safety, but I assure you I can find my own way. I will tell Aro of your concern.'

She ignored the guffaws of Ofellius's men and concentrated on keeping her head upright. She did not want to do anything to provoke the man, but rather to shame him.

One movement of Ofellius's hand silenced the men. 'In due course, you will be returned, but I think to enjoy your company a little while longer. Your wit is quite renowned.'

His minions laughed, but Lydia stood there with a sinking heart. She was right. She was to be held captive. And how would Aro react? She refused to beg. She would reason. She made sure she stood up straight, head held high.

'Whatever problem you have with the Lupan House, this is not the way to get redress. Let the courts decide.'

'What did I tell you, lads? The lady has an unequalled way with words.' Ofellius gave a booming laugh. 'The courts? We shall dispute man to man as we have always done.'

Fear gripped Lydia's stomach. There were so many things she could have done. Her desire for independence had gone too far. Whatever his feelings for her might be, Aro would never jeopardise the Lupan House for her sake. She was a worthless prize. She had to make Ofellius see sense before it was too late for both of them.

'You are making a mistake, if you think having me will make Fabius Aro change his ways. The Sea Wolf will not change for anyone.'

'For your sake, I hope you are wrong,' Ofellius returned. 'Shall we go?'

The man behind her sniggered, causing Lydia's flesh to creep.

'I do not have much choice.'

'No, you do not.'

* * *

'Fabius Aro, we have a problem,' Piso said, coming into the *tablinum*. His brow furrowed. Piso had arrived back from Ostia late yesterday.

'Problem? What sort of problem?' Every muscle in Aro's body became alert.

Piso came forward, twisting his cap in his hands. 'Strabo, the man who escorted Lydia and Tuccia this morning… Rufus found him outside a wine shop. You know the wine shop where you found me the other day—Flora's place.'

Aro's blood ran cold. He knew what Piso was not saying. Lydia was not with Strabo. A thousand different things raced through his brain. Aro forced his lungs to breathe. She had to be uninjured.

'What was Strabo doing in a wine shop near where Rufus lives? It is on the other side of Rome to the Palatine.'

'I understand from Rufus that your wife visited him earlier. She brought a jar of ointment to help with his burns. He was most effusive about it. Some time after she left, Rufus went down to his local for a quiet glass, leaving his granddaughter with his wife and found Strabo slumped on the floor, his drink by his side.'

Aro struggled to keep his temper. 'But where is Lydia, if Strabo was discovered comatose?'

'That is what I wanted to talk to you about.' Piso developed a sudden interest in his cap.

'Out with it, man!'

'She's vanished. Rufus and his wife were the last people to see her.'

Aro resisted the impulse to shake Piso. Getting the information was like getting blood from a statue. Aro felt his blood quicken. He slammed his fist on to the bench, causing it to jump and Korina to whimper.

'Who gave Strabo permission to drink himself stupid?'

'According to Strabo, he was hit from behind. He has a lump the size of a hen's egg on the back of his head. But that could have come from falling off the bar stool. The barmaid, not Flora, another one swears that she saw nothing untoward.'

'Is the barmaid reliable?'

'We've become acquainted. You can never know too many barmaids. Baths, wine and women will all ruin you, but what is life except baths, wine and women?' Piso's eyes twinkled. 'I am thinking of going back there and—'

'*Where is Lydia?*' Aro fought the rage that welled up within him. Out of the corner of his eye, he saw Korina cover her face with her paws and shrink back. Piso shifted uneasily. Shouting would not achieve anything, but it made him feel better. Aro fought for control. 'Do we have any idea of where she might be?'

'No,' Piso replied quietly. 'The barmaid said that men from the Ofellius house sometimes drink there. Not often, but sometimes. The one you laid low in Flora's shop was hanging around like a bad smell outside the wine shop. He sidled off pretty quick once I arrived. As I arrived back here, one of his men handed me this.'

Piso held out a tablet. Aro glanced over it. Ofellius stating he had something of value and offering an exchange. There could be little doubt what this something of value was.

'That should have been the first thing you told me,' Aro said.

'Do you think Ofellius has her?'

'It is a possibility. She was definitely at Rufus's, and then she left. From what you say, no one has seen her and now this tablet arrives, offering negotiations.'

'Gods, I would not wish that on any woman.'

Absently Aro stroked Korina's head. It was all too easy to imagine the scene at Ofellius's hall. Decked in resplendent purple, the finest money and greed could buy, Ofellius would greet him with effusive gestures. They'd chat, skirting around the critical problem. Ofellius would lean forward, snap his fingers and allow Aro a glimpse of Lydia and the bargaining would begin. Aro pressed his lips together. Because he had seen her with her dark hair streaming out over her pillow, heard her voice and felt her womanly curves against his, he would give away more than he intended. Because he wanted to see her smile, and hear her clear voice again, he would sacrifice all.

Aro stood up, wiped his hands on his tunic. He had to stop letting his fantasy run away with his thoughts. He refused to bargain, even for Lydia. If Ofellius had taken Lydia, it would be a fight, a fight to the death.

'What are you going to do?'

'Runners will be sent to see if there is any whisper about Lydia. If Ofellius has her, he will send another note. This one was to whet our appetite.'

Lydia followed Ofellius, pretending to be complacent with her eyes down as a proper matron should, but her muscles tensed, ready to run when the opportunity presented itself. They seemed to be travelling slowly with Ofellius waiting at corners for certain signals before she was hurried across the square.

She said a prayer to Fortunata, asking for her help. Thankfully, none of Ofellius's men touched her. For now, they seemed content to form a phalanx around her.

The streets became more familiar. She spotted a fishmonger Aro and she had passed on their way from the Aventine baths to the temple of Diana. Her throat closed. She could find her way from here.

There had to be a way to break free and escape. She had no doubt that Aro would be furious with her when he found out. He had warned her of the danger. If only she had had an instant more, she'd have returned to Rufus and sent Tuccia back for the litter. Lydia bit her lip. The Fates had certainly given an unwelcome twist to their spindle.

They came into a small crowded market square where a silk merchant had hung out his wares. A litter and two carts blocked the road. Ofellius and his men grumbled to each other, complaining about the traffic.

Lydia's heart thudded. She recognised the colours and bearers. What in the name of Juno was her father doing here? Lydia waved wildly, but no response. It started to head off in the direction of the Forum. A heavy hand closed on her upper arm, propelling her forward. Lydia's throat tightened.

'Lydia, Lydia, what are you doing here? Walking, of all things?' Sulpicia's voice floated over the crowd.

Lydia felt a heavy load roll from her back. Sulpicia had seen her. She was saved. Lydia waved back.

'Hold on, Sulpicia,' she called. 'I will come and join you.'

She shook off her captor's hand and darted towards the litter, daring Ofellius to stop her.

'Thank you for your hospitality, Ofellius.' Lydia gave a

gracious nod. 'But my sister-in-law has a litter and I am rather tired from my journey. She can look after me now.'

Ofellius pursed his lips and his hand made a cutting motion. Two of his men started forward and Lydia thought they might grab her. One of Ofellius's men in his haste tripped over a market stall, sending piles of figs and plums rolling all over the street. The market stall owner and his wife started berating him. Fists began to fly.

Lydia gave a wild look behind her and then sprinted the last few yards to the litter.

'Please,' she said in a low voice to Sulpicia. 'Can you give me a lift?'

'Absolutely delighted to, but, Juno's necklace, it looks as if we are going to be here for awhile.'

Sulpicia moved over a bit and made room in the litter. Lydia hoisted herself into the litter without waiting for it to be lowered and lay staring up at the ceiling, willing her heart to stop pounding.

'Lydia, my dear, you seem out of breath.' Sulpicia put her hand on Lydia's arm.

'I am fine, honestly.'

'Your husband should know better than to make you walk without a guard. These streets are dangerous places.'

'I became separated from my guard.'

'Oh, Lydia, how frightening for you. Are you all right? Were you molested?'

'I am fine now.'

Lydia willed the litter to move and after an age the swaying motion began. She risked a backward glance. The market stall was now in tatters. One of Ofellius's men had just been hit over the head with a roll of cloth and Ofellius looked like he had swallowed a sour plum.

She closed her eyes and lay back on the cushions. Safe.

'Why are you in this part of the city, Sulpicia?'

'I have just been to the temple of the Good Goddess to ensure my baby will be born strong and healthy.' Sulpicia leant forward, her face glowing. 'The augur assures me the baby will be a boy. Publius will be delighted.'

'And my father, how is he?'

'He is well, although his temper is uncertain. You know how he dislikes to lose at anything, and he lost a court case last week. And he has had that despicable trader Ofellius for dinner twice in the last seven days. He even wanted us to dine with him. I soon put a stop to that notion.'

'Ofellius?' Lydia tilted her head. 'What would my father want with him?'

Sulpicia coloured. 'You mustn't think anything about it. You know how I am, always saying things. Forget I ever mentioned it. Now, let me tell you about the divine ribbons I saw…'

Lydia allowed Sulpicia's chatter to wash over her as she took deep breaths and watched the swaying roof of the litter. She was going back home.

A huge lump formed in Lydia's throat as she caught a glimpse of the now familiar façade of the Lupan House. Safety. Home. Aro.

Above all else, she wanted to feel Aro's strong arms about her and lay her head against his chest, drinking in his familiar scent. Somehow winning the wager no longer mattered. She knew as long as Aro was there, she was safe.

The thought surprised her and she forgot to reply to

Sulpicia's observation about the crowds on the Aventine. She made her goodbyes and called for Clodius the porter.

After a short time, he appeared with his dog at his heels. His eyes widened when he saw her.

'I have not been gone that long that you have forgotten my face,' Lydia said with a short laugh.

'Not at all, Lydia Fabia.' He made a low bow. 'As ever, I am pleased to see you. You are a welcome sight.'

'Is my husband within?' Lydia asked. If Aro was here, she might be able to have a quiet word and tell him of her adventure. He had to see that there was something going on. Perhaps, he could warn her father about the follies of doing business with Ofellius and then the whole incident with the fish sauce could be properly investigated. The amphora in Rufus's apartment was from Publius's shipment. She'd bet any amount of money on it.

Without waiting for Clodius to announce her, she swept into the atrium and halted.

The place swarmed with men, some carrying sticks and others she was sure had swords under their cloaks. There was a quiet purpose in their movements. She could pick out Aro's dark head in the centre of the atrium, his back towards the doorway, speaking to Pius.

The sound in the atrium ceased. All movement became frozen. Then Aro made an irritated noise and turned. For a heartbeat, their eyes met. His face lit up, only to be replaced by a stern frown. The quickness of the change made Lydia wonder if the first expression had been her imagination.

She held out her hands, and longed to run to him, throw

her arms about him and feel his solid body against hers. She wanted to tell him that she was wrong and he was right, that she should have taken two men with her, but not here in front of all these men. Her feet felt as if they were encased in concrete. She made a little gesture with her hands.

'Aro.'

Nobody moved.

'You have returned, Lydia.' His eyes glittered dangerously.

'Sulpicia brought me back.'

He lifted his eyebrow at the mention of Sulpicia. 'I had no idea you were visiting your father.'

'I wasn't.'

He was silent at that. He leant over and spoke a word to Pius. Silently the men filed out, leaving Aro and Lydia standing there, facing each other.

'Are you going to tell me where you were?' His face betrayed nothing. His voice was dangerously quiet. 'Or are we to play a game of questions?'

'There is no mystery about it.' Lydia gave a little laugh. She leant forward and dipped her hand in the pool. 'Someone sent word to Tuccia that her grandparents were ill. I took her there as I wanted to make Rufus's acquaintance. I left Tuccia to administer to her grandparents.'

'Did you take a bodyguard?' Again, his words were quiet.

Lydia shifted uncomfortably. She was used to her father's bluster, not this quiet precise way of questioning. How could she tell him of her discovery? Or about what happened afterwards? What if she had been mistaken about everything? The last thing she wanted to do was start a war between two rival trading houses.

'I did.' Lydia answered firmly. 'Strabo.'

'And where is he? Did he return with you in Sulpicia's litter?'

'He disappeared.' Lydia put her hand to her throat, reliving those awful few moments when she had stood alone in the street. 'He had said that the apartment would be crowded and he would wait down on the street. After my visit, he was nowhere to be seen.'

'And didn't you think to return to Rufus's house and wait?'

'It never crossed my mind. The apartment was tiny, barely big enough for four people. He agreed to wait for me. Equally I had no wish to go poking in every wine shop, seeking the man.' Lydia stopped. Her eyes widened. 'You thought something had happened to me.'

'We had received a report, a report which appears to be in error, thank Mercury.'

Lydia's mind raced. She had no way of knowing if Ofellius had meant her harm. He could have been trying to be kind. Perhaps he had wanted to shake her confidence and prevent her from doing something like that again. He had let her go when she encountered Sulpicia. He could have detained her if he had wanted. No, he had simply wanted to give her a fright. And she did not want to risk Aro getting hurt over that.

'Nothing happened. I discovered Sulpicia.'

'And what was your sister-in-law doing in that area of Rome? I would have thought it a little rough for her.'

'She was attending a fertility rite. The baby is due in two months' time, and she wants to be sure it is a boy.'

Lydia waited, but Aro continued to stand there, saying nothing. He was regarding her as if she were a naughty child.

He should be pleased to see her back, but he had a black look. Something was obviously wrong, but once again, he was not going to confide in her. She had had enough this day.

'You will forgive me, but it has been a long day,' she said. 'I desire to use the bathing suite.'

Without waiting for his word of consent, she left the atrium, head held high, refusing to look back.

'What shall I do with the men?' Piso asked as he returned to the atrium. 'Do we go to Ofellius's compound? The men are ready and armed with cudgels.'

Aro turned towards him and shook his head. 'Stand the men down. We don't go to battle today.' He gave a short laugh. 'It appears our old adversary miscalculated. Lydia has returned, unmolested. I have no wish to alarm her further. I will question her later about what exactly went on, but not here, not without giving her time to get her thoughts together.'

'Do you think he captured her?' Piso had a puzzled expression on his face. 'The message was clear. Strabo's head is split open.'

'I think that was the intent. Somehow Lydia escaped. Ofellius appears determined to restart hostilities, but his timing makes little sense. Why now? And why in such a provocative fashion?' Aro chose his words with a great deal of deliberation. He hooked his thumbs in his belt and waited for his captain's response.

'The olive oil scam had been going on for months. It was simply the first time he tried it with the Lupan House. It is odd, though, that his senior captain would have threatened you and Lydia like that. I assume the man has a death wish. But to threaten the wife of a head of a trading house? Whatever happens now, my men and I stand shoulder to shoulder with you. I care nothing for these curse tablets. I am only grateful that you called me back from Ostia before I had left for northern Italy.'

Aro clapped Piso on the back. 'You are a true friend. Thank you.'

'But what happened? Why did he allow Lydia to go? Hermes knows he has kidnapped enough women in his time. He has an unsavoury reputation on Crete. He should know what he is on about.'

'We know the who, but we don't know the why and it is something I intend to find out, Piso,' Aro said with determination.

'Personally, I would like to have seen Ofellius's face when Lydia escaped, and that of his henchmen. Letting a woman slip through their fingers…'

Aro turned away from Piso. His blood ran cold at the thought of what could have happened.

'Luckily, Lydia proved more than a match for them,' Aro replied, keeping his voice steady.

'You approve of what she did.'

'She is a woman you underestimate at your peril, Piso.' Aro looked towards where she had vanished, skirts swinging and her head unbowed. She was a strong woman, his wife. 'And it appears I have done just that. I want you to contact our friend at the Ofellian House and find out exactly who Ofellius is working for. He'd never dare attempt to kidnap a senator's daughter unless he thought he had protection from a powerful senator. He values his own skin too much.'

'What do you intend to do?' Piso asked.

Aro raised an eyebrow. 'Remedy the situation with Lydia.'

# *Chapter Fifteen*

Lydia stripped and left the gown on the floor. She'd find some reason to get rid of it later. She had no desire to remember anything of this afternoon. She had carefully laid a pile of fresh clothes—a dark blue gown, under-tunic and new breast band—on the shelf, next to a pile of white linen towels. Even her sandals were clean.

The flickering light of the oil lamp made the frescoes of Neptune and his sea nymphs waver. Crushed oyster shell had been added to the paint, giving it a shimmering glow. Lydia smiled.

All the time she kept berating herself for being so naïve in how she had handled the situation earlier. She should have done what Aro suggested. She could see that now. The instant she had seen Strabo had vanished, she should have scampered back up the stairs, but, no, she had to prove a point.

The only thing she had done was to show Aro how silly and childish she was. Not the mature and sober Roman matron she wanted to be.

The worst of it was that when she had returned, she wanted to taste Aro's lips. She had wanted him to pull her into his arms and kiss her. She would even be prepared to beg for it, to lose the wager. But it would appear Aro had forgotten or, worse, lost interest.

She gave her body a little shake, reached for the olive-oil pot and started to rub the oil into her skin. So absorbed was she in her own thoughts that she failed to hear the faint click of the door. When the pot was lifted from her fingers, she gave a slight squeak and her hands flew to cover herself.

'Get out,' she cried.

'And spoil the sight?' came the quiet, almost sardonic voice.

Lydia stood still, not daring to move as she felt her body begin to respond to his voice as it flowed over her. She eyed the towel and the distance to it. If she made a lunge, would he stop her? Would he notice the sudden puckering of her nipples? Maybe he would think it was down to the cold.

'Allow me to get dressed. You have me at a disadvantage.'

'You are covered in oil.' There was definite laughter in his voice. She risked a glance at him. He was standing not more than a foot away from her, dressed in his tunic. The dim light of the bathing suite heightened the shadows in his face, making it appear all angles.

Lydia gave an impatient stamp of her foot. 'I know I am covered, but that does not matter. Hand me a towel.'

Aro said nothing, but picked up a *strigil* and advanced towards her. Lydia took a step backwards, reached behind her. Her hand closed on her under-tunic. She drew it over her head, then turned to face him. He stood with an amused expression on his face. Lydia concentrated on breathing.

'What do you intend to do?' she asked, eyeing the cleaning blade.

'To act as your tire-woman. Tuccia is with her grandparents and therefore you are in need of one. I can serve for the short time she is gone.'

'You are many things, but I had never counted a tire-woman among them.' Lydia noticed her breath came in short sharp pants as if she had run very fast. She swallowed hard and concentrated on breathing normally. She refused to think of his hands on her body.

'I can do a passable imitation…if required.'

'I don't recall asking for your help.' Lydia pressed her palms against the cloth covering her thighs. She wanted to appear cool and collected.

'You ought to try, before you refuse me.'

Without waiting for an answer, Aro reached forward and scraped the oil off her skin, a light touch of the blade, but one that sent searing pulses of heat through her.

'It's fine. I can fend for myself.' She made a grab for the *strigil* with one hand while the other prevented her undertunic from gaping. She could see the oil had made the thin linen fabric translucent, clinging to her curves, leaving nothing to the imagination.

'Like you did this afternoon?' The words were lightly said, but the eyes deadly serious.

Lydia gave a slight gasp and looked wildly about her. Who had said something? Had they made it seem worse than it was? She had made an error of judgement, but nothing had happened. She had managed all right on her own in the end.

She pushed away all thoughts of what could have happened if Sulpicia had not appeared when she had.

'What sort of nonsense are you talking about?' Lydia put the offered *strigil* down next to the jug of olive oil, trying to ignore his dancing eyes and the way his tunic moulded to his chest. As she placed it on the shelf, her hand slipped and it went crashing to the ground. She bent to retrieve it. Aro continued to stand in the middle of the small room, arms crossed and a tiny smile playing on his lips as if he knew what was disturbing her. This time, concentrating on what she was doing instead of paying attention to Aro's hands, she managed to place the *strigil* on the shelf. 'I told you what happened.'

A shadow crossed over his face.

'You carefully avoided what happened between the time when you left the relative safety of Rufus's rooms and when you met Sulpicia. We need to talk, Lydia,' he said, each word echoing in the small chamber. 'I need to know what happened. If you do not wish me to act as your tire-woman, then maybe you will tell me the exact circumstances of how your sister-in-law came to bring you home.'

'Is it important?'

'Strabo lies in the infirmary, his head bandaged. The surgeon says he will live,' Aro said in a quiet but determined voice. 'Did you see anything amiss? Any little detail, anything that could help track down his attacker? The men of the Lupan House must be protected.'

Lydia explained again about Strabo, and how she had to flatten against a wall so a couple could descend.

'Would you recognise them again?'

Lydia thought and then shook her head. 'At the time, I was

certain he belonged to the Ofellian house, but now I am not. I have no wish to cause problems. People could get hurt.'

'People have already been hurt.' Aro crossed his arms. 'And you thought nothing was amiss when you came out.'

'Nothing. The crowd seemed heavy at the wine-shop, full of rough men,' Lydia said. 'I had thought I was being foolish, and did not want to cause problems. I will admit to being annoyed that Strabo hadn't waited. I had no desire to linger in that place, hoping my bodyguard would appear. I had no wish to be taken for a loose woman.'

'Go on.' Aro made a little gesture with his hand. 'I want to know everything. Help me to understand.'

Briefly she related her encounter with Ofellius and his men. She watched Aro's face grow graver and graver. Despite the warmth in the room, a shiver passed down Lydia's back. Her hands started to shake. She didn't want to think about what might have happened. She concentrated on retelling the story in a firm voice. If he laid a hand on her or made any gesture, Lydia knew she would be in his arms, but he simply stood there.

'And he let you go? Without a struggle?'

'I suppose he did not wish to make a scene. Sulpicia had seen me. She said that he has had some recent dealings with my father, has even dined with them.' Lydia shrugged. 'My father approves of him so highly, I can't see that he would attack me. My father, despite his illness, still has powerful friends. It was obvious that Ofellius was simply doing his duty as he saw it. I had been concerned, but, thinking about it, it was my over-active imagination.'

'He sent word, requesting a meeting. He wanted to speak

about something valuable I had misplaced. I was sure it was you.'

Lydia moved to the other side of the small chamber. Her heart gave a skip. He considered her valuable. Ruthlessly she dampened down her hopes. She was only valuable because of her father's influence.

'That is why all those men were here.'

'I am hardly one to let an insult like that pass.' Aro put his hands on his hips, the captain of his ship. 'Nobody molests my wife and escapes.'

'It did not come to that.' Lydia pressed her hands together. 'I am uninjured. As I said, it was probably a misunderstanding.'

'If that is what you want to call it, then so be it.' Aro crossed his arms and stared at her, his face stern and unyielding.

Lydia nodded. She was not so foolish as to think it was for her that he would have risked his men. It was the insult to the Lupan House.

'If you have learnt all that you wanted, you may leave.' She gestured towards the door.

'Did you think I was joking when I offered to scrape you down?' He advanced towards her.

Lydia shook her head. Heat infused her body, but the wager still stood between them.

'We have an agreement, you and I,' she said, thinking quickly. 'You were not to kiss me until I begged you.'

'You have asked me twice.' There was a distinct twinkle in Aro's eyes. 'I never said anything about touching you with my fingers.'

He dipped his fingers into the oil and started to rub small circles on her upper arms and the back of her neck. Tiny circles of heat. She knew if she took a step backwards she would encounter the hard wall of his chest.

He continued in a conversational tone as if they were speaking in the atrium rather than in the intimate atmosphere of the bath suite. 'You should recall the exact nature of our wager. I said lips, not hands.'

Lydia swallowed hard. His touch was lighting fires within her. She wanted him. She knew that. She wanted to feel his arms about her, holding her close, but she couldn't tell him that. To tell him would mean he had won. She'd have to give up her freedom.

Freedom. After today, she wasn't sure she wanted it. She had returned, seeking his protection. If any of the men had harmed her, she would have been glad to know that they were punished. She wondered if that made her a hypocrite. Like Sulpicia, did she want everything?

'I can do this myself.' She took the oil from his unresisting fingers.

'It is much easier to bathe if you have help. Someone to scrape your back.' He made no move to recapture the oil, but stood there so close that Lydia could see the stubble on his chin, and the faint white scar across his cheek.

'You are no gentleman,' she said firmly. 'A gentleman would not have come in without knocking.'

A wry smile played on his lips. 'I never said I was, but I am your husband.'

'I never forget that.' Lydia looked down at the gold-and-iron ring encircling her third finger. It was strange in how short a time she had ceased to wonder at its weight and it had become a part of her.

Aro's skin glowed golden in the lamp light. He held out his hands. 'I'll leave if that is what you truly desire.'

Lydia watched the rise and fall of his chest and knew if she sent him away now, she would regret the action for the rest of life. She'd always wonder, what if… She'd worry about the consequences tomorrow, but tonight she wanted to feel his touch against her skin. She wanted to feel how she felt before when they first made love, before he had ruined it. This time, if they coupled, she would know it was because he wanted to, rather than out of a sense of duty.

'Stay.' The word was a harsh whisper, torn from her throat.

'As my lady desires.'

'I am not begging you,' Lydia added quickly. 'I am asking you.'

'I understand that.' His eyes danced. 'If there are any impure thoughts in this room, they come from you and not me. I only seek to help you out in your hour of need.'

Lydia held out her other arm. She'd show him that she was immune to him. It was only one more day, after all. But still it rankled that he was not trying to seduce her. 'You may help me with the *strigil*, but that is all.'

'A condition or a challenge?'

'A statement of fact,' Lydia returned swiftly, but she could not prevent the sharp intake of breath.

The muscles in his arm rippled as he manipulated the *strigil*, scraping the oil off her skin.

'You will not lose, my nymph. In surrendering, we both win.'

'What sort of surrender are you talking about?'

'Unconditional.'

Lydia drew in her breath as the images of what unconditional surrender meant danced in front of her. Her whole body felt infused with fire.

Aro's hands changed. Before they had been coolly impersonal, but now they lingered. A firm touch to the shoulder and her other arm. Sensuous movements.

He dipped his fingers in the oil again, starting to apply the oil to the back of her neck.

'It should be scented with roses,' he murmured. 'Remind me.'

Lydia nodded, unable to trust her voice.

He moved her hair and his fingers made little circles. Servants and bath-house slaves had oiled and scraped her body many times, but never had this sweet languor filled her. She moved slightly and a low moan rose in the back of her throat.

'Stay still,' he commanded. His hand brushed the top of the under-tunic, moving it slightly to reveal her creamy skin. And the tops of her breasts. Her nipples constricted to hardened points. Her throat grew dry. Her body urged her forward, with whispered memories of the other time. She needed to touch him, to feel his mouth against hers. She wanted it, wanted to believe it would not be a surrender.

'Please,' she whispered.

His fingers traced the outline of her jaw, no more than a butterfly touch, and then dropped to his side. His gaze bore deeply into her soul. She wondered if he could see how much she desired him.

Her tongue came forward and licked her dry lips. His mouth was so close, she only had to tilt her face a little bit. Their breath intertwined.

Did she dare? She wanted to feel his mouth. If she took, it was not begging.

Her hand curled around his neck and pulled his face closer. His mouth touched hers gently and then became firm. His tongue sought hers, demanding entrance. She arched her back, feeling the hardness of his chest against her breasts.

Instantly his arms closed about her, holding her firm against the length of him. She could feel his arousal, pressing into her. He wanted her. The knowledge swept through her like a fire, blazing bright. He wanted her as much as she wanted him.

'You will need to undress,' he said against her mouth.

'Why?' She peeped from under her lashes, seeing the hungry look in his eyes.

'So I can continue the bath. It would be a shame if only a little bit of you was clean.'

'Fair is fair. If I am to strip, you should as well.'

He stroked the wisps of hair back from her forehead and clasped her to his chest for a heartbeat. Then his arms loosened and he gave a laugh.

'I am yours to command when you make such requests.'

Within a heartbeat, he stood before her. Naked. His muscles sculpted in warm marble. Lydia reached out and touched the planes of his chest. Her fingers brushed his nipples and felt them grow taut and tight. Her nipples showed answering puckers underneath her tunic.

He drew his breath in sharply, but did not move.

'Are you to be bathed as well?' she asked, pretending to consider the prospect.

'I would need some help.' His voice was no more than a husky rasp.

'It can be arranged.'

'You are overdressed.'

He ran his hands over the thin cloth to where the hardened points of her nipples showed. His thumb and forefinger encircled the nipple, then rubbed, and fire, hotter than a hypocaust, shot through her. She gasped and leant forward, grabbing on to his forearms. He smiled and lowered his head to the tunic, his tongue drawing damp circles around her nipples.

She gave another moan. Her hands plucked at her undertunic. It clung, and she felt his hands slowly lifting it, until she stood before him. The warm air bathed her body.

He said nothing, but reached for the oil. He dropped a trickle on to her breast. The cool liquid slid down, pooling in her belly button. He carefully smoothed the oil over her body, avoiding the dark triangle between her legs. Then he used the *strigil* to wipe her body clean, with long lingering strokes. The longing grew deep in her belly. She wanted more than this.

'Your turn.'

She took the oil from him and dribbled it on to his chest. She made her fingers follow the same pattern his had. The oil flowed over his skin, turning it to a deep gold. She reached behind her and her fingers closed around the *strigil*. Gently she ran it over his chest, feeling the power beneath the muscles. She smoothed the oil over his arms and back, concentrating on each movement and all the while heat from his body warmed her, inflamed her senses.

'I believe I am finished,' she said, hardly recognising her own voice. 'You are completely clean.'

'You haven't done everything.'

She glanced down and saw his arousal. Her hand reached out and touched it. Hard, but silky soft.

His hand closed over hers, held her there. Its pulsating warmth sent flames of fire along her arm. Then he put a finger to her lips and gently eased her down on to the warm floor.

He bent his head and traced a line with his lips to her dark curls. She gasped as his tongue penetrated her innermost place. Her body jerked upwards.

'Shall I continue?' he murmured, lifting his head. She could see the golden light of his eyes.

Her only answer was an inarticulate moan in the back of her throat.

'I shall take that as a yes.'

His tongue returned to her, making lazy trails. Teasing and tormenting. The longing grew within her. His mouth closed around her, sucking slightly, and her world exploded into stars.

Her hands caught his hair, sinking deep in his curls.

'Please,' she begged, wanting to feel all of him, to feel that way she had before. 'Please, I want you. I want you inside me now.'

He lifted his head and a very masculine smile touched his lips. He parted her thighs and the tip of him touched her where his tongue had been. Her body expanded and enveloped the full length of him. Then he began to move. Slowly at first, but with increasing speed as her hips echoed his rhythm. Her breath came in short sharp gasps until she felt the wonderful shuddering release.

In the aftermath of the storm that engulfed them both, Lydia lay in Aro's arms. Her legs intertwined with his, her head resting on the broad expanse of his chest, listening to the now steady thump of his heart. She knew her heart matched his and gloried in it.

'Less than seven days, my dryad,' his voice rumbled in her ear. 'Perhaps the next time you will take me at my word.'

Lydia frowned. She struggled to sit up, but his arms held her firmly against his chest.

'Not this time. You are not storming off in some pretend-outrage. You will admit to losing the wager. You will remain my wife as we married.' He buried his face in her hair. 'I for my part promise to look after you and cherish you.'

'You did not play fair,' she mumbled against his chest, knowing he spoke the truth. She had participated fully in their lovemaking. She had wanted him. Later she would think about what she had lost. In his arms, the question of who was her guardian seemed somehow less important. She knew she was no longer the woman she had been. She did not want to go back to looking after her father and Sulpicia. She wanted to live her own life.

'I merely offered to help you, to serve as your tire-woman. It was you who begged for me to continue.'

Lydia sat up, pulling her knees up to her chest and resting her chin against them, considering the flickering oil lamps.

'You knew what would happen.'

His fingers lifted her chin so that she gazed into his deep eyes. The gold was now mere flecks in a sea of hazel. 'Not knew, hoped. There is a difference.'

'What did you hope to gain by this demonstration?'

His eyes searched her face. Then he gave a little shrug. 'That I keep my promises, however preposterous they may sound.'

'There are other ways to demonstrate that.'

'But few more enjoyable.' He dropped a kiss on her forehead and then his eyes grew serious and he kissed her lips. Lydia savoured the taste of his mouth.

'I will agree with it being pleasurable.'

'We can stay here, but the floor is cooling and I don't want you to catch a chill,' he growled in her ear.

Lydia leant backwards and this time his arms fell away. Despite the warmth in the bath suite, Lydia shivered and wished she hadn't moved. In here everything seemed so simple and straightforward. She reached for her breast band and under-tunic, dressed as rapidly as she could despite her hands fumbling with the sleeves of her gown.

'I told you—you need help with your toilet.' Aro stood up and fastened the sleeves properly, doing so with a practised ease.

'Are you making an offer for the place?' she said with a laugh. 'Tuccia might have something to say about that.'

'Tuccia can look after you when I have to be elsewhere.'

At the mention of Tuccia's name, Lydia remembered the amphora she had seen in her grandfather's apartment.

'You gave her grandfather *liquamen* as a reward for his bravery.'

'I recently purchased a consignment and I know Rufus loves his fish sauce. He did much to save the warehouse from the fire. It seemed a fitting reward.'

Lydia swallowed hard and tried to concentrate on doing up her belt. She had to solve this mystery. Not that it made any difference, but she wanted to know. 'Who sold you the *liquamen*?'

'One of the traders in the Forum sold it to me. He lets me know when something reasonably priced comes in.'

'Are you sure about it?' Lydia felt the belt slip from her hands.

'Does it matter? The bill of sale will be somewhere in my office. Was it a superior fish sauce?' He smiled and his eyes lit up. 'I sent most of it off to Ostia, destined for Corinth, but perhaps Piso will know if an amphora remains. For me, all fish sauce tastes the same—like rotting fish.'

Lydia felt her throat constrict. She could clearly see the markings. She remembered the day Publius had put them on, joking that they would never get lost this way.

Aro ran his hand through his hair, making it stand up. 'Why is it suddenly so important?'

'It had my brother's markings on it. Ofellius swore to Sulpicia that Publius received his cargo in Corinth.'

'I can check the exact date for you. It will be in my office, but it was over a month ago.'

'Then what is going on? Why did Ofellius lie to Sulpicia?' A chill passed over Lydia. She felt as if she was playing a complicated game of *latrunculi* and someone kept changing the rules.

'I have no answer for you.' He bent and kissed her neck. 'I can make a few discreet enquiries. It will take some time, but it would appear Ofellius is playing a very dangerous game.'

'What should I do? Should I tell Sulpicia? She says my father has been doing business with Ofellius. Maybe, if you had a word…'

'It would only make her worry. Trust me. Let me make

some enquiries. In the meantime, rest easy, knowing that Publius has got his money.'

He looked her deep in the eyes and Lydia knew she trusted him. After today, she did not want to have to think about facing Ofellius on her own.

'Now, I was wondering,' Aro said. 'Which would you prefer—a hot meal or a soft bed?'

'Both.'

'I think that could be arranged.'

# Chapter Sixteen

Aro stared out at the night-blackened city. Out there was someone who meant him and Lydia harm. His hands gripped the balustrade so tightly the whites of his knuckles showed. He had nearly fulfilled his vow to his father and now this. Whoever it was had enticed Ofellius to go for Lydia. The most puzzling point was why did Ofellius and his henchmen allow her to go when Sulpicia appeared? There had to be a reason. Lydia had been clever and resourceful, but he suspected there was more to it. If Ofellius had intended to kidnap her, he would have succeeded.

It also bothered him that in attempting to kidnap her they had revealed his weakest point. Elevation to the Senate or indeed victory in any election would mean nothing without Lydia by his side. He gave a wry smile. He hoped he never had to choose between his duty to his father and his feelings for his wife.

A movement in the shadows caused him to crouch, ready to spring. The figure stepped out into the silver moonlight.

'Have you found the remedy? Because from what I know about such things, you are surely not going to find it out here. On your own.'

'We have reached an accord.' Aro stretched. 'You should find yourself a good woman, Piso. It will save you chasing after barmaids.'

'When I find her, I'll let you know.'

'Did you find out anything from our friend?'

'Our friend fell from a boat two days ago. An unfortunate accident, according to Flora's sources. A fitting end for an un-savoury man. I thought you should have done it long ago. I'm convinced he was playing a double game.'

'What else does Flora know, then?'

'You may say what you like, but Flora does something.' Piso kissed his fingers gestured upwards. 'By Hermes, Poseidon and Apollo, the things that woman knows.'

'Quick, man, who is employing Ofellius?'

'You aren't going to like this—Veratius Cornelius.'

'Lydia's *father?*' Aro did not bother to hide his astonishment. 'Veratius Cornelius?'

'The one and the same. One of Ofellius's men is very friendly with Flora's girls. He was babbling on about it tonight. How it all got messed up because the goose got cold feet and appeared.'

Aro felt as if his stomach had been double punched. Rufus had been right all along. He had said not to trust the Veratii. How was he going to explain this to Lydia? And how was he going to explain the need to ensure it did not happen again?

He grasped Piso by both arms. 'Are you sure? You need to be very sure. Pillow talk between a prostitute and her client will not stand up in a court of law.'

'Flora has never been wrong before. What shall I do? Do you want me to arrange for a few of the boys to go and sort Veratius Cornelius out? He must have been the one responsible for the burning of the warehouse. Even Ofellius would not sink so low as to burn a warehouse with the goods still inside. Hates waste.'

Aro's blood ran cold as the full implications of what Piso's news meant. Veratius Cornelius was prepared to sacrifice his own daughter to pursue a vendetta? Something had to be wrong, somewhere. If it was true, he did not deserve a daughter like Lydia. There was no telling what could have happened to her, if Ofellius had succeeded in his plans.

'How could a man want to do that to his own daughter? Doesn't he realise what Ofellius is capable of?' Aro stared out into the blackness, trying to make sense of it.

'Maybe it was why he got cold feet.'

'That litter was not sent by Veratius. It carried Sulpicia, Lydia's sister-in-law, on the way back from a religious ceremony.'

Piso let out a loud whistle. He shook his head. 'It is a mystery then.'

'Before I tell her, I have to be certain.' Aro hit his fists against each other. 'There can be no mistake.'

'Aro?' Lydia's voice floated on the evening air. 'Who are you talking to?'

'Piso. He came back to see how you are faring.'

Lydia emerged from the house into the moonlight. Her hair tumbled about her face. She had thrown a shawl over her shoulders and under-tunic. Aro's body responded instantly to her loveliness. His gut clenched. His wife. The woman he had sworn to protect. Who was in danger from her own father.

'I will be off, then. Once I know more, I will report back,' Piso said in an undertone as he gave Lydia a nod and then vanished into the night.

'It seems late or is it early?' Lydia came to stand by him, her warm body curving in towards him. 'There are no streaks of grey in the sky. Surely Piso can't have to work this early.'

'Work starts early in the shipping business.'

'Business is normally conducted during the day. Only thieves and loose women are up and about at this time.'

'And merchants. The tide waits for no man, my nymph.'

She put her hand over Aro's. 'Tell me the truth, Fabius Aro. Does this have to do with my fright this afternoon? There is bound to be an innocent explanation.'

Aro studied her face, from the pale oval to the line of her brows, straight nose and rosebud mouth. He knew he could not lie to her, but neither could he tell her the truth. He drew her into his arms and rested his cheek against her hair.

'It has something to do with this afternoon. I am trying to discover the reasons behind it and behind all the other attacks. The Ofellian and Lupan Houses have always been rivals, but we have never been bitter enemies, reduced to fighting each other in the streets. It is not good for business.'

Lydia leant back against his arms, her eyes searching his face, seeking reassurance. Aro held his body still. He found he could not whisper false words of hope. She had to see things as they were.

'You are talking about someone other than Ofellius.' Lydia's face was a pale oval in a sea of blackness. 'You think there is someone else involved.'

Aro knew he had reached a deciding point in his life. He

could tell her the truth as Piso understood it and destroy any chance of a relationship with her, or he could wait. For the first time in his life, he hesitated, knowing how much he could lose. It frightened him that Lydia had come to mean so much to him in so short a span of time.

'I have no proof, but I will do. I will put an end to these attacks, Lydia. You must trust me.'

'I do trust you, Aro.' Her hand touched his cheek, smoothing it. 'The hour is late and soon you will be called from your bed. Come, spend some time with me.'

'You must forgive me for not explaining sooner. I had planned to when I found you in the bath.'

'I believe you had other things on your mind.' She gave a throaty laugh.

'May I always be distracted in such a way, my nymph.' He kissed her hair and silently asked the gods for more time.

'Don't even think of it, Korina,' Lydia said a few days later. 'That bit of bread is not for you. Tuccia may have returned yesterday, but it does not mean you will get more treats. You will be as fat as a pig if you are not careful.'

The greyhound buried her nose under her paws, looking mournful. Lydia gave a sigh and gave the last remains of her lunch to the dog.

Because it was such a glorious day, Lydia had decided to have her lunch outside while she waited for Aro to return. Today he would have his position confirmed by the censor, a ceremony which women were forbidden to attend. She had invited her father to dine with them after the ceremony, but he had declined, giving worries about his health as an excuse.

Lydia was disappointed, but Aro had told her not to worry, that their celebration could be all the more private.

He had left slightly earlier than planned as there had been a disturbance in the night at the warehouse.

A sudden tramping of feet and Gallus, her father's porter, came into the garden, hotly pursued by Aro's porter. Clodius looked hot and flustered.

'I am sorry, my lady, but this infernal ruffian would not wait. He insisted on speaking with you.'

'It is all right, Clodius, the man is known to me.'

'Lydia Veratia, you must come at once. Your father requires your presence.' Gallus drew himself up importantly.

'The Lady Lydia *Fabia* may have other matters she has to attend to, as I explained to you before.'

Lydia did not miss the slight emphasis on the name. Both porters stood toe to toe like rival cockerels, trying to face each other down. Lydia wasn't sure whether or not she wanted to laugh or cry. Which family she belonged to did not change what was inside her. She was still herself.

'Gallus, what is wrong? Why does my father need me?'

'It is the Lady Sulpicia. She has taken a turn. Veratius Cornelius requires you to come at once.'

Lydia frowned. Sulpicia's baby should not appear until next Kalends at the earliest. She tried to remember what the midwife had said when Sulpicia had first consulted her.

'Has my father summoned the midwife?'

'She will be there directly. She said sometimes babies decide to make their appearance early. The Lady Sulpicia is asking for you.'

'If she is asking for me, I will go. I made a promise.' Lydia stood up. Her mind raced. There were so many things that had to be done. She had no idea how long she'd be there, looking after Sulpicia. Aro would have to understand.

'My lady, Fabius Aro specifically requested that you be here when he returned today. The cook is preparing a special meal, and the musicians are arriving. All is in readiness.'

'He will understand. This is an emergency. Sulpicia would not have sent Gallus otherwise. Tuccia, you take care of Korina…no, I will take her with me. She can keep my father company.' She stopped and looked at Gallus. 'It is an emergency, isn't it?'

Gallus's cheeks reddened. He drew a line in the dirt with his sandal. 'Veratius Cornelius gave me to understand it was.'

'There are no men to spare. You will have to wait until some men arrive from the warehouse. I can't allow you to go out unprotected. Fabius Aro gave explicit orders.'

'When did he give this order?'

'This morning before he left. He said that you were not to venture out on your own today, and to have you wait for him.'

'I will not be out on my own. Gallus is here. He can take me.'

Clodius glanced over at the other porter. His expression showed that he did not have much confidence in the plan.

'Fabius Aro will not like it,' he repeated, shaking his head. 'I can tell you now. You might wish to risk the Sea Wolf's wrath, but I will not.'

Lydia put her hands on her hips. 'If he knew what was happening, he would agree with me.'

Clodius looked unimpressed. Lydia pushed a tendril of

hair behind her ear. She would get nowhere by arguing with Clodius. What she had found with Aro was too fragile to trust to a disgruntled porter. She had no wish to repeat the misunderstandings of the first days of their marriage.

'Very well, take me to him. I will inform him myself.' Lydia drew herself up to her full height. 'Surely you can have no objection to that.'

Lydia noticed the stillness before they had even arrived at the warehouse. Instead of the bustle and hum, everything was silent. One or two workmen hung around the yard, but it was as if the whole place held its breath.

'Is it because of the censor?' she asked in a hushed tone.

'It's them curse tablets, I reckon. It has been this way for the last few days. Despite Fabius Aro's reputation, they are taking their toll. People are beginning to whisper that the Sea Wolf has lost his touch.' Clodius spat on the ground and made a sign to ward off evil.

Lydia swallowed hard. The curse tablets, the ones that had started when she married Aro. Exactly who was her enemy?

'The curse tablets mean nothing,' she said with a laugh. 'Fabius Aro had augurs and diviners in to purify the place.'

'It may be, but people are whispering. They say that he may even lose the election because of the whispers. The gods have started to desert him.'

A chill passed over Lydia. This election to the Senate meant everything to him. He had married her to secure the necessary votes in the tribes. The censor would see he had the support. Lydia thought back to her blithe words to the fixer at the baths—he won't need you, because the people will be behind him.

'That is nonsense. Wine-shop talk. I am sure Fabius Aro would agree with me.'

'Agree with you about what?' Aro's voice boomed. 'What would I agree with you about, Lydia?'

Aro appeared in the entrance way. Instead of looking flawless in a gleaming white toga, droplets of sweat clung to his brow and several patches of dirt clung to his tunic as if he had been shifting stone or amphorae. His eyes looked weary.

Lydia raced over to him, feeling as if a burden had dropped from her shoulders. She'd explain, then she'd go to Sulpicia. She had no desire to have any disagreement between them, but she had to go.

'It's Sulpicia. Gallus says the baby is coming and she is asking for me. I promised her when we married that I'd return when the baby was born. She is frightened, Aro, oh, so frightened. It is the least I can do—to be there.'

Aro smoothed the hair away from her forehead, before resting his forehead against it.

'I thought Sulpicia's baby was not due for days,' he said, releasing her. 'Next Kalends, I thought you said.'

'Babies have a habit of coming when they are ready. Please give me leave to go.'

He looked away from her then. 'I can't, Lydia. I fear it is a trap.'

'A trap? What are you talking about?' Lydia's body went cold and she wrapped her arms about her waist. 'What sort of trap?'

'There have been rumours that your father is in league with Ofellius and trying to discredit me. I fear you might be in danger.'

'My father? What sort of nonsense is that?'

'Ofellius's behaviour was strange that day he tried to kidnap you.'

'I escaped.' Lydia pushed aside thoughts about how he had not tried very hard to recapture her. They were unworthy. 'My father would never have tried to harm me. I am his daughter.'

'I am sure he did not have the least intention of harming you.'

Aro placed his hand on her sleeve and the warmth from it travelled up her arm, infusing her body with the memories of the nights they had spent together.

'Then why would he do it?' Lydia shook her head. 'I refuse to believe it. My father would never ever put me in harm's way. Whoever told you that seeks to injure my father.'

'I wish I knew, but until I do, I must ask you to refrain from going to his house.'

'Do you have any proof? Or is it merely market whispers?'

'If I had solid proof, I would have told you sooner. You must believe me, Lydia. I have no wish to blacken your father's name.'

'But you believe it to be true.'

'Yes.' The word was drawn from his breast.

Icy fear clenched Lydia's stomach. There had to be a mistake somewhere. There had to be a simple explanation for all this. 'Have you spoken with my father about it?'

'Until I have solid proof, I have refrained from doing anything out of respect for you and your father.'

'You have condemned him without speaking to him. We are not talking about one of your business rivals. We are speaking of my father.'

'Which is why I am trying to be cautious, Lydia. Someone wanted you kidnapped, and I am trying to discover with all due speed who that someone was. I never make accusations lightly.'

Lydia drew in her breath, concentrated on not losing her temper. She had to stay calm, but Aro also had to see sense. She was pleased he wanted to protect her, but she would be safe in her father's house.

'Aro, I made a promise to Sulpicia. I have to go. I have to go now, not when you can spare the men or when it is convenient to you. I must be there for her.'

Lydia drew away from his hand. A deep chill had pervaded her inside. Surely Aro could not be jealous of her family. He could not be asking her to turn her back on Sulpicia in her hour of need.

'If you are worried, come with me to my father's. It will not take long and, once you see I am safely there, you can go.'

Aro ran his hand through his hair, making it stand up straight. 'I could say the same thing to you. Why can't you wait until I have the time to take you? The ropes holding the amphorae were cut this morning. Someone wanted a nasty accident to happen. It is only through good fortune that no one was injured. I have to make sure everything is safe. I have a duty towards my men and the Lupan House. Then I need to present myself at the Campus Martius before the sun crosses the rostrum.'

'And I have a duty towards my sister-in-law! She is giving birth!'

'You need not shout. I heard you the first time,' Aro said, an irritated look appearing on his face. 'I will take you after I have sorted things out here. Then I can stay and wait for you.'

'Why? Don't you trust me to return?' Lydia raised her chin and stared directly into his eyes. She refused to show that that one remark had cut through her. Despite what they had shared, he had no trust in her.

'I never said that.' An indulgent smile played on Aro's lips, infuriating Lydia all the more. 'Calm yourself. Listen to yourself, Lydia. You are in no state to go and help Sulpicia. What do you know of birthing? Let the midwife take charge.'

'I can hold her hand. She asked for me!' Lydia gritted her teeth. She refused to lose her temper. The worst of it was she knew Aro was right. She had no idea of the birthing process, but it made no difference. She had given her word. She refused to let Sulpicia suffer alone and frightened. She drew a deep breath and concentrated on keeping her voice calm and reasoned. 'I promised her. Can't you understand?'

Aro's eyes softened. Lydia felt her heart beat faster. He had understood. He would let her go.

'Can't you understand that my wife's safety is of paramount importance to me?' His voice was silky soft, cajoling her. 'I am only asking you to delay a little.'

Her stomach dropped to the tops of her sandals. He was only humouring her. He would find another and yet another excuse. He did not intend to let her go.

'I need to go now.' If only she could make him see. She had to go now. Every breath she took was a reminder of her failure to keep her promise. 'I have to go now. I am going with or without your leave.'

'And I forbid it.' His hand closed around her arm. 'You are my wife and you will obey me in this.'

'Never.'

'You will obey me. You will do as I say. We married *cum manu*. I am your guardian as well as your husband.'

Lydia drew herself up. Anger washed over her in a great wave. Forbid her? She thought they were beyond that. She had thought things were different between them. All she could see stretching out before her was a lonely life. She could never exist in such a relationship. With one furious motion she took off her ring and threw it at his feet. It fell to the ground with a small clang of metal hitting stone.

'I regret I cannot be the wife you want. I thought for a time I could, but I can't. What we had is no more.'

She turned and started to walk towards the entrance, her heart breaking. She knew if she looked back and saw any softening, anything, she'd run into his arms, so she did not allow herself. She concentrated on putting one sandal in front of the other.

'My lady, my lady, where are you going?' she heard Gallus call.

'I am going to keep my promise.'

Aro watched the ring bounce in the dust at his feet. He took a step towards Lydia's fast-disappearing skirts, but then stopped. He did not run after women. Instead, he bent down and picked up the ring, cleaning it carefully.

'Shall I go after Lydia Fabia?' Clodius asked.

Aro closed his eyes and shook his head.

\* \* \*

A sense of weariness swept over Lydia as she approached her father's house. At first she had been too angry to think; then she had worried that Aro would come after her; then she worried that he wouldn't. But he didn't. He failed to even send one of his men hurrying after her.

Their marriage to him meant less than fixing the ropes on the amphorae. He had never said that he loved her, only that he intended to protect her. He would do the same for any who belonged to the Lupan House. She was no different. And the irony of it was that she loved him. If he had come after her, she might have flown into his arms and forgotten all her principles. But he hadn't. He had only cared about appearances. Lydia's throat closed and she quickened her footsteps.

She was pleased when the familiar gates of her father's house appeared.

The house seemed very quiet, unnaturally so. None of the servants were about. She supposed they were behaving this way out of respect for Sulpicia.

She'd first check on Sulpicia and then she'd see her father and explain about what had happened this morning. Then later, much later, she'd allow herself the luxury of tears. Now the place inside her felt too raw and hollow. How could she love a man who denied her the right to fulfil her promises? Why had it happened? And how could he believe her father would ever do anything underhand?

Lydia tapped on Sulpicia's door and heard Sulpicia's voice bidding her to enter. Rather than sitting on a birthing chair or groaning, Sulpicia sat at her dressing table, applying the last bit of wine dregs to her cheeks, chatting away to Beroe, the tire-woman.

'Sulpicia, I came as quickly as I could. Tell me I am in time.'

Sulpicia turned with a start. 'Lydia? Why are you here?'

'You sent Gallus with a message, summoning me.'

'Not I.' Sulpicia gave a tinkling laugh and waved a bracelet bedecked arm. 'I haven't seen Gallus all morning.'

Lydia ran her tongue over her lips. Rapidly she went back over Gallus's message. He had told her that Sulpicia was giving birth. Someone had lied to him. Someone had wanted her here and not in the safety of Aro's house. The worst thing was that she had believed Gallus. The room seemed to sway.

'Lydia, my dear, whatever is the matter? You look green. Doesn't she look dreadful Beroe?'

'You didn't send for me? The midwife is not here?'

'Do you have a fever, Lydia?' A worried frown appeared between Sulpicia's brows. 'Maybe you are anxious about the censor?'

'I am perfectly fine,' Lydia said through gritted teeth. 'But why did someone feel the need to send for me?'

Sulpicia stood up and went over to Lydia. She put an arm around her and Lydia allowed her to lead her to the bed. Lydia sank down.

'My back ached this morning. My feet are swollen. I bear a certain resemblance to a beached whale, but Beroe has assured me these are good signs. The baby should not be here for days, Lydia. You know that. There was no need for *me* to send word.'

Two bright spots appeared on Sulpicia's cheeks.

'You know who sent for me,' Lydia said quietly.

Tears sprang to Sulpicia's eyes. 'Cornelius. He wanted me to write the note, but I refused. I hoped you wouldn't come, that you'd realise I would never ask Cornelius to do such a thing, and when I did send for you, it would be a note in my own hand. Gallus is too…too volatile. He is apt to forget things. You have always said that.'

'Of course I came. I made a promise.'

'Cornelius said you would. We argued about it. It is one of the reasons why I am in my room. He has become impossible since this sudden friendship with Ofellius.'

Lydia fought the urge to scream. Her father knew her all too well. He had used her and her sense of duty. She had been so intent on fulfilling her promise to Sulpicia, so sure of her own righteous behaviour, that she had refused to listen to Aro's words of caution. Instead of showing what a wonderful person she was, she had shown the contempt she had for his protection. His love. She had been so concerned about fleeing Aro's bonds that she had not realised he was trying to protect her.

All she wanted now was a chance, a chance to apologise and to start over again. There had been something between them. Maybe, just maybe, they could salvage something from the wreck of their marriage. From now on, she'd listen with her heart.

'Lydia, where are you going?'

'I have to go back.' Lydia paused, her hand on the door. 'I have to go home and find Aro, and apologise.'

'You can't do that.' Sulpicia reached out a hand and grabbed Lydia's arm. Her eyes were wild. 'Tell her, Beroe. Tell why she has to stay here.'

'Why not? There has been a dreadful mistake.' Lydia held out both her hands, palms upwards.

'Cornelius only listens to Ofellius. He lured you here. Ofellius has surrounded the house. He intends to keep you here. He intends to ruin Aro. When he is finished, he said the Sea Wolf will be no more.'

## Chapter Seventeen

Aro's study was silent and cool after the heat of the yard. Tightening his jaw, Aro put Lydia's ring on the necklace and looped it around his neck. He held his father's ring in his hand, looking at its blue stone. Then, deliberately, he walked over to the strong box and tossed the ring in. He placed his snow-white toga with its broad purple stripe on top of the box. Becoming a senator was nothing compared to being Lydia's husband. The vow he had given his father was less important than the vow he had given his wife on their wedding. She might have tossed the ring away, but he was not going to let her toss away their marriage that easily.

'Aro?' Piso's voice jolted Aro from his thoughts. 'What are you doing, sitting here in the gloom? You should be at the Campus Martius. The censor has begun his roll call.'

'Deciding my plan of attack.' Aro stuffed the necklace inside his tunic and stood to face Piso.

'You have already heard about what is happening?' Piso

shook his head. 'I don't know how you do it. The gods must whisper to you.'

'What nonsense are you spouting now, Piso?'

'Rufus's grandson has come up with the proof. Veratius and Ofellius are working together. He's become friends with one of the lads from the Ofellian House. Seems they were in school together as boys. This lad sent word he couldn't meet our lad because he was wanted for important duties. Could be several days.'

'Important duties? Sometimes, Piso, I wonder if you have not taken a knock too many in those wine shops you favour.'

'Ah, but you haven't heard. Ofellius has his henchmen waiting outside Veratius's house. They have been told to expect trouble. The lad was given a badge to wear. It is the same insignia as the knife you showed me the other day.'

'When did this happen?' Aro asked. Every muscle became alert.

'This morning. According to Rufus's lad, they had to hide in the shadows until a certain person arrived and then they were to wait outside, in case of trouble.' Piso paused. His expectant smile fading a little. 'Aro, are you all right?'

'Veratius has hired Ofellius as a bodyguard.'

'But why?'

'Lydia left this morning. Her father sent word Sulpicia was in labour. And so she left to fulfil her promise.' Aro opened the strong box, took out a dagger and tucked it in his sandal.

'And you let her?'

'I did not have much choice in the matter.' Aro slammed his fist against the table. 'It would appear her father knew his daughter very well.'

'You mean…'

'I had suspicions when she came to me with the request. I should have gone with her, but instead I chose to quarrel and nurse my injured pride when she stood her ground. I believed—I hoped—her father would keep her safe.'

Aro reached down and tucked another dagger into his belt.

'It's a trap, Aro. You must not go there. Ofellius will use it as an excuse. Lydia will find a way to come back to you—'

'Call the men!' Aro bellowed, cutting Piso's words short.

'What are you going to do?'

'We are going to give Lydia a chance for her freedom, and we are going to end this dispute between the Ofellian and Lupan Houses for all time.' He clapped Piso on the back. 'What are you waiting for, man? We are going to war.'

'Father, can you tell me why—?'

Lydia stopped in the doorway to her father's study and stared. She had expected to find Veratius Cornelius alone, but instead he was deep in conversation with Ofellius. She glanced towards where her grandfather's dagger normally lay. It was not there. A chill swept over her. Lydia forced her back to remain upright. She refused to give in to panic.

'Father, why are you not at the Campus Martius, giving your support to Fabius Aro?' Lydia pointed to Ofellius. 'Why is this man allowed in the house? He attempted to kidnap me a few days ago. And a few days before that one of his men accosted me with a knife stolen from this very house.'

'What is this all about, Ofellius?' Her father looked startled. 'Did you try to abduct her? You know I had words with you about that when I gave you the knife. My daughter is not to be harmed.'

Lydia's insides knotted as the full horror crashed in on her. Her father had known. Her father was working with Ofellius. Aro had been right. She looked at her father's study with every shelf crammed with figurines and vases. She had always thought this was the safest place in the world.

It wasn't.

Ofellius's man had not stolen the knife. Her father had given him the knife. He had put her in danger. A great well of despair opened up inside her.

'It was a misunderstanding,' Ofellius said. 'I discovered your daughter wandering the streets alone and tried to do my civic duty and return her to you.'

'My home is not here,' Lydia said in desperation. 'My home is on the Aventine with Fabius Aro, my husband.'

'He might not be much longer,' her father said in a solemn voice.

Lydia twisted her belt around her hand. What exactly was her father up to? He could not know about the fight she had had with Aro. She had to play for time. She had to hope she could find out a way of returning to him, and explain the situation.

'You were the one who sent the curse tablets?' she asked, staring hard at her father. Her mind reeled, shied away from what her father had done. 'Why did you want to ruin my husband? It makes no sense.'

'The curse tablets will stop when he gives you up as a wife,' her father replied calmly. 'Once he realises that the augurs misread the signs at your marriage, he will allow you to go free. Ofellius here has helped implement my plan. It came to me several days ago. I will let him have his seat in the Senate, if he gives up my daughter. I am trying to save you, Lydia.'

'For too long the Sea Wolf has ruled the waves,' Ofellius growled. 'It is time he learnt humility.'

Lydia's jaw dropped. Everything swayed. Her father, the one person she did not suspect, was the force behind the attacks.

'What do you want from me?' she whispered.

'I want you to leave your husband and come back here.' Her father put a heavy hand around Lydia's wrist. 'Things have not been the same without you. You keep this house running far more efficiently than Sulpicia. Nobody looks after me in the same way. She orders the sort of food she wants and takes no notice of me. Besides, I know it is what you want. You didn't really want to marry Fabius Aro. I saw it in your eyes.'

Lydia pushed her father's hand away from her. 'You have no idea what I want! You only want me here for your own selfish reasons, reasons that have nothing to do with my happiness!'

'Control your temper, Lydia.' Her father pressed his fingers together. 'While you may think you have feelings for this Fabius Aro now, all that will change in time. You will thank me in time.'

'I will never thank you.'

'I am not an unreasonable man. You can stay here or else I will withdraw my support for Aro's candidacy. How many will vote for a man who has been abandoned by the gods? And abandoned by his father-in-law? Jupiter Maximus, I should have bargained better. Ofellius opened my eyes on the day of your marriage.'

'You have no right…' Lydia struggled to breathe.

'He had no right to take my daughter from me.'

Lydia closed her eyes, willing herself not to lose her temper. She had to escape from here. She started towards the door.

'Where are you going, Lydia?' her father asked. 'I have not dismissed you yet.'

'Back to where I belong.' Lydia forced her back to remain upright. She refused to let Ofellius or her father see how frightened she was.

'And how will you travel, my daughter? The streets of Rome are notoriously dangerous.'

'I might prefer to take my chance.'

'Think carefully, Lydia. Let's not be hasty,' Ofellius said with a smirk on his face. 'You don't have to answer your father straight away. You may sleep on it, consider it and mull it over. Ask yourself—what do you have to gain with defiance?'

'Lydia, my dear, also consider this—what will Aro do if he discovers the choice you are making? What will you do when he discovers you have denied him the opportunity to become a senator? How will he want you then? You will lose everything. My door will not be open to you then.'

Lydia stared at her father, seeing him through new eyes. It was not just that his right eye drooped a little at the corner or that he seemed to be talking out of one side of his mouth only. It was something much more fundamental than that.

She had made so many excuses for his behaviour since his illness, but now she knew he had changed. Her father, the one she remembered, would never have asked her to behave in such a fashion. Because his own father had had such a disregard for promises, he had been determined to instil in his children the need to keep your word.

'You brought me up to always keep my promises,' she said, gazing directly at her father, trying to find the gentle man she knew was in there. 'Would you have me break my solemn vow to Fabius Aro, then, Father?'

Cornelius waved his hand. 'He left me no option when he insisted on marrying you *cum manu*. I would not have you tied for life like that. I would have failed your mother, if I had allowed that. That is why I enlisted Ofellius's help. We devised this plan. He can have his precious place in the Senate, but not my daughter.'

'It is a pity you never thought to ask me what I want.'

'I am your father. I know what is best for you.'

'The woman is mistaken. Enough talk,' Ofellius growled. 'As we agreed, Veratius Cornelius—she may continue as Fabius Aro's wife or he can become a senator.'

'He doesn't need you or anyone else to be a senator.' Lydia faced the pirate with blazing eyes. 'It will be the people who decide!'

'Brave words, but foolish,' Ofellius said. 'And what happens then? When he loses? How will he look at you then? Don't you agree, Veratius Cornelius?'

'Lydia, it is your choice. Be grateful I am offering you this choice.'

Lydia shook her head. This was not her father, not the man she remembered. He had to be somewhere in there, but how could he do such a thing to her if he truly loved her? How could he ask her to make such a decision? She had been blind, completely blind. And her words to Aro, proudly proclaiming that her father had nothing to do with the curse tablets or the incidents, how hollow they sounded now. And how foolish.

In some ways it should be easy—Aro would never want her back after she had thrown the ring at him today. Even now, he might have gone to the censor to register the divorce. The bitter irony was not lost on her.

'Father—' She held out her hands, beseeching him one last time.

'I think my wife would rather I made up my own mind.'

Lydia spun around and faced the door. Her heart skipped a beat. Aro!

She took a half-step towards him, and he held out his arms. Within another step, she was gathered close to him and heard the reassuring thump of his heart. Her hand went to his face, touching it to make sure he was real.

'You came for me.'

'Did you really think I would let you go that easily?' he whispered in her ear.

Her father recovered first. 'How did you get in, Fabius Aro? This house is well protected.'

'For future reference, Veratius Cornelius, when you station guards, it is better if you station them around the entire house. You left the rear entrance exposed. I was able to climb up and in the open window. Scaling walls may be a skill from my youth, but it is not forgotten. Sulpicia was slightly surprised, but informed me where I might find Lydia once she and her tire-woman had recovered from the shock. Now, if you gentlemen will excuse me, I think it is time I took my wife home. She has had a long day.'

Ofellius advanced, blocking their way. 'Shall we settle this man to man?' Ofellius said. 'You have insulted this family long enough.'

Aro dropped Lydia's arm and turned to face his fellow merchant. 'With pleasure, but it is not I who have insulted this family, but you.'

Lydia stifled a scream. There was an air of unreality. She wanted to beg her father to stop this, but he grabbed her arm, holding her back.

'It is in the lap of the gods,' he whispered, motioning for her to keep quiet.

'Let me and my wife pass, Ofellius, and we will settle this later—in the courts. We are not on the high seas here.'

'Brave words for a man who is about to die,' Ofellius sneered. He reached out and shoved Aro backwards, throwing him off balance. And then he grabbed a dagger and held it out.

Aro took a step back, balanced on the balls of his feet, crouched, his hands ready.

'I believe I explained before what would happen if you or your men harmed one hair of my wife's head. You don't listen, do you, Ofellius?'

'You talk too much, Fabius Aro,' Ofellius said, starting to come towards him.

Aro looked to his left and right, checking, mentally preparing for the assault. It had come to this, finally. He had not sought the confrontation, but he welcomed it. Ofellius had to understand that Lydia was his wife and no man would take her from him. He had allowed the insults to go on too long.

Ofellius charged forward. Aro shifted his weight at the last breath, grabbed the outstretched arm and spun Ofellius around. The dagger dropped to the floor.

'Did you know that I was taught how to wrestle by an Olympic champion?' he remarked at the look of surprise on Ofellius's face.

Ofellius broke free, retreated to the other side of the room, breathing like a bull. He charged forward again. This time, he caught Aro around the waist and dragged him down. He brought his knees to his chest and levered the large man up. Ofellius flew backwards, got to his feet, and then charged again, this time managing to land a punch on Aro's jaw. Aro gingerly felt his face, and then waited for the next assault. Patience, he told himself. Wait for the opening.

'Father, you must do something, Aro could get killed,' he heard Lydia say from a distance away.

'And would that be a pity, child? It would solve all our problems.'

'It would solve nothing. You don't know him as I do. Aro is the most noble man I have ever met. The world would be a much greyer place at his passing.'

Renewed energy surged through Aro. He crouched low, ready.

Ofellius started forward.

'Watch out, he has another dagger!'

'I see it.' Aro pulled his own dagger from his belt.

Aro and Ofellius circled each other, Ofellius probing with the dagger. Sweat trickled down Aro's back. He had to wait. He had one chance.

Each breath Lydia took seemed to take an age. She willed Aro forward. But the two combatants seemed evenly matched. Suddenly Ofellius struck. Forwards and up. Aro dropped to the ground.

A scream echoed through the chamber and Lydia realised with a start that it was hers. She fought against her father's arms. 'Let me go. Can't you see he is hurt?'

'Not so immortal after all, Sea Wolf.' Ofellius aimed a kick at Aro's body.

A hand snaked out, grabbing Ofellius's legs and sending him crashing to the floor. Ofellius's head hit the side of the table.

'You were always too sure of yourself, Ofellius,' Aro said, standing up.

Lydia jerked herself free of her father's grasp, grabbed her father's Grecian vase and brought it down on Ofellius's head. He gave a groan and lay still. Aro gave a low whistle and Piso appeared with two other men.

'You called, Sea Wolf?'

'Ofellius is in need of attention. Please give it to him.'

Piso's face broke into a wide smile. 'With the greatest pleasure.'

'All secure out there?'

'They were no match for us.' Piso gave a bow. 'And they call themselves sailors—pure waterfront mob, these lot. Gods, you wonder where they learnt to fight. Your servant, Lydia Fabia.'

Lydia stared at Aro, hardly knowing what to say.

'Do you realise how expensive that vase was, daughter?' her father asked in an irritated voice.

'Do you realise how precious my husband is to me, Father?' She turned and faced her father with her hands on her hips.

'I believe it is time this war between us came to an end, Veratius Cornelius.' Aro held out his hand to the older man. 'My men are outside and they are in no mood for leniency. They take more exception than I do to the good name of the Lupan House being blackened. But explain all to your daughter and I will spare you and your house.'

'You will denounce me to the censor.' Veratius Cornelius looked white and shaken. 'Ofellius warned me of this. When I am no use to you, you will ruin me and cast off my daughter.'

Lydia looked at her father with tears in her eyes. Her father seemed to have shrunk. The lines on his face were etched deeply and his eyes watered.

'Father, Ofellius lied to you. He stole Publius's shipment of fish sauce and sold it on the open market. Aro has the bill of sale. He has lied to you about everything. He did not want to right some wrong. He used you as a way to destroy Fabius Aro. Why would Aro denounce you? What purpose would it serve?'

'Are you sure of this, daughter? Did Ofellius steal the fish sauce?'

'I can prove it. In this office is the tablet Ofellius sent saying he had shipped the entire lot, but in Rufus's house is an amphora with the markings Publius used. Aro has a bill of sale.'

'I have brought it with me.' Aro reached into his belt and drew out the small tablet. 'Half of the amphorae are still in my warehouse. They were what Ofellius sought to destroy in his attack.'

'Ah, woe is me. What have I done? I believed that pirate.'

Veratius Cornelius buried his face in his hands. Aro went over and raised his face.

'You are my father-in-law. An evil man took advantage of you and your illness,' Aro said quietly. 'Lydia has assured me that you would never hurt her and I must believe her.'

'I would never hurt my daughter. How could I? I love her.' There were tears in her father's eyes. 'I just want her to be happy. But Ofellius told me how unhappy you were, daughter.'

'He lied, Father.' Lydia reached out and caught her father's hand. 'He wanted to destroy Aro and so he lied. He played on your anger and your outrage. He used you. If you had but spoken with me, I would have told you. I am very happy and content. I wish to stay as Aro's wife. He is a good man.'

'Yes, I see that now. I have wronged you, Fabius Aro. I spread false rumours about you. All because I wanted my daughter back.'

'I will always be your daughter, Father.' Lydia bit her lip. She had to say it before Aro left. 'Just as I will always be Aro's wife…if he will have me.'

'Lydia…' Aro's fingertips touched her cheek '…you have given me more than I could hope for.'

Lydia looked and saw a trickle of blood. 'Father, quickly fetch a doctor. Fabius Aro is hurt.'

'Yes, of course, daughter, and I will go to the censor and explain. He is an old friend and may disregard the fact that the sun has gone beyond the rostrum.'

'There is always next year for the enrolment,' Aro said quietly. 'All that matters is my wife is safe and back with me'

'I will get your wounds bound.' Her father gave a bow and

hurried from the room, calling for Gallus and the other servants.

Lydia stood, staring at Aro, trying to determine how badly he was hurt. After everything she had said to him, he had come to her rescue. Words deserted her.

'It is a mere scratch, I assure you,' Aro said, holding out his hand.

'You do not need to play the hero with me, Fabius Aro. Now, let me see how bad the wound is.'

His fingers caught hers. 'I will live, Lydia, but I have no desire to live without you.'

Her breath stopped in her throat. She concentrated on the tiny trickle of blood.

'I thought I might have lost you,' she whispered. 'I couldn't bear that.'

Aro squeezed her hand back. 'I have something that belongs to you,' he whispered. He reached inside his tunic and pulled out his chain. On it was her ring.

Lydia stared at the chain. Instead of the familiar gold ring with a blue stone, the iron-and-gold *arra* ring was fastened to the chain. 'Where is your signet ring?'

'In the strongbox at the warehouse where it belongs. I plan to give it to our firstborn son.' Aro smiled down at her. 'Nothing matters if you are not by my side. It doesn't matter if your father withdraws his support. I will be a senator when the Fates decree, but I will be nothing without you by my side.'

'I was wrong to throw your ring away.'

Aro knelt in front of her. He captured her hand and slid the ring on to her finger.

'Lydia Veratia, will you come back to me? Stay at my side and grow old with me? If you desire, I will give your hand back to your father, but say you will stay with me. Because without you, my life isn't worth living.'

'How long have you felt this way?'

Aro drew her into his arms and rested his chin against the top of her head. 'I knew you were the one for me the day I first met you. I had come all prepared to denounce the Veratii and turn your father in to the censor, and instead I found the sort of woman I wanted to share my life with. You were truly a huntress of Diana's come to life.'

'Truly? I didn't even like you then.'

A dimple appeared in his cheek. 'And do you like me now?'

'I love you, Fabius Aro—' Lydia stopped. She had to say it, because otherwise it would be between them and she did not want any misunderstandings. 'I can never be the sort of wife you want. I am not interested in spinning and gossip drives me mad. I will probably disobey you as often as I obey you.'

'Say you will stay with me and I will give your guardianship back to your father, if that is what you desire.'

Lydia shook her head. Something she had longed for had ceased to matter. 'I trust you to look after my interests as well as, if not better than, my father.'

'You humble me.' Aro raised her hand to his lips. 'I do solemnly swear that I will never be autocratic again.'

'Be mindful of making promises you can't keep.' Lydia gave a gentle laugh. 'Before the next Ides is out, you will be autocratic and demanding as ever.'

He sobered at this, but she gave his hand a squeeze. His face broke into a wreath of smiles.

'And,' she added, 'I wouldn't have you any other way, my Sea Wolf.'

'Yours and no other.'

He bent his head and she tasted his mouth, glorying in his kiss.

After a long while he said against her lips 'Do you know what they say about wolves?'

'What do they say?'

'A wolf mates for life.' He pushed her hair back off her forehead. 'I will have no other but you.'

Lydia laid her head against his chest and sighed contentedly.

'Aro, Aro!' Piso charged in to the room and then stopped, turning pink cheeked at the sight of Aro and Lydia embracing.

'I thought I gave orders not to be disturbed.'

'This arrived from the censor.' Piso held out a scroll. 'I knew you would want to see it.'

Aro broke the seal and read the scroll. A huge smile came over his face. 'By popular acclamation, I am enrolled as a senator!'

Lydia reached up and smoothed a lock of hair from his forehead. 'It would appear you will have the need for that purple-striped toga rather sooner than you had anticipated. You have achieved your heart's desire.'

Aro's arms tightened around her, holding her close.

'As long as I have you in my arms and safe, my dearest love, that is the only thing that matters. All else can wait.'

Aro bent his head and allowed the scroll to fall from his fingertips.

\* \* \* \* \*

# Historical Note

*Sine manu* versus *cum manu* marriage—in other words, who had control of a woman's fortune and served as her guardian. It is somewhat surprising to learn that by the end of the Republic most marriages were *sine manu*. Control of a woman's property and right to divorce stayed with her father or legal guardian, it did not pass to her husband. As there was no bar on women inheriting property and no system of primogeniture, a marriage *sine manu* ensured a family's wealth would stay with the birth family. Marriages in the early republic were almost exclusively *cum manu* and there were cases of terrible abuses by husbands, including the murder of one wife for daring to take the keys to the wine cellar. Thus, to give women and their families more rights over the disposal of the dowry, the marriage *sine manu* was enacted. The move towards marriage *sine manu* coincided with a decrease in a father's rights over his children. It was supposed to strengthen marriage, but in fact led to a higher divorce rate. The marital freedom which most women at the end of the Roman Republic (the time period in which this novel is set) enjoyed under the *sine manu* marriage system would not be repeated in the Western world until the twentieth century as Jerome Carcopino points out in his excellent book *Daily Life in Ancient Rome*. Also, as Romans during this period believed that upper-class women needed to be educated in order to teach their sons, one discovers a number of interesting and strong women, from Caesar's mother Aurelia and Clodia Metellia (the inspiration for Catullus's love poetry whose passion for lower-class vowel sounds changed the Roman accent for generations) to Sempronia, who was widely admired for her wit, wide reading and personal culture, and Attia, the rather more shadowy mother of Augustus.

If you want to read more about Roman marriage or women, Jerome Carcopino's *Daily Life in Ancient Rome* and Robin Lane Fox's *The Classical World* are both excellent places to start. Other books I have found useful are:

Broadman John, Jasper Griffin and Oswyn Murray (eds), *The Oxford History of the Roman World* (Oxford University Press 1988) Oxford

Carcopino Jerome, *Daily Life in Ancient Rome* (Yale University Press 1967) New Haven

Grant, Mark, *Roman Cookery: Ancient Recipes for Modern Kitchens* (Seriff 1999) London

Holland, Tom, *Rubicon: The Triumph and Tragedy of the Roman Republic* (Little, Brown 2003) London

Lane Fox Robin, *The Classical World—An Epic History from Homer to Hadrian* (Allen Lane 2005) London

Rauh, Nicholas K., *Merchants, Sailors & Pirates in the Roman World* (Tempus 2003) Stroud

Woolf, Greg (ed), *Cambridge Illustrated History: Roman World* (Cambridge University Press 2003) Cambridge

MILLS & BOON®

*Look out for next month's*
*Super Historical Romance*

# HIS LORDSHIP'S DESIRE
*by Joan Wolf*

**Napoleon's troops defeated, Wellington's Spanish
campaign is over. Now a dedicated English soldier
enters a very different kind of war: a battle for
the woman he loves...**

Alexander Devize, Earl of Standish, is summoned home
to his duties. Waiting for him, he believes, is Diana
Sherwood, the headstrong beauty with whom he shared
one unforgettable night. But she has other intentions...

Diana is a soldier's daughter and will not be a soldier's
wife! Alex's wild and reckless passion may haunt her
dreams – still, she's determined to find herself a proper,
steady gentleman. But she's reckoned without Alex's
readiness to risk all in a fight he will not lose!

"The always-awesome Joan Wolf proves she is a
master in any format or genre."
— *Romantic Times BOOKreviews*

## On sale 4th May 2007

*Available at WHSmith, Tesco, ASDA, and all good bookshops*
*www.millsandboon.co.uk*

# THE STEEPWOOD

# *Scandals*

*Regency drama, intrigue, mischief...*
*and marriage*

### VOLUME SIX

*The Guardian's Dilemma* by Gail Whitiker

In order to save his young stepsister from a fortune-
hunter, Oliver Brandon places her in a ladies' academy.
However, he realises that the schoolmistress may not be
as respectable as she appears...

*Lord Exmouth's Intentions* by Anne Ashley

Vicar's daughter Robina Perceval has relished her season
in Town, but what of Daniel, Lord Exmouth?
A widower, with two daughters to raise, it would
appear that he's in search of a wife.

## On sale 6th April 2007

*Available at WHSmith, Tesco, ASDA,*
*and all good bookshops*

*A young woman disappears.*
*A husband is suspected of murder.*
*Stirring times for all the neighbourhood in*

# THE STEEPWOOD
# *Scandals*

### Volume 5 – March 2007
*Counterfeit Earl* by Anne Herries
*The Captain's Return* by Elizabeth Bailey

### Volume 6 – April 2007
*The Guardian's Dilemma* by Gail Whitiker
*Lord Exmouth's Intentions* by Anne Ashley

### Volume 7 – May 2007
*Mr Rushford's Honour* by Meg Alexander
*An Unlikely Suitor* by Nicola Cornick

### Volume 8 – June 2007
*An Inescapable Match* by Sylvia Andrew
*The Missing Marchioness* by Paula Marshall

# 2 FREE

## BOOKS AND A SURPRISE GIFT!

We would like to take this opportunity to thank you for reading this Mills & Boon® book by offering you the chance to take TWO more specially selected titles from the Historical Romance™ series absolutely FREE! We're also making this offer to introduce you to the benefits of the Mills & Boon® Reader Service™—

- ★ FREE home delivery
- ★ FREE gifts and competitions
- ★ FREE monthly Newsletter
- ★ Exclusive Reader Service offers
- ★ Books available before they're in the shops

Accepting these FREE books and gift places you under no obligation to buy, you may cancel at any time, even after receiving your free shipment. Simply complete your details below and return the entire page to the address below. You don't even need a stamp!

**YES!** Please send me 2 free Historical Romance books and a surprise gift. I understand that unless you hear from me, I will receive 4 superb new titles every month for just £3.69 each, postage and packing free. I am under no obligation to purchase any books and may cancel my subscription at any time. The free books and gift will be mine to keep in any case.

H7ZED

Ms/Mrs/Miss/Mr .................................................Initials ................................
BLOCK CAPITALS PLEASE

Surname ........................................................................................................

Address ........................................................................................................

...............................................................................................................

.......................................................Postcode.........................................

**Send this whole page to:**
**UK: FREEPOST CN81, Croydon, CR9 3WZ**